Praise for J.B. Cheaney

The Middle of Somewhere

Kansas Notable Book

Texas Bluebonnet Award Nominee

Florida Sunshine State Young Readers Award Nominee

Indiana Young Hoosier Book Award Nominee

"The main characters are particularly well drawn and believable, and readers will root for both children as they attempt to overcome the obstacles placed in front of them. Fans of Jack Gantos' Joey Pigza series are sure to appreciate Ronnie and Gee's excellent adventure."

—*Booklist*

"Cheaney provides plenty of 'oh-my-gosh' scenarios with Gee's escapades...crafty, descriptive first-person narrative."

—*Kirkus*

The Playmaker

A *Booklist* Top Ten First Novels for Teens

"Twists and turns will keep readers in suspense throughout the tale while the exciting climax will bring some answers and unexpected connections. Informed by solid historical and literary scholarship, this well-written adventure novel is a winner."

—*School Library Journal*

"Fans of Susan Cooper's *King of Shadows* (1999) will enjoy this challenging, well-researched coming-of-age tale that will enrich theater, literature, and history courses."

—*Booklist*

SOMEBODY
ON THIS
BUS
IS GOING TO BE
FAMOUS

J.B. CHEANEY

sourcebooks
jabberwocky

Published by Sourcebooks Jabberwocky, an imprint of Sourcebooks, Inc.
P.O. Box 4410, Naperville, Illinois 60567-4410
(630) 961-3900
Fax: (630) 961-2168
www.jabberwockykids.com

Library of Congress Cataloging-in-Publication data is on file with the publisher.

Source of Production: Worzalla-USA, Stevens Point, WI
Date of Production: June 2014
Run Number: 5001937

Printed and bound in the United States of America.
WOZ 10 9 8 7 6 5 4 3 2 1

To Vicki and Leslie
in memory of long Saturday afternoons
on the porch
with a cup of coffee,
a slice of pie,
and a manuscript.

Prologue
Storm of the Decade

L ast night's weather forecast predicted rain.

This isn't rain. This is like somebody upstairs furiously hurling buckets of water at the vehicles creeping along the highway below. Minutes before, Patrol Car 38 was one of them. Then a gust of wind slapped it like a huge hand, the rear end shimmied, and the car swung around in a one-eighty that landed it on the yellow line. Front tires spun on an angry stream of water that hadn't been there a moment before.

The patrolman notices his hand shaking a little as he adjusts the radio knob. "Gonna be a busy morning," he mutters to himself—meaning, *Get a grip.* The wind is still tugging at his car like it might want to flip it over just for fun. He thought it was a tornado at first. But no funnel cloud twirls up, just a mighty gale, like you'd read about in the Bible or see on a Weather Channel special called *History's Worst Wind Disasters.* Shingles and branches dance in the current, and up ahead he sees a squarish piece of debris, maybe ten feet across, cartwheeling over the open field. Somebody's roof?

The radio fizzes and sputters: "Szzppppt!"

Broken phrases and bitten-off words start popping up in the static.

"Dispatch...Seven oh...fficers on 81 East...(*Squawk!*) Calling...Vehicle off a bridge on...(*Scriiiiiiitch!*) All available...47 West, report of...(*Crackle!*)...rd County, 215 south... school bus...Repeat...all officers...(*Pip! Pip! Pip! Scriiitch!*)"

The officer sits up straighter and leans closer to the radio: a school bus on Highway 215? That's his territory. For the next few seconds, the radio tells him nothing but noise, then, "—way 67 eastbound, semitrailer sideways—"

He grabs the transmitter and jabs the button: "Dispatcher 7. Dispatcher 7. This is Car 38. What's the location of school bus on 215? Over."

It takes a few tries, but he finally gets an answer: "Car 38. Area of Drybed Creek. That's all we know. Over."

"I'm on my way. Over." He clicks off, replaces the transmitter, and puts the patrol car in gear. Pulling forward, he circles the convenience store and heads out the way he came in. School bus off the road—every parent's nightmare. He's a father—he tries not to imagine any details as he turns south, flips the siren, and speeds down the highway as fast as he dares, fans of water spraying up from the wheels and LED lights sizzling through the rain.

* * *

The rain has slacked off to a steady downpour—not buckets but hard fat drops, driven like nails. "Holy cow!" gasps the patrolman, gazing down at so-called Drybed Creek, now a gray, spiky torrent, studded with tree limbs and shingles and pieces of pipe. Where's the bridge? And where's the school bus? As he slows down, a hand pokes from the window of the pickup parked beside a bluff on the other side of the road. It's pointing to the right.

The hand belongs to an old fellow in overalls. His mouth is stretched wide in a shout, but the patrolman can barely hear him over the roaring water. "It went off over there!"

Car 38 pulls over on the narrow shoulder. The patrolman grabs a poncho from the backseat and jerks it crookedly over his head while opening the door.

A movement from uphill catches his attention. A kid—a boy—limping down the road. *Down* the road? Where did he come from? Then a shout makes the officer turn around: another kid, trudging *up*. All the patrolman can make out is a white face, but its terrified expression strikes like lightning.

He steps back from the patrol car, waving his arms so they can see him. Are they both from the bus? How did they get so far away from it? Where are the rest of the passengers?

The red-white-and-blue lights scream through the water: *Danger! Danger! Danger!*

August
(Nine months earlier)

The light on top of the patrol car blinks sternly, like it's seeking out perpetrators of a crime. Spencer Haggerty, on his way to catch the school bus, pauses for a second—like the way his mother always jerks her foot off the accelerator when she sees a patrol car. What is it about the police that makes you feel guilty, even if you're not?

Jay is running toward him over the common, bounding across the street as the patrol car rolls toward the end of the loop and signals a right turn. "You missed all the excitement!"

"Huh?"

"There's been a robbery, dude! A *crime!*"

"Really?" Their boring subdivision, a crime scene?

"Spencer!" shouts his mom from the doorway. "Did you remember your physics camp report? And your scientific calculator?"

"Yes! Bye, Mom!" She can't see his eyes roll.

"How about your socks?" Jay asks, grinning. "And your underwear? Did you remember your tighty-whities?"

"Shut up." Spencer, a redhead, blushes easily.

"Oh, and your brain. Did you remember your outstanding brain?"

"Who was robbed?"

"Poppy—he came over while we were having breakfast, majorly ticked off. He'd already called the cops and everything, but it probably won't help. Wait'll you hear what was robbed."

"You mean *stolen*. Your grandparents were robbed. What was stolen?"

"Good boy—you remembered your brain." Jay taps his friend's skull. When his hand gets smacked aside, he laughs. "A wheelchair. That's all—a stupid wheelchair!"

"Who uses a wheelchair?"

"Remember last winter when my grandma slipped on the ice and broke her tailbone? They bought it so she could get around easier when they went to Florida. It's been folded up on the sunporch for months. So this morning, Poppy went to let Panzer out through the back door, and somebody'd broken in! The window screen was cut and everything. They looked around, but all they could find missing was the wheelchair."

Spencer frowns at something that doesn't sound right. "That's an oxymoron," he says.

"A what?"

"Two words that don't go together, like to *find* something *missing*. How do you find it if it's still missing?"

Jay punches him good-naturedly on the shoulder. Since he's grown bigger and stronger over the summer, it actually hurts. "C'mon, Mr. High-school-reading-level. You know what I mean."

They've almost reached the gazebo at the entrance to Hidden Acres Subdivision where the school bus stops. All around the loop of asphalt that ties the neighborhood together, kids are emerging from their houses or drifting across the common. The dusty late-summer light falls pale and sad, as though sorry to be going.

Igor Sanderson catches up to them, dragging his brother. Or that's what it looks like at first, but really he's trying to shake off Little Al, who's clinging to him. "Thanks a lot," Igor growls at Jay.

"You're welcome. What for?"

"Calling the cops. They totally freaked out my mom."

"That wasn't me who called—it was my grandfather."

"Whatever." Igor pauses at the steps of the gazebo.

"So how'd they freak out your mom?"

"They came over to ask questions. She looked out the window and lost it." Igor tosses his backpack to the ground, throws up his hands, and runs around in a circle. "*It's the cops! Go see what they want! I'm not here!*"

The little kids on the other side of the gazebo laugh. They always laugh at Igor.

"No offense," Spencer asks politely, "but does your mother have a criminal record?"

Igor stops. Then he shrugs. "She's just nervous. She's always nervous around strangers, 'specially when my stepdad's away on a job. Buzz *off*, Ally." He bats at his brother's clinging arm, explaining, "It's his first day of kindergarten."

7

"It'll be fun," Jay tells the little boy.

"It's the start of your academic odyssey," Spencer adds as he climbs the three steps to the gazebo—and nearly hits the floor after stumbling over a foreign object.

It's a foot, in a size 11 Adidas.

The foot belongs to Bender Thompson. "Watch it, freak!" is all Spencer can think to say.

"Looks like you're the one who ought to be watching," Bender remarks. Then he points a finger at Little Al with narrowed eyes. "You too. You could be the one they pick for the first-day-of-school human sacrifice. Just before lunch."

Little Al's jaw drops and he grabs his brother's arm again. "Leave him alone!" Igor yells at Bender, puffing out his chest a little.

Bender is almost thirteen and starting seventh grade, with a body mass that could make almost two of Igor, but he's not in a fighting mood. He merely takes a roll of paper from behind his ear and blows imaginary smoke.

"So, Igor," prompts Jay. "What happened with the cops?"

"Mom finally came out and talked to them." Igor rises on his toes and dances a couple of steps back. "But we don't know anything." He clutches his hands together as though pleading. "*Honest, officer! We don't know anything! Please let us*—Hey, what got stole, anyway?"

Jay opens his mouth, but before he can get a word out, Shelly Alvarez arrives in a rush as though blown by an excitable wind. "Omigosh! The police just came to our house! Did you know there was a *robbery*? Who called the cops?"

Bender speaks up. "Somebody who heard this screeching sound from your house—a sound like a cat getting skinned alive?"

Shelly tosses her long black hair. "Just wait. Wait until I do my breakout concert at AllStar Arena. No free tickets for *you*."

"I'm *so* not devastated," says Bender.

"That's because you didn't see my breakout performance at the county fair last July."

"What—you mean during the cow competition?" The other boys can't help but laugh, because Bender is pretty funny sometimes.

"Dweebs," comments Shelly with a big fake smile.

Miranda Scott joins them from the east side of the subdivision. "Did anybody see that police car that just went by?"

"Tell them about the county fair show, Mir," Shelly commands.

It sounds like a command, but Miranda treats it like an honor. "You mean on the main stage? It was awesome. She did this one song with sparklers—"

"It's called 'Razzle-Dazzle,'" Shelly explains, but before she can go on, Kaitlynn and Simon Killebrew arrive—Kaitlynn mouth first, as usual.

"Guess what!? There was a robbery last night! My dad told the police he saw a black pickup early this morning when he was loading the van to go to work, but it was still dark then so it might not have been black, maybe dark green or blue. He just called my mom and said a cop came by his shop! It must have been serious—does anybody know who got robbed?"

"Me," says Bender. "Somebody stole my reputation."

The other boys roll their eyes, and Spencer says, "Who'd want it?"

Bender glares as Kaitlynn squeals, "*Panzer!*" She runs over to a russet-colored dachshund being walked by Jay's grandfather. The old man pauses, puffing angrily behind his cigar, to let Kaitlynn scratch his dog's ears. She chatters on: "It's the first day of school, Panz! Don't you love the fall? Hot chocolate and leaf piles and Halloween?"

Panzer yaps in reply as Mr. Pasternak tugs on his leash. "I'd like it better if I wasn't being robbed in the dead of night," the old man growls.

"*Robbed!?*" squeaks Kaitlynn. "So it was *you*? My dad said—"

"Is that the bus?" says Mr. Pasternak as a downshifting engine can be heard over the rise. He doesn't seem to be in the mood for Kaitlynn's conversation.

"Here's the bus!" Kaitlynn leaps to her feet and runs to the gazebo to join the others. There's one more by now: Matthew Tupper, the other seventh-grader. He waited until the last minute to show up, lurking by the rose of Sharon bushes like somebody's lost shadow. The Tuppers have lived in the neighborhood for over a year and still don't act like they belong. Maybe being the only African American family makes them a little standoffish, though nobody will admit that.

The yellow school bus curls over the top of the rise like a caterpillar, coughs tiredly, and rolls toward the crowded gazebo. Meanwhile, across the common, Bender's mom screeches out of the Thompsons' driveway in her Suburban, a coffee mug in one hand and a hairbrush in the other. She's late for an appointment, as usual, but hates getting behind the school bus because it goes so slow and makes so many stops and there are not many good places to pass it on the twisty highway. Every school year begins a nine-month game of chicken between her and the driver.

The bus stops with a squeal of brakes. A split second before the STOP sign flips out on its metal arm, Mrs. Thompson's Suburban roars by. The driver frowns and shakes her head before she smiles and opens the door. "Hi, squirts! Welcome aboard!"

Her name is Teresa (Terry) Birch, but she's known as Mrs. B. And she always says "Welcome aboard!" like her bus is a cruise ship. Every year she wears a different hat that indicates where she went during the summer. This year, it's a yellow bucket hat from Dripping Springs State Park, Oklahoma.

Hidden Acres Subdivision is her first stop, so the bus is empty when the littles get on and take the front rows. The fourth-through-seventh-graders can sit where they want in the back seven rows. On the afternoon ride home, when the bus is packed, everybody has assigned seats. Mrs. B allows this one perk for big kids in the morning only.

Bender boards first, after the littles. "How were the drips?"

She frowns, then realizes he's talking about her hat. "I'll never tell," she answers. "Move on back, Bender. Hi, Kaitlynn—keep moving, dear, you can tell me later—Hi, Jay, hi, Spencer, hi, Igor *(not even grown-ups can remember Igor's real name)*, hi, Shelly, hi, Miranda—Stop shoving, boys! Matthew, are you riding today?"

Matthew is always last. "Thanks for joining us," Mrs. B remarks while looking over her glasses at the rearview mirror. "Boys! Settle down and let's get this show on the road!"

Bender heads for the very back seat and flops, noticing the same crack in the vinyl, the one with the curled edges that annoyed him last year. He wrinkles his nose: the 409 smell doesn't quite cover the aroma of old potato chips lingering in the creases. Matthew, two seats ahead of him, stares out the window. Spencer and Jay grab a seat together. Igor slips a whoopee cushion under Miranda as she sits down: *thwpppp!* She springs up and angrily throws it back at him. Igor nearly chokes himself laughing, even while pretending to be knocked out with birdies circling over his head. Mrs. B would normally be yelling at him by now, but this being the first day, she's giving everybody a pass. Miranda's frown turns to a smile when Shelly asks, "Can I sit with you?"

The door snaps shut and the motor lumbers up to speed, leaving Hidden Acres behind in a haze of road dust. The bus climbs back over the rise and down the little valley and rolls to the stop sign where Mrs. B carefully looks both ways before turning south on the highway.

Kaitlynn wants to know what everybody did for summer vacation, because her family just returned from a *fabulous* two weeks at Yellowstone and Glacier National Parks. Matthew shrugs when she asks him, and Bender claims he had to change his name and go into the witness protection program for two months.

Jay took a road trip to North Carolina with his grandparents, followed by a week at Pop Warner football camp. Spencer can top that: a physics camp in St. Louis that you had to have straight A's and three teacher recommendations to get into. Spencer plays down that part, but everybody knows he's brilliant.

Shelly is already thinking about next summer: "There's this two-week program in Glendale, California—right next to Hollywood. It's called Shooting Star camp. This really cute guy who plays bass in a band called Schrödinger's Reptile—he caught my act at the fair and he said I should definitely try to get in. So I sent for the application."

"You're bound to get in," Miranda says. "Just send them a DVD of your fair show."

"Oh, that was amateur," Shelly says. "For a real demo, I've got to rent a studio—"

"Hey!" Igor breaks into the conversation. "We went to Disney World. In Florida. The whole family." He jumps up and begins singing "It's A Small World After All."

"Sit down, Igor!" Mrs. B calls from the front.

The bus is slowing down, signaling a turn.

Kaitlynn sits up so quickly her glasses bounce. She stretches her neck and twitches her nose like a rabbit. "We've never stopped here before!"

Mrs. B has made a right turn, and a green sign flashes by: Farm Road 152. For about a quarter of a mile, the bus shudders down a gravel lane pitted with washouts, coming to a crossroads. Three mailboxes are lined up on a board at the southwest corner of the intersection, the names on them so faded they can't be read. No houses in sight, but at the opposite corner sits a neat little three-sided shed, with a peaked shingled roof and a bench inside where one can wait for the bus on a windy or rainy day.

But no one is waiting there.

Mrs. B pulls even with the shed. Then, with her signal beeping, she backs into the crossroads. After a short pause, she heads out the way they came, up the bumpy gravel road toward the highway.

"What's up with that?" Bender yells from the back seat. "Is there a new kid on the route?"

"Supposed to be," Mrs. B replies. And that's all she'll say, even though Kaitlynn wants to know who the new kid is, or at least what's its name, and is it a girl or a boy and what grade is it in? Mrs. B doesn't say, only gooses the accelerator after reaching the highway. Before long, everybody forgets about the new stop, and the robbery and the police car, because it's the first day of school and other thoughts crowd their minds. Such as:

I need to set my own goals this year—but how?

Does Penelope Gage still hate me?

Did Mr. Kennedy ever figure out I'm the one who let the gerbil out of its cage and it died under his desk and stunk up the whole science room?

Am I going to do something great this year?

Can I sneak into school without catching the eye of Jeremy Castle, who promised to beat me up the next time I cross his path?

How can I get somebody important to notice me?

How can I get Coach Baker to not notice me?

Why doesn't everybody just leave me alone?

It's only eight miles to school, but with all the curves and hills and stops along the route, the trip will take twenty-five minutes on average. So the riders who got on at Hidden Acres are stuck with each other for nearly an hour each day, round-trip, and everyone thinks they know all they need to know about everyone else. But they're wrong.

Because somebody on this bus is going to be famous.

September

Shelly Alvarez is sure she's going to be famous someday. "Oh baby baby, I need your looove!" she belts out, standing in the aisle at the center of the bus as she swings her long black hair.

It's the third week of school. Last night, fall rode in on the back of a strong west wind, and everybody is wearing jackets this morning. The air snaps, putting an extra decibel in Shelly's voice. "I need your love toniiiiiight!"

"I need you to shut up right naowwwwww!" Bender howls from the rear of the bus, the last syllable sounding like a wolf with its tail caught in the emergency door.

Shelly laughs as she drops into her seat. "Just wait till I get back from Shooting Star Camp. I'll probably add a whole octave to my vocal range."

She doesn't hear his reply, because Miranda just asked if she's met the new girl yet.

"Nope." Shelly bounces up again and stretches over the

empty seat in front of her so she can tap the new girl on the shoulder. "Hi. I'm Shelly Alvarez, but I go by Shell. That's my stage name. I don't plan to use the Alvarez. Just Shell, as in, 'Did you guys go to the Shell concert Saturday night?' 'Yes! Omigosh, it was *awesome*. I love the way she sings "Destiny Street"—"Oh I'm motoring down—ninety miles an hour!" And what they did for a finale was—'"

"Everybody sit down!" Mrs. B yells over her shoulder.

"I'm…Alice?" the new girl says. She has pale hair and pale eyelashes that give her green eyes a startled look. She takes a deep breath and rattles off, as though she's said this many times before, "I'm staying with my grandma, Mary Ellen Truman, in the stone house on top of—"

"Gotta sit down. Catch you later." Shelly wiggles her fingers and drops back in her seat beside Miranda. "Okay, I met her."

Miranda is giggling. "Shelly, you're insane!"

"It's *Shell*, remember. I'll probably change that, though. *Shell* is over too quick, you know? You miss it if somebody's talking fast. Like, 'You guys gototheShellconcertlastnight?' Did you hear the name? No!"

"What about using your middle name?"

"Are you serious?"

Miranda smiles and raises her shoulders, like an apology. "I think it's pretty."

"*Guadalupe?* First, it's too long. Second, it'll be shortened to Lupe, which comes out Loopy. No way." Miranda smiles and shrugs again. "Maybe I need three syllables, like yours. Only your name is a little—no offense, but kind of old-fashioned? I'm thinking something sweet, like Caramel."

"Or...spicy, like Cinnamon?"

"Or spiky, like Porcupine?" That voice comes from behind them. Their two heads turn to Matthew, who's sitting in the middle of the seat and looks surprised he said anything—especially the kind of remark that usually comes from Bender.

"Who asked you?" the girls say, almost together, then burst out in giggles as they turn back around.

"That was perfect," says Miranda. "Like we're thinking together."

Shelly nods, but she's already miles away from this seat in the middle of the bus—years away, really, under the hot lights of some big arena where they have championship basketball games and figure skating. But tonight: *Ladies and gentlemen, please welcome:*

CARAMEL!

Screams, cheers—a beam of light spikes the electric figure with the long swingy hair and silver miniskirt, sweeping up the crowd in a big hug before snatching the mic and—

Wait a minute. Caramel wasn't the kind of word you could shout over and over. Car-a-*mel!* Car-a-*mel!* Besides, there were two different ways to say it. Maybe two syllables were better, and stick with something that everybody said the same way. Like Brandi. Bran-DEE! Bran-DEE! Bran—

"Pipe down back there!" Mrs. B yells from the front. Shelly blinks, as though her fans were raising a ruckus outside her own head. But the driver is yelling at Igor, who has thrown up his hands and screams like he's on a roller coaster as the bus starts down the long steep hill toward Drybed Creek. He's done that for three days in a row.

"Do you think Igor's too young for fifth grade?" asks Miranda.

Shelly glances across the aisle where Igor is leaning forward, resting his chin on the seat ahead of him, his tongue flopped out and eyes crossed for the littles. His dark glossy hair comes to a widow's peak in the middle of his forehead, and his snappy gray eyes are fringed with long dark lashes. "He's too young for second grade," she says. "But he's kinda cute."

"Cute?!" Miranda sputters. "I wouldn't think he was cute even if…if I found him on a Hello Kitty lunchbox."

Shelly laughs, but soon she's time-traveling again, this time to the past—to the magic moment last May when she pulled triumph from tragedy at the Spring Talent Fling.

The Fling is always held on the last day of school, when everybody has their minds on swimming and summer camp and hanging out for days on end. Shelly was scheduled for last on the program, after the audience had fidgeted through a few hundred (not really, but it sure seemed like it) lip-sync acts and piano pieces and even Davy Blair playing "Twinkle, Twinkle" on his violin. She had to admit, that took some guts—to keep playing even after kids had started throwing pencil erasers at him.

By Shelly's turn, the natives were really restless. She asked Mr. Manchuso, who was manning the sound system, to bump it up. The thump-thump-thump of the intro got everyone's attention. Then she *electrified* them by cartwheeling out in her silver-sequined leotard (ordered from Footlight Magic Dancewear). She grabbed the mic and busted out with "What's Got Into You?" (No lip sync for Shelly—her dad said she could raise the roof on a barn without the aid of electronics.) But she was only seven bars into the song when the sound cut out.

Like, totally. She learned later that the cord to the main speaker jack had disconnected somehow—maybe an accident, like somebody kicked it while running backstage. Shelly suspected sabotage, even though she couldn't prove it. But that's not the great thing.

The great thing was, she didn't miss a beat. She found the beat *inside her*—the drums, the keyboard, the bass, the reverb. She felt the pulse in her boot heels as they stomped the stage, her long hair swinging like a curtain. She *kept on singing*, and a few kids in the front row started clapping in rhythm, and then more and more, as a kind of fever swept through the room. When the speaker got reconnected and the sound blasted out, right on the beat, her audience went *crazy*. By the second refrain, they were on their feet, clapping, stomping, hollering "Whoo-ot!"

She could have taken four or five bows and an encore if Mrs. Jasper hadn't cut it short. "A star is born," the teacher said, though she didn't sound exactly thrilled. Like Shelly might let triumph go to her head.

It went to her heart. She should have freaked out when the music stopped, but she didn't. That's because there was no stopping the music inside, pumping through her so strong she could sweep a cafeteria full of kids right along wherever she went.

She was so *there* she never wants to be anywhere else.

That's what people don't understand: they think she's just a show-off. Uncle Mike, who surprised her once while she was practicing in the backyard, can't stop calling her Shelly Vanilli, after some old one-hit-wonder rap duo. Eventually, even her dad said something about letting it go to her head. And Evan…ew. She'd prefer not to think about Evan. It's a good thing Mrs. B makes the younger kids sit at the front of the bus, in case Shelly's tempted to commit little-brother-slaughter on the route. Not that she wasn't tempted other times, like a few weeks ago, when he stole one of her costumes and made a wig out of black yarn and put on a show after dinner with a broom handle for a microphone. And his friend Simon Killebrew pretended to be all the fans, screaming and throwing themselves at the stage. Dad thought it was pretty funny. Even Mom laughed, though she hasn't been feeling well lately.

Her parents are always telling her not to take herself so seriously. She'd like to know how she was ever going to go pro without taking herself seriously? Show business is hard work, and she'd better start right now, figuring out how to get auditions and—

"*What?*"

"Sorry." Miranda shrinks back a little. "I just asked if you think Bender's going to get in trouble this year."

"He's always in trouble. Why should this year be any different?"

"Do you think he's cute?"

Shelly makes a barfing noise. "If anybody's cute on this bus, like real-guy cute, it's Jay." Jay's grown two inches over the summer, and his face is squaring up, with a strong jawline and black eyebrows and a nose that's getting beaky.

"I agree!" Miranda agrees. "And he's nice too. Mostly. It's too bad about his eyes."

Shelly glances back at Jay. "What's wrong with his eyes?" They're blue, with a twinkle.

"Didn't you hear? He started copying down page numbers wrong from the whiteboard, so his parents made him get his eyes checked, and he's going to have to wear glasses."

"So what's wrong with that? He'd look good with glasses."

"But he wants to play junior varsity next year!"

"I *know*. It's all he talks about, being a running back. So how hard is it to see who he's throwing the ball to?"

Miranda pauses. "I think the quarterback throws the ball. The running back—"

"—catches the ball. Riiiight. Okay, that's too bad." Shelly spares a moment of sympathy for Jay, who like herself, has ambitions. But her own plans need attention too.

Because she finally talked her parents into letting her apply for (drumroll, please) Shooting Star Camp in Glendale, California, which is an extremely big deal. *Two weeks of intensive training with industry professionals*, according to the website. Ever since she heard about it, she's been pestering her parents.

Well, "pester" is the way they put it. But she's just trying to make them see how important it is: "Meadow Ballinger went there! And Justin Riley said he got the training to launch his career from there! It's a golden opportunity!" It also costs $1,700, which made her dad spit out a mouthful of coffee when she told him. Does she know how much a high school Spanish teacher makes? Even when added to what a Staples store manager makes? And how big a bite her dance and voice lessons take out of that?

But finally—finally!—the 'rents agreed to let her apply, just to see if she gets in. The competition is so tough they think she won't. But she'll show them. An amazing demo, good recommendation letters, and performance credits would all be factors in getting in. That's why she needs some gigs—

Across the aisle, Igor pops up and twists around, holding a sign. It's actually just a piece of notebook paper sloppily hand-lettered. Because of what Shelly has just been told, she knows it's meant for Jay: IF U CANT C THIS UR GOING BLIND.

From the back, Jay's rolled-up jacket, sleeves fluttering, shoots directly at Igor, who ducks in time. "Igor, sit down!" yells Mrs. B.

"But I didn't—"

"Sit *down!*"

"It was Bender's idea!"

"Do you want me to stop this bus?"

Shelly sighs. It's hard getting famous while stuck on a school bus for an hour every day. But she doesn't yet know how hard it can be.

* * *

Exactly one week later, she knows.

Mrs. B is just about to pull the door shut on Tuesday morning when Shelly stomps down the street, her backpack bouncing fiercely with every step. She hears the driver mutter, "Take your time, dearie," as she stalks down the aisle and drops beside Miranda.

Bender sneaks up a couple of rows, grabs a granola bar that's sticking out of Igor's backpack, and uses it as a microphone to belt out, "Baby baby, I'm sooo mad!"

"Hey!" yells Igor as Shelly swings her own backpack at Bender and the granola bar spins off into oblivion.

"Everybody *sit down!*" hollers Mrs. B. "Or this bus ain't goin' nowhere!"

"Promise?" says Bender.

"But—" Igor, meeting the driver's eyes in the rearview mirror, sits.

"What's the matter?" Miranda murmurs to Shelly.

Shelly is almost too mad to talk. But she has to or else explode. "So Jay thinks he's got it bad? My career is *over*."

"What?"

"Okay, so it might be. It's the worst."

"What's the worst?"

"The worst thing that could happen."

"What happened?"

"The worst!"

"But what *is* it?"

Shelly pauses, biting her lip, then takes a deep breath and spits out, "My mom is having a baby."

"Oh!" Miranda says in surprise, adding in confusion, "Is that bad? I mean," she hurries on, as Shelly glares at her, "I thought you were going to say your parents were getting divorced or you had to move to South America, but babies are…Igor has a baby sister who just started crawling and she's *so* cute. I went over to watch the little ones last Saturday when Igor's mom had a bad headache. I changed the baby's diapers and everything. It's not so bad. If you have to babysit sometimes, I could help, or…"

Shelly moans. Miranda doesn't understand, being an only child and not destined for stardom. "It's like this. They tried to make it this rah-rah we're-so-happy big deal, but I *know* they didn't plan to have a baby now. Or ever, probably."

"But…why is it bad for you?"

"Two things. Number one, they're going to need my rehearsal room so they can put the crib and changing table and all that junk that goes along with a baby in there."

This hurts: her rehearsal room (which the 'rents insist on calling "the spare bedroom") is the only place she can work out her routines in private, where not even Uncle Mike could barge in. There's a mirror on the closet door and enough space to turn cartwheels and practice her signature slow-mo headbang that makes her hair spray out like a fan. And now they were going to fill it up with stuffed animals and diapers. Ick.

But that's not even the worst thing. "The worst thing is, my mom's going to quit her job in February so they'll have

25

time to train another manager before the baby comes. That means no money to spare, just when I need tuition for camp. Oh, and I also have to buy the camp workout suit and leotard and T-shirt…" Here, she has to stop and catch her breath. She cried her eyes out the night before, after a supersize blowup with her parents. It's amazing she has any tears left. "So," she chokes out, "there's no way we can afford Shooting Star Camp."

"Oh, Shelly!" That finally gets Miranda's sympathy. "Are you sure?"

Shelly sniffs, sucking it up, forcing herself to recall the logical steps her dad had ticked off on his fingers last night. "My mom quits in February and isn't going back to work for at least a year. Baby's due in March, and there're gonna be bills the insurance won't cover. No money left over. End of story."

"Maybe next year, then?"

"But camp is every *other* year! That means I won't get another chance until I'm fourteen, and all the kids who got to go this year will be way ahead of me and they'll know each other and the coaches and agents and…"

She's getting worked up again, like last night, when her dad had stopped being reasonable and ordered her to her room: *And don't come out until you're ready to apologize!* Seeing nothing to apologize for, she didn't come out until this morning.

"Are you sure there's no way?" Miranda looks really sympathetic now. It makes Shelly glad to have her for a listening friend. "Like, maybe if you could raise half of the money? I could help you do a bake sale. I like to bake."

Yeah, it's easy to see that. Miranda is kind of round. "But half of seventeen hundred dollars is eight hundred dollars I have to raise!"

"Actually…I think it's eight hundred fifty."

"Whatever. How many cupcakes with sprinkles does that add up to? A *lot*."

"Well…maybe a car wash?"

"Right." Shelly catches herself biting her nails, a habit she's trying to break. "Maybe a thousand-dollar scratch-off ticket."

"When did you say the baby was due?" asks Miranda.

"What? Oh, I don't know. Sometime in March, I forget the date."

"Do you think they'd let me watch it sometime?"

"Sure, come on over and watch it anytime you want. But I don't think babies do much at first."

✳ ✳ ✳

Next morning, when Shelly gets on the bus, Spencer is telling everybody he got accepted into space camp for the following summer. His good news would have made her feel worse about her bad news, but today her attitude has done a one-eighty turn. She has a plan. Cheerful as a chickadee, she slides in beside Miranda. "Hey, what are you good at?"

Miranda blinks in surprise. "Uh…not much. I can cook, like when my mom works late at the nursing home and I have to—"

"No, I mean in school. What's your best subject?"

27

"Oh. Language arts, definitely. Remember I won the school-wide spelling bee last year?"

"Right." Actually Shelly doesn't remember anything about Miranda from last year, except that she hung out with that snotty rich kid, Penelope Gage. "That's perfect, because I can't spell. I've got a plan—you want to hear it?"

"Sure!" Miranda's face brightens.

"This morning, Dad told me he looked up the camp website and found out that they give scholarships. A *limited number*. And I might get one if I bring my grades up and do some volunteer work and have my teachers and youth pastor and glee coach write letters saying I'm the greatest thing since spandex."

"That's…that's terrific," says Miranda, trying to be tactful. "I guess the main thing is the grades." Shelly's grades aren't the best.

"That's what my dad says. I'll still have to raise money because the scholarships are only good for about half of it. I go, 'Okay, so like if I get a scholarship for half the tuition, will you guys pay the rest?' And he goes, 'Half the rest. No more than *half*. You earn one-quarter of the total—that's about five hundred, because we have to pay airfare—and that'll tell us that you're really serious about this.' Like I can't just *tell* him I'm really serious. Anyway, I'll need to bring my grades up a little, so I was wondering if you could help me out with language arts stuff? Like, after school sometimes?"

"Okay. Sure!" Miranda beams, like she was just asked to ride the homecoming float holding a dozen roses. Shelly's thinking it's sweet that she wants to help when Kaitlynn pops into the seat in front of them. "I heard you were going to try for a scholarship to Star Camp!"

"*Shooting* Star Camp," Shelly corrects her, glancing at Miranda who raises her eyebrows. "How'd you hear that?"

"Your mom told my mom. And congratulations about the baby! Babies are fun. Except when they have colic and cry all night like my brother Steven did for the first three months."

"Weren't you sitting somewhere else?" Shelly asks. Kaitlynn's wheels are always spinning so fast she doesn't have a clue how uncool she is, with her stuck-out ears and headbands and skirts that ride low on her skinny hips.

"Just let me tell you my idea. If you want a scholarship, you need lots of service projects. So why don't you run for Youth Court? I'll nominate you."

Shelly opens her mouth with an automatic *no*, then hesitates. That's actually a good point, about service projects. Youth Court is made up of five sixth-graders (plus two alternates) who meet once a week to hear complaints that kids bring up against each other, like bullying, fighting, stealing, and things like that. Candidates have to be nominated by two classmates and a teacher, and the campaign runs from mid-October to the first Tuesday in November.

"I want to run for Youth Court next year," Kaitlynn is saying, "but I can't this year, so I'll manage your campaign. It'll be good experience for me, and it'll help you get a scholarship even if you don't win. I've got a great idea for a campaign song—"

"Please," Shelly interrupts. "Nobody writes my songs but me. So I'll think about it, okay?" She turns deliberately to Miranda. "Now, my other bad subject is math, unless you count social studies and science. Do you know anybody who's good at math? Like, somebody on this bus?"

Miranda glances around then leans in and lowers her voice—even though, with the groan of the bus as it slows to make the turn onto Farm Road 152, a secret-service listening device couldn't have picked her up. "Actually, Bender is really good at math."

The back tire hits a pothole on the gravel road, making Shelly's next word jump out like a scared rabbit. "Bender?! He's *good* at something?"

"Shhhh!" Miranda wiggles her fingers but it's too late. The subject under discussion creeps up and slides into the seat behind them while Mrs. B isn't looking.

"Did I hear my name?"

"Did you?" Shelly turns around and flutters her eyelashes. "I was talking about *blenders*. And how your head would look in one." His head is large, and usually there's a lock of dark hair flopping over his wide forehead that always looks dirty. The hair, that is.

"Haw haw." Bender glances out the window at the little shed that swings into view when the bus backs up. "What's up with this stop?" he yells at the driver. "It's been three weeks now, and there's never anybody here!"

"Sit down, Bender!" Mrs. B calls back, even though he's not standing up.

He heaves a mighty sigh and throws himself back into his usual seat. From there, he carries on the dispute with Mrs. B as she pulls away from the shed and starts back up the gravel road. "We average two minutes and forty-three seconds a day doing this! Do you know how much that is for the whole year?"

"How do you know he's good at math?" Shelly asks Miranda.

Miranda stares at her. "Didn't you hear what he just said?"

"...Four hundred eighty-nine minutes!" Bender is saying as he tucks a rolled-up strip of paper behind his ear. "That's eight-point-fifteen hours of extra sleep I could get if we didn't have to make this stupid stop!"

"Thank you for the update, Bender," Mrs. B says while looking both ways at the stop sign. "Now go back to sleep."

"He says that kind of stuff all the time," Miranda murmurs. "Some of the kids think he uses a hidden calculator but I think he mostly does it in his head."

"What if he's just making up numbers?"

"You mean you never noticed?"

"*Please.* I'm working on a career. I've got to stay focused. Besides, there's no way I'm asking *him* to be my math tutor. I'll just skip math—can't be good at everything, right? What do you think I could do for volunteer work? Hey, doesn't your mom work at a nursing home?"

"Uh-huh. She's a physical therapist. She's at Sunset Hills two days a week."

"Perfect. Ask her what I can do to cheer up old people. That's always a good volunteer thing. I know!" Shelly sits up straight as she answers her own question. "I could put on a show!"

* * *

"What kind of show?" Shelly's mom asks when she springs the idea next morning at breakfast.

"My kind."

"Could I have eggs and bacon?" Evan asks. "Cereal just makes me hungry."

Mrs. Alvarez groans. "Sorry, sweetheart. I can barely tolerate the *words* eggs and bacon these days." She's having what she calls morning sickness, another complication of having a baby that Shelly finds totally gross.

"Please, Mom?" Shelly pleads. "Miranda already talked to her mother and they can set it up for next Thursday after bingo."

"I don't know, Shelly," says her mom. "These are senior citizens. They're into Frank Sinatra and Perry Como, not Claire."

"Can't I at least have some sausage?" Evan whines. "Or cheese fries?"

Mrs. Alvarez gags and makes a dash for the bathroom. Dad takes over. "How about you just do something short and simple. Like 'The Good Ship Lollipop.' That was cute when you did it for the Elks Club."

"That was ages ago! I was, like, seven years old! I'm so not that performer anymore!"

Her dad takes a deep breath. "Shelly, the whole point behind volunteer work is that you're doing it for somebody else. Not just to get something for yourself. If you're going to do this, then put on a show they'll like."

"Okay, okay. I'll pick the music tonight."

"Not more than twenty minutes," he warns. "They get drowsy in the afternoon."

"*Okay*," Shelly says again, wondering how anybody could get drowsy while she's onstage.

* * *

Miranda's the one who has to take Shelly's overstuffed gym bag to the gazebo and wrestle it onto the bus next Thursday morning. That's because Shelly smuggled all the contents—costume, Mylar curtain, Mylar pompoms, and two box lights—to Miranda's house the night before. Her parents insist she doesn't need lights and props for a nursing home show where most of the audience will be asleep by the end. So they think.

"Are you moving to town, Miranda?" asks Mrs. B as the girl struggles up the steps with a bag that looks like it might be holding a janitor-sized vacuum cleaner and maybe the janitor too.

"No, I—"

"That's my equipment," Shelly explains, boosting the bag from the rear. "I've got a gig."

"What's a gig?" Igor asks from behind where the boys are waiting.

"It's some kind of noose, I think," Jay says. Self-consciously, he adjusts his glasses. It's his first day to wear them, and he keeps glancing around to see if anybody notices. Shelly thinks he looks dignified and serious, like the president of the United States in a movie.

"No, she means gag," says Bender. "She needs a gag."

"Shut up, Bender," Shelly snaps.

"A 'gig,'" explains Spencer, doing his learned-professor imitation, "is a term used by musicians of the popular sort, meaning an engagement, or in the vernacular, a 'job.'" His dad is a musician—Shelly's guitar teacher, in fact.

"Everybody move along," says Mrs. B. "Find a seat."

Shelly and Miranda find one together, parking the gym bag on the seat in front of them.

"Hey, Jay," Igor calls from the back. "Look."

Everybody looks where Igor is pointing out the near window. Jay's grandfather is standing in front of the gazebo, Panzer's leash looped through his arm while the dog noses in the grass. The old man is holding a sign: *IF YOU CAN READ THIS YOUR A GREAT RUNNING BACK. KNOCK 'EM DEAD JAY PASTERNAK III, MVP.*

"Oh," sighs Miranda after a moment. "That's really sweet."

Shelly nods, meanwhile wondering if Mr. Pasternak usually wears his house slippers to walk the dog. Jay bites his upper lip and releases the catch on the nearest window. Forcing it down, he sticks out his fist with the thumb up.

"Okay," says Mrs. B in a tone unusually gruff. "Let's get this show on the road."

Speaking of show… Shelly shares a glance with Miranda,

knowing they both see Mr. Pasternak's sign as a good omen: *Knock 'em dead!* (Though not too dead, since it's a nursing home.)

"Hey, I just thought," she says as the bus rolls toward the highway. "You can do my intro."

"You mean, 'Here's Shelly'? I think the activity director's going to do that."

"No, I mean you could do some kind of opening act. Like all the pros have a warm-up band to get the crowd pumped. You could sing 'The Star-Spangled Banner' or something."

Miranda actually turns pale. "Or I could throw up or something. I *hate* to get in front of a bunch of people."

"Okay, okay." Shelly is feeling a little nervous herself. This is the first show she's ever done all on her own, and she's thinking it might be nice to have someone to share the glory. Or blame. But she should have thought of it before now.

"Shelly?" Miranda asks. "Are you scared?"

"Scared? No—it's just a show. I've done lots of 'em."

* * *

But not quite like this. For one thing, they don't have the time or equipment to set up her Mylar curtain properly or her box lights at all. Charlotte, the activity director, doesn't seem to understand why she needs a Mylar curtain, so Shelly tries to explain: "It's one of my signatures. Every performer has a signature, to kind of say who they are and get the show off to a good start. I have to burst through the curtain and get the audience all jazzed."

"Honey, it'll take a lot more than a long silver fringe to get this audience jazzed," Charlotte says. But she finds a roll of duct tape and a couple of brooms so the girls can prop up Shelly's signature between two folding chairs. Meanwhile, Charlotte and a volunteer put away the bingo cards and rearrange the residents.

What Charlotte will not do is give a proper intro. Instead of *Ladies and gentlemen, please welcome…SHELL!*, Charlotte merely says, "Shelly Alvarez was very sweet to come over today and sing a few songs for us. Let's give her a warm Sunset Hills welcome."

And how, thinks Shelly, was anybody going to get pumped over that? But she nods to Miranda over at the boom box, takes a deep breath, and bursts through the Mylar curtain to the opening strains of…the weather report: "…CLOUDY with a fifty percent chance of showers…"

"Sorry," says Miranda after turning down the volume. "That's the radio."

Shelly feels her face burning as she backs through the curtain, followed by a few titters from the audience. "I thought you had it figured out!" she hisses at Miranda.

"I did!" Miranda hisses back. "I do. It was just a mistake—I said I was sorry."

Shelly sighs impatiently. "Ready *now?*"

Miranda nods, pressing her lips together. At the signal, she pushes the play button, and Shelly bursts through the curtain to the crashing chords of "Bleeding Heart." Only the chords don't crash because the volume is still turned down. The unexpected quietness throws Shelly off-stride, literally—she bumps the curtain frame slapped up with duct tape and brings it down.

Miranda cuts the sound again. "Sorry." Her face almost matches the bright-red chili peppers on her Sedona, Arizona, T-shirt.

Members of the audience are beginning to murmur in sympathy: "That's all right, honey." "Poor little thing."

Shelly would almost rather they laughed at her. She grabs the mic off its stand and speaks into it: "Ladies and gentlemen, I'm going to start with Claire's latest hit, 'Bleeding Heart.'"

She's a trouper. She puts everything she has into "Bleeding Heart," leaving the audience so stunned at the end they can barely clap. Except for the guy over by the window, who isn't old, so he must have been kind of mentally handicapped or something—he stomps and pounds the arm of his wheelchair and shouts, "Yeah! Rock 'n' roll!" until the ladies nearby manage to shush him: "That's enough, Larry!" "Larry! Pipe down!"

Shelly goes into "Fantasy Land," followed by "Razzle-Dazzle," where she wanted to light a handful of sparklers and twirl around the stage area (a big hit at the county fair last summer), but Charlotte has already said No way. Shelly anticipated that; it's why she brought the silver and purple pompoms. She's head-banging through the final riff when Charlotte, who'd left after the intro, suddenly appears at the back of the room and shouts, "That's great, Shelly, we really appreciate your coming. Now maybe you could finish up with something a little quieter?"

There are two more songs on her program, neither of them especially quiet. But Shelly can take a hint. She signals to Miranda to change the CD, and she finishes with "The Good Ship Lollipop," which gets a nice round of applause. Larry stomps and shouts "Yeah!" just like the other time, so she guesses he's not a Claire fan.

"That was very nice, thanks again," Charlotte says before wheeling a resident out of the dining hall. No invitation to please come back, like they'd begged her at the county fair.

In other words, she bombed. She's never bombed! And yes, it was mostly old people who weren't into that kind of music—but still, it bites.

Without a word, Miranda helps gather her stuff. Carrying the gym bag between them, they walk three blocks to the pediatric clinic where Miranda's mom is working today. They find seats in the almost-empty lobby, both so devastated—for different reasons—they don't notice the girl sitting across from them. She's the kind of girl it's easy not to notice.

Miranda speaks first. "...Alice?"

The girl looks up from her book, blinking. "Hi."

"What are you doing here?" That sounds a little rude, especially coming from Miranda, but Shelly doesn't even care enough to ask. The sooner she gets out of this nightmare, the better.

"I'm...waiting for my grandma." Alice's finger flicks one corner of a page in a way that gets on Shelly's nerves.

"Oh," Miranda says. "Is she a patient?"

Miranda must be pretty shook up too, Shelly thinks, to ask if Alice's grandma is a patient in a pediatric clinic.

"No," Alice says. "She's here with my—I mean, she's a volunteer." Abruptly, Alice returns to her book.

Shelly picks up a copy of *Highlights*, barely noticing a few minutes later when Mrs. Truman pushes out a boy in a wheelchair, and Alice jumps up as though she can't wait to leave. Shelly knows the feeling, but just as the sliding door opens and shut behind her, she wonders if she missed an opportunity.

Mrs. Truman, Alice's grandmother, once owned all the Hidden Acres property before selling it to Jay's grandfather for development. She's probably loaded—maybe Mrs. Truman would consider contributing to a worthy young performer's scholarship fund? Shelly doesn't get too far with that thought before Miranda's mother bustles into the waiting room with a smile as bright and wide as her polyester hips. "So, how did it…"

Her voice dwindles to nothing as she gets a good look at their faces.

Nobody says much on the way home. Miranda is probably feeling terrible. Which she should, after ruining the show.

"Do you need any help with your stuff?" she asks as they pull up in front of the Alvarez house.

Not from you, Shelly thinks but only shakes her head. She drags the gym bag out of the car and down the side of the house so she can sneak it in the back door. Hearing voices in the kitchen, she stashes it behind the washing machine to unpack later.

The voices belong to her mother and Uncle Mike—her least favorite relative. Like, all she needs to make this day just perfect is him. Mom puts on a smiley face when Shelly walks in. "Hi, honey! How was the show?"

"Fine." She crosses to the fridge to get a glass of orange juice, which she read somewhere is good for the throat after a performance. "They really liked the Lollipop song."

"What did I tell you?" The over-bright tone in her mother's voice tells Shelly (a little too late) that she's interrupted an argument.

"Did you do a show today, Beanpot?" That's Uncle Mike.

Shelly closes the door of the fridge and slowly turns. "I really, really hate it when you call me that."

He's the kind of guy who used to be cute—she's seen his high school pictures—but now he's sort of gone slack. Everything hangs on him: his jeans, his stubbly chin, his hairy belly peeking under a T-shirt that's too short. "Hey," he says, throwing up his hands. "It's a compliment. Little Mexican Beanpot—means you're cute and peppy and kind of brown—"

"That's enough, Mike," Mom interrupts. "Or I'll have to ask you to leave."

"Don't bother. *I'm* leaving." Shelly stalks through the kitchen and into the hallway—without the orange juice. The voices sharpen and speed up behind her until she cuts them off with a slam to the door.

She queues up Claire's latest album on her iPod, throws herself facedown on the bed, and sings into her pillow:

You think you know where I come from
but you don't have a clue;
Think you've got me on a string, but baby;
I've got a bead on you.

Claire probably understood about rotten relatives—she grew up in Arkansas with a house full of rowdy siblings. Had to fight her way to the top. She got her start in country and western, but fortunately all she kept of that phase were her signature white cowboy boots. Maybe Claire had a sucky nickname too. Shelly slams the mattress with her toes, remembering how Uncle Mike picked her up at school one day in third grade and nearly ruined her life by yelling across the front lawn, "Heeeeey, Beanpot!" That was all it took for her to get stuck with Beanpot for the next two years. Accompanied by farting noises.

Shelly clenches her fists. *They don't have a clue.* Claire overcame a lot to get where she is. *If she can do it*, Shelly thinks, *so can I. So can I!*

Her mother is knocking on the door even before the song is over. "Sorry about that," she says, sticking her head inside.

Shelly doesn't turn over. "Was it your fault?"

"In a way. I should have shown him the door as soon as he asked for a loan. Or as soon as I said no the first time."

"Must've made him mad. He hasn't called me a Mexican beanpot since I was eight." It was because her ears used to stick out like jug handles, and because her face was round and kind of brown.

"He's just a bigot, Shelly. And a has-been. His great-est days were in high school, when he got to run with the Molehill gang—"

"The Molehill gang?" Shelly pulls out one of her ear buds and turns over to look at her mother.

"Just the crowd he hung out with. They were into pranking. Their last one got him expelled—but never mind. The point is, Mike's not worth a second of your time."

"I know. I'm focused." But it's okay to feel bad once in awhile, isn't it? Sheesh.

"Good," her mother says. "Oh—I'm going to run a load of laundry after dinner. If you have anything to throw in, get it now."

As the door clicks shut, Shelly remembers what she'd left in the utility room. She'd better sneak those box lights into the garage before getting more unwelcome questions about the show. While her mother is putting dinner together, she quietly unpacks the gym bag and notices, for the first time, that one of her Mylar pompoms is missing.

✳ ✳ ✳

The next morning, Mrs. B is yawning her head off and doesn't ask about the gig. Bender does, but Shelly is used to ignoring him. Though she makes a point of not sitting with Miranda, she feels a tiny bit better. It's Friday, thank goodness, and by Monday, her flop will be ancient history. Besides, every enter-tainer has horror stories about bad acoustics or equipment malfunctions or tornadoes or whatever, and now she does too. Just like a pro.

Because she's sitting alone, Shelly pays a little more attention to what's going on outside the bus. Because she's bored, she can understand why Bender gets so bent out of shape when Mrs. B turns off on Farm Road 152. Because she's on the right side, she notices the little shed when the bus backs up alongside it, and suddenly her hands are clapped to the glass and her eyes are staring so hard they could pop right out of her head. It's like that guitar chord at the end of Claire's latest CD, when you think the last song is over: claaaaang!

On the corner post of the shed is a metal bracket, the kind people put on gates and doorposts to hold a flag. Stuck in the bracket is a purple and silver pompom, exactly like the one she left at Sunset Hills.

October

B ender was born to fame—just not his.

It started in kindergarten: "Are you Thorn Thompson's brother?" That's when John Thornton Thompson, otherwise known as Thorn, was the league soccer champion and the youngest representative ever to go to Boy's State Leadership Camp. By the time Bender got to fifth grade, the questions sounded skeptical: "Are *you* Thorn Thompson's *brother*? The guy who led his team to the state basketball championship and was a National Merit Scholar and is now at Dartmouth College on a full scholarship—are you sure you're related to him?"

But it's obvious: Bender is the image of Thorn but stamped after the inkpad was nearly dry so the image is paler and completely washed out on some of the lines. He's not so much overweight as puffy, with a face not ugly but forgettable. He doesn't do sports, and his grades are only so-so. While Thorn streaked through the Centerview school system in a blaze of glory, Bender just serves his time, count-ing the days until he can graduate. Counting hours too: by the time he graduates from high school, he figures he will have spent 1,848 hours on a school bus.

He did the math in fifth grade. First, he palmed a stopwatch from Mr. Finagle's office while getting a lecture for sneaking into the girls' locker room during a gym class and stuffing all the socks in the shower drains. Then he used the stopwatch to time bus rides to and from school, every day of the week. Then he divided by five to get the average number of minutes on the bus every day, multiplied by five days per week, thirty-six weeks in the school year, for eleven years, K–10 (by eleventh grade, he planned to have his own car and never set foot on a bus again). That made a total of 1,848 hours, which broke down to:

two months,

two weeks,

two days,

and fourteen minutes,

plus a few seconds, which he seldom counts. Seconds would matter if he were calculating a voyage to Jupiter, but for the next four years, he just wants to use up that time in ways that resemble Thorn Thompson's career as little as possible.

* * *

"Hey!" Igor blurts, stumbling to one side as Bender bumps him away from the back seat.

"I saw that, Bender," calls Mrs. B from the front, her eyes piercing the rearview mirror. "Igor, let it go—just find a seat."

Igor probably would have let it go on his own, since he's about three sizes smaller and two grades younger than Bender. But when Mrs. B tells him to, he has no choice but to do the opposite and punch Bender in the stomach on his way up the aisle. Bender's arm whips back so hard it nearly knocks Igor down. "OW!"

"Fight! Fight!" cheers Spencer.

"Boys! Do you want me to stop this bus and come back there?"

Igor says no, Bender says yes, but it's kind of under his breath. Mrs. B has never Stopped the Bus and Come Back There, but she's always threatening to. He kind of wants to know what would happen if she did, but maybe not today.

Matthew sits in the next-to-last seat, directly ahead. Bender studies his smooth dark neck and the sharp line made by his close-cropped hair and imagines drawing the hairline a little lower with a Sharpie pen. Would Matthew even notice? The guy seems to be in a world of his own most of the time.

Shelly has plopped down a few rows in front of Matthew while Miranda stops just past the middle. They haven't been speaking to each other for a week, ever since Shelly's nursing home gig—which, everybody gathers, did not go well. She's been huffy lately: probably arguing with her folks about Shoot the Star camp (as Bender calls it). Today her nose is so far in the air she doesn't notice he's sitting less than sixty inches behind her.

Bender takes the rolled-up paper from behind his ear and

clicks his mechanical pencil until a two-centimeter piece of graphite breaks off. Cupping his hand carefully around the paper tube, he sucks the lead inside, takes a breath, and spits it out.

Shelly whirls around, a hand on the back of her neck. "Bender!"

He's already unrolled the blowgun and is staring out the window looking bored. "What?"

It's perfect: just the right amount of irritation, not overdone. He's a pretty good performer, just not in a show-offy way like her.

"You plinked me!"

"*Plinked* you? How?"

Mrs. B is negotiating an S-curve and can't spare a glance in the mirror. That tiny piece of lead is invisibly rolling on the floor and nobody can prove anything. The perfect crime. He glances around and catches Jay nudging Spencer with a little grin. Bender frowns: *What are you smilin' at, punk?*

With both hands in his lap, he rerolls the strip of paper, breaks off another piece of graphite, and loads up his blowgun. It's intended for Jay, but at the last minute, he changes his target and swings over to Matthew.

Plink! Matthew puts a hand on his neck, on the hairline that Bender had contemplated lowering—but he doesn't turn around. What's with that kid?

Suddenly he notices the new girl, one row up on the opposite side. For the first week or so she was telling everybody her name—what was it, Alison? Or Alice?—and that she lived with her Grandma Mary Ellen Truman in the old stone house at the top of the hill, blah blah blah. That might have been interesting, because the Truman house was said to be haunted at one time. Old Mr. Truman's first wife had died there, and so had he—making one wonder about foul play from the second wife. But the second Mrs. Truman is so ordinary, with her bridge tournaments and golf dates and volunteer work, she gives haunted houses a bad name. Kids didn't even bother to make up stories about it anymore.

Her granddaughter Alison-or-Alice has a way of disappearing, like some wizard master gave her a cloak of invisibility. Her cloak is a book—she disappears into books. But right now, she's looking at Bender.

He backs up against the window and points his blowgun at her threateningly. Mrs. B picks that exact moment to glance up in the mirror and catch him taking aim. The gun isn't loaded but may as well be.

"I see that, Bender!"

Shelly spins around. "Aha! I knew that was you!"

Mrs. B makes him move to the front of the bus and surrender the weapon, which is stupid because it's just a rolled-up piece of paper. Mrs. B realizes that, of course, and knows he can make another one just by tearing off a strip from his notebook but takes it from him anyway. "Sit right there." She nods at the first seat while signaling for a right turn.

He considers reminding her of all the time they're wasting because she insists on making this stop—two minutes and forty-five seconds of his life every day that he'll never get back—but nothing he can say will discourage Mrs. B because he's already said it. He settles down to a bumpy ride on the gravel road. Soon the shelter will appear to which they pull even, pause, back up, head out—

Wait a minute! He sits up straighter. He sees something: a flash of red disappearing over the rise beyond the shelter. It was a person, he's sure of it: some kid or grown-up wearing something red, like a jacket. Or more likely a cap. Lifting his eyes, he notices, for the first time, a house. It was hidden by trees before, but now that the leaves are falling he can make out a roof, a corner, faded siding, peeling paint. He turns to Mrs. B, noticing her eyes twitching from the house to the road as her jaw sets like a trap. She saw the flash of red, just like he did. "Is that who we're supposed to pick up?"

"What?"

"The person wearing the red cap or whatever it was."

"Probably just a cardinal." Mrs. B keeps her eyes resolutely on the gravel road as the bus snarls into low gear for climbing the hill.

Bender glances behind him. Matthew is gazing out the opposite window, Shelly is singing to herself, and Miranda is trying to ignore Kaitlynn. Igor is in the middle of a game of keep-away with his Yankees cap, tossed by Jay and Spencer during that dead space while Mrs. B is scanning the highway before making a turn. Then Bender notices the new girl watching him again. Immediately, her eyes flicker away. The bus lumbers onto the highway. "Turn around, Bender," Mrs. B commands.

He turns around, facing forward again. What was that red thing? As bright as a cardinal, but bigger. He knows it was a person, and what's more, he's sure Mrs. B knows it too.

He doesn't realize it then, but at that moment, his nibbling curiosity opens its jaws and clamps down hard.

***

Ever since he was old enough to remember anything (which would have been at approximately three years, five months, two weeks, and four days), his head overflowed with numbers. He figured out how to multiply before any math teacher even brought up the subject; his times tables were no sooner said than memorized. Numbers were friendly and practical. For instance, if you took thirteen steps to the mailbox every day and thirteen steps back, that was twenty-six, and if 2,810 of your steps made one mile, you'd walk thirty-seven miles per year just going to the mailbox. Wasn't that worth knowing?

Bender is the one who goes to the mailbox because he used to get postcards from his grandmother, who traveled a lot. When he was in fourth grade, she took her last journey, as his mother put it (meaning she'd croaked), but the habit is so ingrained Bender still takes those thirteen steps to the mailbox every day, as though he might get a postcard from the great beyond.

One time, when she was visiting, he figured how fast her plane must have been going to get her from London to Kuala Lumpur in ten hours, twenty-three minutes. That was after she'd told him the approximate distance in kilometers. He was only ten years old, and he never even picked up a pencil except to write down the time in minutes. He did it in metric, which of course is easier to calculate, but his grandmother gave a little gasp when he told her the figure.

Then she fished a calculator out of her purse and started punching buttons. After a few seconds, she raised her head and stared at him. "Does your father know he has a potential Einstein in the house?"

He shrugged, not knowing what a potential Einstein was. And anyway, his father isn't around much. He's an insurance claims adjuster. Wherever there's a flood or tornado or hurricane, Dad has to go figure out what the property damage is and exactly how much the insurance company will pay. Numbers—with dollar signs attached—make up Dad's job, and when he comes home he retreats to the woodworking shop in the garage and measures and cuts wood for furniture his mother then has to figure out where to put. He made the bunk beds in Bender's room, for when friends sleep over. Which they never do because they don't exist.

Anyway, with all the numbers crowding his work and his hobby, Dad tunes them out during his downtime. That's why Bender has never shared his potential. All that figuring he can do in his head stays there, except for the numbers that leak out on the bus, when nobody's listening.

* * *

The first Friday in October, Shelly bounds onto the bus after almost everyone has boarded, whips out a couple of drumsticks, and beats a tattoo on the back of the front seat.

"Excuse me?" says Mrs. B.

"Attention, everybody! I hereby announce my candidacy for Youth Court! With liberty and justice for all!"

"What?" Spencer springs up from his seat. "*I'm* running for Youth Court!"

"Nothing like competition," smiles Shelly. "Please make room for my campaign manager."

Miranda squeezes past her and starts handing out fliers, even to the kindergartners who can't read. "Vote for Shelly," she says. "Vote for Shelly. Vote for—" Apparently they're friends again, and Miranda looks happy as a pig in slop, as Bender's mother likes to say. Sweet.

Spencer, on the other hand, is almost spitting. "How come you're so civic-minded all of a sudden? You couldn't care less about Youth Court! This is just résumé enhancement, right?"

"Whatever." Shelly smiles even harder. "Now for a preview of my campaign song—"

"Oh no, you don't," Mrs. B cuts in. "Time to motor. Sit!"

Everybody sits, but Spencer is so hot you can almost see steam coming off him. Bender grins to himself—it looks like an interesting ride for a change. He waits until the bus has reached the highway before raising his hand. "I have an announcement too: my vote is for sale."

Kaitlynn turns around to tell him he doesn't have a vote because he's in seventh grade and junior high kids don't have anything to do with middle-grade youth court, blah blah—and he says, "Didn't you ever hear of voter fraud?"

Spencer spins halfway around and points at Shelly. "That's exactly what I mean! She'll turn this campaign into *Entertainment Tonight!*"

"Chill, dude," says Jay beside him.

Shelly turns her head and flutters her eyelashes at Bender. "Just for you, a special solo."

"See? She doesn't even care!" Spencer yells.

They continue the argument, Shelly insisting she's always cared about justice and Spencer demanding she prove it, all the way to Farm Road 152 and down the hill. The bus backs up as usual, the three mailboxes scroll by—

Wait a minute.

The center mailbox has something tucked between the flag and the box: a large sheet of white paper or maybe poster board, rolled into a cylinder that sticks out about fourteen inches from the mailbox, like a giant cigarette or—

Bender feels a sting on his neck and claps his hand over a small, damp lump. A *spitwad?* From where? Across the aisle, Matthew is staring out the window, Alice-or-Alison is buried in a book, and Igor is bouncing in his seat, calling out, "Vote for Shelly! No, vote for Spencer!"

Igor owes Bender one—actually several. But so does Matthew. Which of them blew the spitwad? The bus makes a jerk and pulls forward, redirecting his attention to the back window. That tube of paper stuck in the mailbox looks like a giant blowgun.

Everybody knows his habit of rolling up pieces of paper after writing on them, but nobody knows why. He writes numbers he sees, like the mileage from St. Louis to Chicago or the capacity in gallons of a ten-foot-diameter wading pool. Then he invents word problems for them (in his head) and solves the problems (also in his head). But nobody knows that. Or do they?

The paper is stuck on the mailbox exactly like he sometimes tucks the rolls of paper over his ear. What if it's a sign? What if there were special numbers written on that paper that only he could understand? Or is that totally crazy?

Bender's thoughts come thick and fast as the bus climbs toward the highway. Who put—Why is it—What is it—Could it be for him?

Vote for Shelly! Vote for Spencer!

The faster his thoughts come, the more they jab at him like tiny bat claws. He can't just sit here. He can't let this go by—it might be really important! The bat claws dig into his brain until he can't stand it: *Out! Out!* they tell him. *Get off the bus, check it out.* His eyes lock on the rear door.

Emergency exit. Do not open. Yeah, yeah. Alarms will go off, all that. No way can he *sneak* off the bus. But if he hits the ground running, he'll be all the way to the mailbox before Mrs. B backs up; he can grab the paper, and if there's anything on it, he might even have time to stuff it in his jacket.

The bus is at the highway, right blinker on. Bender eyes the handle of the emergency door; it's actually no stranger to him. He's imagined opening it many times, just to see what would happen. He's even checked out the mechanism and located the safety latch underneath the handle. But now that he has a reason to open it, his nerves are jittering: does he dare? Does he have the nerve to *act* on some of the crazy thoughts he's had? Nobody's looking. Mrs. B's head is turned to the left, waiting for a van to pass. If he listens closely, he can imagine the right turn blinker chanting, *Now! Now! Now!*

Or maybe that's his pounding heart—*NOW!*

The bus wheels crunch as Mrs. B presses the accelerator. Bender jumps for the handle, pushes the safety latch, jerks the handle up, swings the door open, and leaps.

The alarm bells in his head are so loud he can't hear the real alarm. So far so good—

But his plan to hit the ground running doesn't work out too well. There's a technique to landing on one's feet, which Bender has never practiced. Instead of running, he stumbles and falls, moaning as pain shoots from ankle to hip.

The bus rolls back, and for a terrifying second (he'd never thought old Big Yellow could look so HUGE), he thinks it might just roll over him. Then Mrs. B sets the brake. Faces appear around the edge of the doorway: Alice-or-Alison, Jay, Spencer, Kaitlynn, Shelly's little brother, Evan, and Kaitlynn's little brother, Simon, all with wide eyes and open mouths.

Igor pops through the crowd. "Cool! I wanna do it too!" He jumps out the door like Bender had planned, only better: he lands on his feet and takes off running.

"IGOR!!" yells Mrs. B, who has pushed through the crowd. "Come back here, NOW!"

Igor freezes in mid-stride, then starts running backward in slow motion. Meanwhile, Bender groans again, partly for sympathy. But he isn't getting any from the driver. With hands on her hips and her puzzled, angry face cocked to one side, she demands, "What the Sam Hill do you think you're doing?"

She enlists Jay's help in getting Bender back on the bus and tosses an Ace bandage from the first-aid kit for him to wrap his ankle with. It's definitely sprained, maybe even broken. He feels it swelling, throbbing against the bandage until he can hear it in his ears. Just outside of town, he glances up at the billboard where his mother beams down at him: *Myra Bender Thompson—Your Go-to Gal for Home or Investment!* Her head perkily tilted to one side, she holds a house in one hand while the other sweeps over a map of the county, like she's ready to get you any little property your heart desires. In real life, he can't remember ever seeing her smile at him that way.

* * *

Certainly not today. When she picks him up at school, she's mostly interested in letting him know she had to pass one of her appointments off to another agent in the office, and if the other agent makes the sale, she gets nothing (she's number two on sales but closing in on number one). "What did you jump from? The nurse told me but I must have heard wrong. The emergency door of the bus?"

They go straight to the clinic to get his ankle X-rayed. No fractures, but his lower leg is swollen to the size of a watermelon by then. "Take it easy for a while," the doctor tells him. "Use an ankle brace for a day or two, then support socks for a week. What did you say you jumped from?"

* * *

"What were you thinking?" His mother says once she's slammed the car door and buckled her seat belt.

"I…always wanted to try it. See what would happen."

Her sigh is more like an explosion as she puts the Suburban in reverse and shoots into the parking lot, screeching the brakes as a van honks behind her. "Just to see what would happen, huh? I used to know somebody like that. In high school. Always pulling stunts to see what would happen— until he went too far."

"Went too far how?"

"People got hurt."

"Like who?"

"I don't want to talk about it, okay? It's not the point."

He wonders why she doesn't want to talk about something as far away as high school. "What is the point? People getting hurt? I'm the only one who got hurt this time."

His mother appears to struggle with what to say next as she taps an agitated rhythm on the steering wheel with one finger: one-two-three, one-two-three, one-two-three-four. "You were hurt—thank God, it wasn't worse—but other people were inconvenienced, like me. Next time you start wondering what'll happen if you do something, just use your imagination."

He knows that's all the sympathy he's going to get. "Are you gonna tell Dad?"

She stomps the brake pedal at the edge of the parking lot, jerking them forward in unison. With her head turned to watch the right-lane traffic, she says, "Why should I? It would just give him another excuse for not coming home."

That statement has an odd ring. "Why…why wouldn't he just come home after he finishes the job?"

His mother makes a left turn—slowly, for her. "No good reason. That's just it. Sometimes I think he makes up excuses to stay away longer."

She glances at him, and the look is like an open door. The voice too. Sometimes he gets the sense that if he asked a serious question, like *What do you mean by that?* she'd give him a serious answer. As if she would like to talk to him. Sometimes he thinks he should walk through that door, answer that voice—but he can't. He doesn't know why. Watching the minivan ahead of them, he remarks, "Get Thorn to call him. He'd come home if *Thorn* asked him to."

She stomps the brake pedal again as the minivan signals a turn. "For your information, *Thorn* is not a miracle worker."

"Coulda fooled me," he says.

A few days later, Miracle-boy himself emails from college: Hey, little bro. Mom says you jumped out of the back of a school bus. What's up with that?

Thorn almost never emails him. Bender doesn't reply.

* * *

Mrs. B decides that Bender should sit in the front seat of the bus, across from her, for an entire week. So she can "keep an eye on him." It's the seat reserved for notorious school bus criminals, and he qualifies, but he's okay with that. Sitting this close, he can see all the numbers and gauges on the dashboard.

Because of the times he's occupied this seat in the past, he already knows the average speed Mrs. B drives and the exact mileage to various points on the route. But now he gets to clock the distance to the mystery stop and check if Mrs. B's rate is any faster or slower. No to the latter. After a week of jotting down odometer readings, he has a precise answer to the former: 2.83 miles.

He's read somewhere that an average adult can walk one mile in twenty minutes. Given that he's not an adult (though he might be average, especially compared to a certain spectacular individual whose initials are JTT), he should still be able to cover a mile in twenty-five minutes, and two miles plus 0.830 shouldn't take much more than an hour. Or one hour and ten minutes, max.

He will pick a day when both parents are out, play sick, wait until the school bus leaves, and hike to the mystery stop. What he'll do when he gets there, he leaves to inspiration. The plan is so simple it almost bores him, but as he's already discovered, simple plans are more likely to succeed than the other kind.

✳ ✳ ✳

During the last half of October, Halloween shares equal time with the campaign for Youth Court, which in previous years attracted no more attention than a Red Cross fund-raiser. But Bender has to admit, Shelly has given this race a lot of pizzazz. She teaches her campaign songs to the littles and belts them out on the bus, both coming and going. Such as:

> *I'd like to teach the school to sing in perfect harmony.*
> *I'd like them all to vote for me upon November three.*

Sometimes Bender joins in from the back, just to irritate Spencer. The genius didn't expect this kind of competition, but he sucks it up and makes up for his lack of musical ability with computer-generated campaign signs like *Spencer for the people! The people for Spencer!* Jay, his manager, makes up a cheer and launches it every time the Vote-for-Shelly choir pauses for breath:

> *Two! Four! Six! Eight! Who do we appreciate?*
> *Three! Five! Seven! Nine! Who's the brain that's really fine?*
> *Spencer! Spencer! Spencer! YAAAAAYYYY!*

Sometimes the campaign gets so rowdy Mrs. B actually pulls over on the side of the road until the noise level drops.

Meanwhile, Kaitlynn wants to know about everybody's Halloween costume. For a week, she agonizes out loud (in-between campaign songs) before deciding to be a willow tree. Miranda is going as Cruella de Vil (though Bender thinks she has a few too many pounds on her for that) and Shelly grandly announces she will be a Supreme Court justice. Spencer (groaning loudly at Shelly's choice) says he's going as a mad scientist. Jay will borrow his grandpa's old helmet and jersey (like last year), and *voilà*; instant football hero.

"A nearsighted football hero?" Bender asks. Jay scowls at him.

Igor will be a spider and Matthew a shrug—at least, that's what he does when asked—and Alice-or-Alison looks confused, as though not sure what Halloween is.

And Bender? "A garbage bag."

Jay says, "Yeah, *right*," while Igor holds his nose and waves away imaginary fumes. But little do they know, including Bender, how true that will be.

✳ ✳ ✳

As it turns out, Halloween looks like the best day to carry out his plan. Mr. Thompson is in Arkansas adjusting flood claims, and Myra Bender Thompson will be showing houses to a new client from Pennsylvania. The client has only one day to look, so they're planning an early start.

When the alarm goes off in Bender's room that morning, he lies awake for a few seconds. Then he moans. Last night, "Tornado Tim" Blair, the weatherman on Channel Five, predicted a 60 percent chance of rain beginning around midnight and continuing through the morning hours, with a low of thirty-four degrees which might climb to the forties by noon. Bender had wondered if he should call off his plan but decided that 60 percent didn't mean anything when predicting the weather.

Right now, however, the chances of rain are 100 percent, and he can tell by the trembling drops on his windowpane that thirty-four degrees is *cold*.

He considers dropping the plan, getting up, and going to school instead of pretending to be sick and taking a hike. Or better yet, just pretend to be sick, stay where he is, and sleep the whole miserable morning into oblivion.

But...

It isn't that often that both parents are out when he leaves for school. And from now on, the weather is only going to get worse, or at least more unpredictable, until spring. It's now or never, sort of—put up with a little misery today or let the mystery drive him nuts every time Mrs. B backs up beside the empty shed on Farm Road 152.

With a long sigh, he launches phase one of his operation: unwrap the onion he cut last night and hold it over his face until his eyes and nose well up. Then turn on the heating pad under his blanket and put it to his forehead. After a few minutes, he stuffs the onion and heating pad out of sight and calls out, "Mom! I'm sick!"

He almost overdoes it, bringing his temperature on the scanning thermometer up to 103.4. His mother is wondering if she should call the doctor, but Bender suggests he might feel better with more sleep. Besides, she has houses to show.

"Okay," she says doubtfully, tapping a finger on her cell

phone. She's ready to walk out the door in a navy blue pantsuit and the low heels she wears when she's going to be on her feet a lot. "I'll call at noon to see how you're doing. And you call if you need anything…"

Half an hour later, he tears a garbage bag off the big roll of industrial-grade bags his father uses for the weekly pickup. He slits the bag up one side, making a poncho in case the rain decides to pour instead of drizzle. Then he plunges into the elements.

Cutting across the common, Bender almost collides with Panzer, Mr. Pasternak Senior's dachshund. At the other end of a leash is Mr. Pasternak Senior. Both seem to materialize from behind a tree. "Whoa! Sorry…" Bender says, frantically trying to come up with a story for the questions the old man is bound to ask.

But Mr. Pasternak just nods irritably and says, "Watch where you're going, buster! Kickoff is at two o'clock sharp." It seems odd for him to be out walking in the rain, and Panzer doesn't look too happy about it. As for what he meant by kick-off time, Bender doesn't stop to wonder. He's off like a shot.

In less than a minute, he's across the loop and on the road, covering ground like Thorn Thompson setting a new cross-country record.

This stretch along Farm Road 216, from the gazebo to the highway, will be dicey. Anybody driving it is bound to see him in the open field, likely to know who he is, and even more likely to stop: "Bender? Did you miss the bus? Do you need a ride to school?" He plans to run alongside the road where the ground is a little lower and hit the dirt if he hears a vehicle. But the landscape is rougher than he expected, with all kinds of dips and—car coming! He drops immediately, and the garbage bag balloons over him, settling on his head.

The vehicle rolls on by. He doesn't dare look up to see who it is.

But then it hits him—he has the perfect disguise! What could be more ordinary, less worth looking at, than a plastic bag along the road? True, it's bigger than your average bag, but if he keeps well to the side of the highway and listens carefully for the sounds of an approaching vehicle, he'll have plenty of time to cover himself and drop to the ground undetected. So the garbage bag is his Halloween costume after all. Ha!

Twenty-three minutes and twelve seconds later, he's learned a few things.

Such as, "average walking speed" means a healthy adult walking briskly on a level path with no obstructions. Getting *to* the highway is the easy part. Now that he's here, he has to stay inconspicuous, which means *off* the highway. No way can he duck under barbed wire, circle trees, and step over gullies at three miles per hour. After slipping on patches of mud and wet grass, he also learns that garbage bags don't really keep the water out. Once he's hit the ground a few times to hide from passing vehicles, even industrial-grade plastic leaks like a cotton sock.

Finally, an hour later, Bender learns that a mile is really long. Five thousand, two hundred, and eighty feet, and he has to fight for every inch of it (that would be 63,360 inches).

Being thirteen sucks, he thinks—not for the first time. These golden years from twelve to fifteen, that his dad sometimes wishes he could go back to, are a freaking POLICE STATE! Shuttled from school to home and back again, having his head stuffed full of stuff somebody else decided he needs to know, while what he really wants to know he can't find out, and when he finally makes a prison break, the land itself seems to be against him—

He stops. Where is he?

Where is anything?

It's not raining anymore, but that's no help because he is wrapped in a fog so thick it's blurred his sense of direction. While he was stumbling along, it sneaked up on him and threw its cold wetness over his head. And now…he's trapped.

Okay, forget about the mystery stop; forget about everything but home, his own bed, his electric blanket. He's clutching that pathetic garbage bag in a desperate effort to conserve heat, even though the dampness has worked all the way to his goose-pimply skin. He clenches his teeth to stop the chattering, listening for sounds from the highway. Once he can determine which direction it is, he'll head straight for it and hitch a ride home. No matter who stops for him, even if it's a serial killer. Even if it's his mom.

Well, maybe he's not *that* desperate.

After another fifteen minutes or so, though, he almost is. The fog packs him like cotton, so tight he can't move. Or rather, any place he moves is exactly like the last place, and if he wanders, he'll only get more lost. The silence is so thick no sound can penetrate, or just barely. How did he get so far away? From everything? Even the ground under his feet seems spongy and uncertain. *Where am I?* doesn't even register, because he's lost all sense of *where.* What if there's no *where* here? Is that a reasonable question?

He shakes his head fiercely. Miles to the shed: 2.832. Miles to town: 7.59. Circumference of the earth: 24,901.55 miles. Total surface area: 197 million square miles, or 510 million square kilometers, rounded to the nearest hundred thousand. Somewhere on that vast expanse is *him.* "Hey!" he shouts at the top of his lungs to whoever might be around to hear. "HEY!"

His voice sinks into the cotton, like it never was.

Maybe he, Charles Bender Thompson, never was.

Too weird. He can feel the fog erasing him, like the mistake he suspects he is. Oops. Let's redo that, or pretend he never happened, make him smaller and smaller...

He opens his mouth but no sound comes out. Instead, a sound goes *in*: a motorized sound, like a vehicle on a road— and it seems to be coming closer.

"Hey!" he shouts. Then he runs—or stumbles, with his gimpy ankle—over the bumpy ground in the direction the sound seems to be coming from. "Hey, stop!"

He jumps over a rut and skids on loose gravel. It's a road! He can follow it, once he figures out which direction. Except that the sound is catching up to him, and he knows something has to be done, but his head is fuzzed up and slow and—

Out of the fog charges a Halloween nightmare: two glaring eyes and gleaming chrome teeth!

"Stop!" he screams. The creature stops, right after knocking him over like a bowling pin.

* * *

"Hey?" speaks a voice somewhere over his head. Bender jerks upright and his brain wobbles. Once his vision clears a little, he can make out a man standing over him—a man with a long stubbly chin and stiff brush-cut hair. On the gravel, a vehicle is idling.

It's all coming back to him now: he has just run like a panicked possum to the middle of a road, where he stopped long enough to get hit by a truck.

Brilliant.

"Hey, kid? Are you okay?"

Do I look okay? Bender wants to reply, but his teeth are chattering again. His eyes are chattering too, or that's what it feels like: he's seeing in fast-shutter speed. He squints, finds something to focus on: a metal buckle on the man's belt. It's a bird, a big bird—eagle? With wings spread? He tries to speak, but what comes out is, "D-d-d-d—"

The man spits out a four-letter word and crouches on one knee, bringing the eagle closer—along with a long-bladed knife strapped menacingly to his belt. He pulls Bender's eyelids open, glares at the pupils, grips his wrist while feeling for his pulse, aims questions at him like arrows. "What's the day of the week?"

"Th-Th-Thu—"

"Got it. What's your name?"

"B-B-Bender."

"What's your mom's maiden name?"

"Bender."

"No, I asked—Wait a minute." The pressure on his wrist relaxes as the man sits back on his heels, eyes wide. "Was your mom Annie Bender, by any chance?"

Bender just stares back, vaguely recalling that his mother's full name is Anne Myra Bender Thompson. But that doesn't seem to have any relevance here.

"*Crap!*" the man says, making him jump. Doesn't he have a blanket in his truck or something? The motor is thrumming briskly; bet it's warm in the cab. "Don't tell her you saw me. Don't tell anybody. You've put me in a helluva moral quandary, you know that? No, you don't. Listen—Man, what to do? I'm in kind of a hurry, but… Listen, what's the story here? What are you doing out in the fog?"

Funny he should ask. Bender feels like he's been in the fog all his life; fog is his natural state. "W-w-w—"

"Yeah, that's easy for you to say. Ha-ha, forget it. Let me try again—where do you need to go?"

This one's easy. "H-home."

"Home. Don't we all? Well, okay, is it close? Just nod, yes or no."

Bender nods.

"Okay, lost boy, into the truck. Point me in the right direction, but if I start to think this is a trick, I'm letting you out, no matter where we are. Got that?"

If there's a trick, it won't be on his side of the equation. All his life, Bender has been told not to take rides from strangers. But somebody who's shared a moral quandary with you (sort of) isn't exactly a stranger, is he? The knife doesn't give him a nice cozy feeling, but whether it's smart or not, Bender knows he's going to accept the offer.

November

Miranda will never be famous for anything, except maybe for who she's friends with.

Last year, it was Penelope ("Don't call me Penny!") Gage, whose father is president of First Republic Bank and who lives in the biggest house in town. Back in fourth grade, before Miranda had even met Penelope, she and her mother would drive by the house while it was being built, watching it change from a cleared lot with a poured foundation to a proud stone and timber mansion. They would ask questions of each other as the house progressed: How big will it be? How tall? What style? Where would the windows go?

The answers came over time: 1) Very. 2) Two and a half stories. 3) Rustic lodge. 4) Everywhere. The double doors in front opened to an entrance hall with cathedral roof and three chandeliers, but Miranda wouldn't know all that until fifth grade, when she got to be friends with Penelope.

It's kind of interesting, how that happened.

Two of the fifth-grade classes were in the library on a sleety afternoon last January when the fire alarm went off. The whole school groaned, as if the building had reared up on its foundations and exclaimed, "What the—?" They were only supposed to have drills on nice days.

Except it wasn't a drill. It was a real fire, started in the cafeteria kitchen after lunch when the staff was taking a break. When somebody finally noticed, things got a little confused and the alarm went off and the fire department got called. By the time three hundred kids were shivering on the sidewalk in a freezing rain, the fire was already out.

How Miranda's class got there was a little confusing too: they were in the library, and Mrs. Russell was in the restroom and Ms. Henderson was just outside sneaking a cigarette and Mrs. Jenks was under the checkout desk, trying to figure out where to plug in a computer cord. The kids lined themselves up in front of the outside door with no adult supervision. In the shuffle, Miranda found herself standing next to Penelope, who was holding a book. "I've read that!" she blurted.

Penelope glanced at her then stared forward again. "Is it any good?"

"It's kinda sad." Miranda could have said that more people died than she expected, but it was a good book anyway. One of the best she'd ever read, in fact, if you went by how many Kleenexes it took to get to the end. But she didn't say anything because Mrs. Russell, who had dashed back from the restroom, was directing the bulky line forward. Besides, Miranda wasn't sure how cool it was to get so totally into a story you had to keep a Kleenex box nearby. Soon, icy raindrops were stinging her face.

Penelope took the Lord's name in vain as she stuck the book under her jacket and pulled up her hood. "If this is a drill, it's the stupidest one ever. My dad's going to call the school board and complain."

Miranda surprised herself. She knew Penelope's dad was a bank president, and Penelope was probably the richest kid in town. And who was Miranda? Nobody. All the same, she opened her mouth and said, "My dad's going to call city hall."

By the time they got to the playground fence, two fire trucks had arrived to prove this wasn't a drill. While they shivered in the schoolyard, the two girls amused themselves playing My Dad knows more important people than Your Dad: "Mine is going to call Channel Ten News!" "Mine is going to call our senator!" "Well, mine is going to call the president!"

They giggled, and then Miranda surprised herself for the second time that afternoon: "Actually, my dad won't even know about it. He lives in Arizona."

Penelope didn't say anything for a minute. Then she squeezed Miranda's hand. It seemed kind of natural at the time, because all the kids were huddled so close together they looked like a giant mushroom under the drippy sky. But Miranda couldn't help thinking that she'd let a piece of her real self slip in a very dorky way—like when you bend over and the elastic of your underwear rides up over your jeans. But Pen's squeeze seemed to tell her it was okay.

A lot of calls were made that week: to city hall and the

school board and the fire department and the county health extension office and the mayor. But among those calls was one made by Penelope to Miranda: "Want to ask your mom if you can come over after school on Friday?"

Come over?! To that huge, glassy, rustic-lodgey house she and her mother used to guess about when they drove by?

When Mrs. Scott came to pick Miranda up after work that Friday, she seemed a little nervous about meeting Mrs. Gage. Penelope's mother didn't act snotty, but she had an edge. So did Penelope, for that matter: both were thin, with narrow faces, sharp noses, and glassy-green eyes, whereas both Miranda and her mother were roundish (okay, over-weight), with round faces, curly brown hair, and big dark cow's eyes.

Mrs. Gage invited Mrs. Scott in for a cup of herbal tea, but Mrs. Scott said no, she had tons of stuff to do at home. "I know the feeling," Mrs. Gage said, already closing the heavy front door with its beveled glass. "Thanks for letting Melissa come over. See you later."

"*Miranda*, Mom!" Penelope's voice came muffled from behind the door.

Penelope was sometimes hard to be friends with. She usually ignored Miranda when boys were around, and she accepted an invitation to go to a concert for Miranda's birthday but can-celed the day before with a lame excuse. They always ate lunch together, and half the time, Penelope unloaded on Jayden or Jordan or Jenn—or her brother or her brother's girlfriend or even her mom. Or she would talk about college and how she couldn't wait to get out of this boring little town where the most excitement was Rodeo Days.

"You know who I can't stand?" Penelope asked at lunch on the next-to-next-to-last day of school.

Just about everybody, Miranda thought, but she didn't say it.

"Shelly Alvarez, that's who. She thinks she is so hot. You should have seen her after school yesterday, at the Talent Fling tryouts."

"How did your ballet go?"

"Let me tell you. I spent at least twenty minutes getting ready but only got to dance for, like, two minutes! I was just warming up when Mrs. Jarvis stopped me. 'That's great, Penelope, we'll put you on the list, and, Dylan, are you ready?' Dylan's doing a stupid lip sync. They should ban all the lip syncs next year—they're boring and they don't take any talent whatsoever."

"I agree," Miranda agreed.

"But when *Shelly* gets onstage, she's got her *tech crew.* Pul-leese. Mr. Manchuso is doing the sound for her and Barton Joy is doing lights, and she gets to go through her whole song."

"Ewww," said Miranda.

Penelope stabbed her organic roasted veggie wrap with a fork. "Then Mrs. Jarvis talks up how great everybody is but there's a few she has to leave out because of time."

Miranda gasped. "Pen! She didn't cut *you,* did she?"

"Of course not!" Penelope looked outraged at the very idea, and Miranda almost apologized. "Most of the fourth-graders get cut, but she still leaves in a *bunch* of lip syncs, and Daniel

Kenner's lame magic show comes next to last, and guess who's last? The act Mrs. Jarvis thinks is so great she puts it there to wrap up the whole show?"

"Uh...Shelly?"

"*Shelly.*" Penelope took a savage bite out of her veggie wrap. "I should've just left. I should've not signed up for the stupid show, but my mother made me."

Miranda thought she remembered Penelope's mom advising against it, but maybe she'd heard wrong. Penelope went on, "If I'd brought my Firebird costume—which makes that silver outfit of Shelly's look like a pillowcase—and *lights* and everything, it would have been a totally different story. That's mostly what Shelly has going for her, anyway: tech support."

"Uh-huh."

"If you pull the plug on her, she's nothing."

"Right."

Penelope suddenly put down her veggie wrap and sat up straighter. "Wait a minute. I have an idea. What if we actually *pull* the *plug*?"

By "we," she meant Miranda.

What if Miranda slipped backstage just before Shelly's turn ("The back door is open all the time") and sneaked over to the sound equipment, and while Mr. Manchuso's back was turned ("He's always reading comic books—*X-Men* is his favorite"), she could knock out the plug to the speakers ("It'll look like an accident! If you move fast enough, they won't even know it's you!").

Friendship is easy if all you have to do is nod and laugh at the right times. But when you have to actually *do* something, it's like being called up to give an oral book report, when all she wanted to do was read the book. (Mr. Cavendish in the fourth grade was always making her stand up and read her reports because he thought they were so good. So she started writing crummy ones, just to make him stop.)

Miranda stalled. "Why can't you do it? Since you'll be backstage already."

"Because I'll probably be changing. That costume takes a lot of time to get out of—it's got all these tricky hooks and stuff. Can't risk it."

But you can risk me, Miranda thought.

Penelope was going on: "…after all these months and coming over to my house and taking you shopping, I ask you to do this one thing as a friend—how can you say no?"

Easy, Miranda thought. *Just two letter sounds, en and oh.* But somehow it wouldn't come together. And neither would *yes*.

"How will I know which plug?" Miranda felt her throat going dry.

"I'll figure it out ahead of time and mark it somehow. I'll even loosen it up, so it'll be easy to knock out. Nobody will see; they'll all be watching *Awesome Shelly*. And as soon as the speaker cuts off, it'll take them a while to figure out why. You'll have plenty of time to get away. Come on, it'll serve her right."

Miranda wasn't sure about that—she had nothing against Shelly, who could be annoying but wasn't mean. Besides, they lived in the same subdivision and sometimes talked. And besides, wasn't it kind of…like…wrong?

"Please?" Penelope asked.

Miranda blinked. Had Penelope ever asked anything with a please?

"Okay," she heard herself saying—and dropped into a simmering pot of misery for the next forty-eight hours.

On the outside, she looked the same but was really a virtual human, trying to act normal while a snake wrapped around her quick-beating, mousy little heart. *Why did I say yes? Why couldn't I say no?* This was lots worse than an oral book report. *What if they catch me? And I'm so clumsy they're bound to. What will I say?*

On the morning of the Spring Fling, even her mother noticed: "What's the matter? Do you have to do a speech or something?"

"Bye, Mom," she said mechanically, walking out the door.

In the end, Miranda did the right thing in the wrong way, maybe. That is, she didn't do anything.

She literally sweated through the lip sync and piano solos and barely noticed Penelope's ballet. When Daniel Kenner came out in a red-lined cape to begin his magic act, Miranda was supposed to raise her hand and ask to go to the bathroom so she'd have plenty of time to get backstage before Shelly's turn. But by the time Daniel concluded his act and bowed low to thunderous applause, Miranda still had not moved.

When Shelly bounded out in a silver flash, Miranda didn't join in the whoops and screams and was as surprised as anybody when the sound cut off. But when Shelly sang on, all alone, carried by self-confidence and determination,

Miranda was one of the first to join the clapping, and the rest was history.

So was her friendship with Penelope.

* * *

Of course, Penelope's still around.

A week after screwing up Shelly's nursing home gig, Miranda picks up the phone at home to hear a voice from the past: "Back to eating lunch alone, aren't you, Scott? That's how Shelly repays her *friends*." Penelope hangs up without waiting for a reply, not that Miranda could think of one.

Her former friend knows where it hurts; more than anything, Miranda dreads eating alone. Lunch period feels like the Cafeteria Table at the End of the Universe, and she's considering asking Mrs. Jenks if she could get a library pass for that time.

Penelope spoke too soon, though: Shelly's not perfect, but she doesn't hold a grudge. The very next morning, she takes a seat next to Miranda as though nothing happened and asks her to manage her Youth Court campaign. That afternoon, they write the fliers—Miranda types them on the Alvarezes' computer, and Shelly imports a publicity photo of herself with her head cocked and one hand behind her ear. They print five dozen, which Miranda hands out the next day:

> Shelly Alvarez hears you!
> A sympathetic ear, a caring heart,
> She's the one who'll take your part.

Miranda also writes the campaign speech, and during the last week of October, Shelly delivers it flawlessly to the faculty meeting and the homeroom representatives. On the first Tuesday in November, all the candidates give their speeches to the general assembly of fourth, fifth, and sixth graders, with the voting to come right after.

There's no polling data, but Miranda is confident about her candidate's chances. Especially if you take Spencer's reaction as a kind of reverse indicator. Other sixth-graders are running, but the chemistry between those two makes it seem like a one-on-one matchup. The more Shelly charms, the more Spencer scowls; his speeches get louder, quicker, and angrier as the campaign goes on, in spite of Jay reminding him to chill. Miranda knows Shelly will win, right up until the last day and the last speech—actually the last minute of the speech.

Shelly has been hitting all her points about how everybody deserves a second chance and she's made mistakes in her life and knows how to be sympathetic and see both sides of an issue. The audience is eating it up, especially in comparison to Spencer's rant about right and wrong and being impartial and making sure perpetrators get justice—who wants that?

But *then*: "I'm honored to be your candidate for Youth Court," Shelly says, looking up from her notes. "I've learned so much by the experience, and the most important thing I learned is…I'm not the best person for this job. I'd like to resign my candidacy right now, and hereby throw my support to Spencer Haggerty!"

She smiles and returns to her seat onstage in total

silence—everybody is stunned until Mr. Pearsall starts the applause. Miranda feels like a popped balloon, and Spencer looks like he's been stabbed in the back, even though Shelly has handed him a victory: when the votes are counted, he picks up enough of hers to win a place on the court.

"I knew it didn't mean anything to you," he snarls while waiting in the bus line that afternoon. Jay shakes her hand and says she ran a good campaign—though Miranda actually ran it! To all of Kaitlynn's why-why-why questions, Shelly says she didn't feel worthy of the honor this year.

Miranda gets an honest answer, at least: "Youth Court is great for political types, but I've got too much to do in the afternoons. The campaign will still look great on my scholarship application."

A résumé enhancement, just like Spencer said.

But that's just Shelly. Next morning, she takes a seat next to Miranda on the bus and says, "Did you see *National Talent Search* last night?"

It's hard to stay mad at her. She sparkles when she's happy, and it has nothing to do with her looks—except for her thick, shiny, almost-black hair, Shelly's not that beautiful. But she draws you, as though she's always about to lean in and whisper, *Guess what?*

So in spite of her disappointment, Miranda can't help but be glad she caught part of *NTS* before going to bed. "You mean with that Vietnamese girl?"

"*Yes!* Ohmigosh, she was so pathetic, I would have voted three thumbs down if they let me. I wanted to put a note on the website that they shouldn't allow…um…"

"Asians?"

"No…"

"People of other cultures?"

"No! I mean non-Claires. People who aren't the least little bit like Claire shouldn't be allowed to do Claire songs."

"Oh." Actually, Miranda thinks that being not-Claire is a mark in the Vietnamese girl's favor, but she'd never say it.

"Can you believe her singing a *slow* version of 'Saturday Night Lights'?"

"Yeah, that was pretty bad. I didn't even know what the song was at first."

"Exactly." Shelly studies her fingernails and chips the bright pink polish. "Hey, are you entering the language arts fair this year?"

Miranda, who is expecting the conversation to ride on awful Claire imitators all the way to school, has to reverse her mental wheels and make a sharp turn. "Uh…I guess so. Yeah."

"I was wondering if you could, like, help me with it? Dad said it would be a good way to build up my portfolio for the scholarship. Especially since language arts is so—artsy. So I was going to try and put together a few poems or something. Poems would be good, especially if I'm going to write my own songs."

She leaves a pause, so Miranda says, "That's a good idea."

"Right, so…I was wondering if you could read some of my stuff."

"Oh. Sure! I'd be glad to." At least it's something she's good at.

They agree on a regular time to meet and read their stuff to each other: Tuesday after school, four-thirty to five. That way, Shelly can catch the last half-hour of *Dance America*. They'll take turns reading and then make helpful suggestions for each other.

But by the middle of the month, they haven't met at all. "Weren't you supposed to come over yesterday?" Miranda asks on Wednesday morning.

Shelly claps a hand to her head. "I can barely do my regular homework—how can they expect me to pump out poems and book reports and compare-and-contrast?"

"But you wanted to enter the language arts fair. And I said I'd help, if we could—"

"I know, but I've been getting all kinds of great ideas on *Dance America*, and I have to practice them right away or I'll forget, and then the hour's over and I've got to get started on my homework."

"We could do it on another day…"

"Um…don't think so. Because of dance lesson on Monday, and guitar on Thursday, and voice coach on Wednesday, and Friday being the day my mom makes me stay home and help clean up for the weekend—that'll only get worse after the baby comes. How about I just give you what I write and you can tell me what I ought to change?"

Miranda agrees to that, even though she was hoping they could discuss ideas. Mrs. Evangeline, her language arts teacher, has great suggestions that might be good for Shelly.

"Don't ever tell me you don't have anything to write about,"

Mrs. Evangeline likes to say. "Every writer starts with the same thing you have: experience. A good writer can make an interesting story or poem out of *anything*."

Miranda has been thinking she might be a good writer. Especially after writing a short story called "Yes or No?" based on her friendship with Penelope (with some details changed), that came back with an A. In the margin, Mrs. Evangeline wrote: *This is exactly what I'm talking about! Please let me help you make it even better.*

So she's been making it better, and they've decided the story should be her main entry in the language arts fair. "But you have time to write one or two more," Mrs. Evangeline told her. "Why not try some poetry?"

"What about?" Miranda has an idea poetry is about boyfriends, which she doesn't have.

"Anything at all. Look out your window."

She didn't mean literally, but at the moment, Miranda is thinking of poetry subjects while looking out an actual window. They're backing up to the empty shed on Farm Road 152. She glances back; Bender is gazing at it like always. He's kept very quiet since being out sick the whole first week of November—with pneumonia, Miranda heard. It's funny, how everybody seems to take this stop for granted now—Kaitlynn is telling Mrs. B about this great idea she got for a project, Alice is reading, Matthew is staring into space, Spencer and Jay are arguing, and Igor is trying to pop the little kids with Halloween candy corn without Mrs. B catching him.

It's a drippy day ("Try to include plenty of concrete details," Mrs. Evangeline says), with the smell of smoke and wet leaves in the air. Beyond the shed's mossy roof, Miranda can see a line of bare trees (what kind of trees?) like a gray fringe against the gray sky (Good!). The shed seems to huddle in the rain like a...like a (figure of speech here)...an abandoned tricycle? Maybe. What does it remind her of? Something that shouldn't be alone. Something that hides and is afraid to show itself, even though the bus comes by every day and knocks on its door. No, no door, but it's like the bus is hoping somebody will be inside even though the shed stays empty, day after day. Or else it's afraid—

Kind of like her, maybe.

She was afraid to be herself with Debbie Hawthorne in the fourth grade and with Penelope Gage in fifth and ended up losing both of them. What's her problem? She tries to be a good friend and go along and make the other person feel good about themselves...

The bus pauses after backing up. As though waiting for some little girl or boy to appear, who never does. *Like me*, Miranda thinks again. I'm waiting for *me* to show up.

"Hel-*lo*?" Shelly snaps her fingers. "Did you hear what I said? I've got an idea for a poem, so how about I write it and you fix it?"

"Okay." Miranda is so deep in thought it's hard to climb out. "Sure, whatever."

From somewhere in the back rows, a voice shouts, "Stink bomb!"

A heavy object flies out and hits her on the back of the head. "Ow!" The object hits the floor: a running shoe.

"Igor!" Mrs. B yells. "Was that you?" The bus is at the top of the hill; she slams it into park and turns around. "Whose shoe?"

"Mine," Jay says. "My gym shoe. He sneaked it out of my backpack."

"I was aiming at Spencer!" Igor claims. "He was razzing me. But then we went over a bump and—"

Mrs. B points to the right front seat. "Up here." As Igor slouches forward, muttering about how it wasn't his fault, she continues, "This is the third time this month, buster. Next time, I'm going to pay a little visit to your folks…"

Miranda rubs her head and nods absently as Shelly asks, "You okay?" The big yellow bus groans onto the highway, and suddenly, as though the shoe had knocked an idea loose, Miranda knows what her poem is going to be about.

* * *

Igor doesn't apologize until the following afternoon, when she's walking to Mr. Pasternak Senior's house to return a multi-blade paper cutter her mother borrowed from Jay's grandma. Igor is sitting on the curb in front of Pasternak Junior's. He doesn't seem be doing anything in particular, but it's a chilly overcast day, and if you're going to do nothing, you'd want to do it someplace warmer.

"What's the matter?" she asks.

"Nothing. I'm waiting for the trash pickup." He rumples

his clothes and throws himself back on the driveway, eyes crossed and tongue sprawling. "I'm roadkill."

"Stop being stupid," she snaps, still irritated about the shoe.

"Okay." He sits up and brushes himself off. "I'm waiting for Jay to get home from track practice so we can play *Horror Castle*."

"But it's *cold*. Why don't you wait at home?"

Igor stares at the gray sky as though the answer is up there. "Because...my mom's having one of her bad days."

"What does that mean? She kicked you out?"

"Sort of." He lifts his narrow shoulders. "She gets over it pretty quick. She'd let me in right now if I went back. But I'm not ready."

"Oh." Miranda doubts the story, first because it comes from Igor and second because she likes Mrs. Sanderson, who is girlish in a way most ladies outgrow by the time they have four kids. And she's devoted to her family, as Miranda knows from babysitting for her a couple of times.

Igor sneezes, then digs around in his jacket pocket and pulls out two Kleenexes. He stuffs the ends into each nostril so they're hanging out of his nose like ropes of snot. "I'm having science problems."

He probably doesn't even know he meant *sinus*. Miranda heaves a disgusted sigh and continues on to Pasternak Senior's. Fifteen minutes later, on her way home, Igor is no longer on the curb. She knew he was faking all along.

✳ ✳ ✳

What is it?

A little shelter built of worn gray boards,

A friendly bench to sit on, a sturdy roof to keep off the rain.

The bus rolls sadly by the empty bench—

Who is it?

"It doesn't rhyme," Shelly says, the day after Miranda has finished her poem and typed it up. Shelly finished hers too; it's in the notebook on her lap.

"Mrs. Evangeline says poetry doesn't have to rhyme. In fact, sometimes it's better if it doesn't."

"How come you centered it like that?"

"Because it's a kind of poem called diamante. That means 'like a diamond.' So the middle line's the longest, and the beginning and end are the shortest."

"Oh." The bus stops to pick up Pat and Pat, the Henderson twins, who edge down the aisle to the middle seat.

"Do you...um...do you like it?"

"Like what?" Shelly is staring at the top of Alice's head. Alice is on the seat directly in front of them, bent over a book as usual. Her pale hair gleams like spun silver in a low beam of sunlight. "Oh, the poem? I guess so. I never thought too hard about who's supposed to be waiting at that shelter. Now you've got me wondering."

That's a good thing, Miranda decides. She would have liked Shelly to say something nice about the poem itself, but maybe it's good that the poem makes her think about something besides dance music and costumes. "Where's yours?"

"Here." Shelly opens the notebook and thrusts it at her. "I haven't had time to work on it much."

Miranda scans the page, over which Shelly's sprawling print seems to sprawl more than usual:

> You are my everything, my everything.
> I long for the day when you give me your ring.
> You are pizza and candy and diamonds and boats.
> Your roses, roller skates and root beer floats.
> When I'm thinking of you I go all catatonic
> On Friday please call me I'll meet you at Sonic.

"So?" asks Shelly. "What do you think?"

"It's…got real stuff in it. That's good. Mrs. Evangeline says you should write about what you know."

"You mean like Sonic? I got the idea when my dad and I stopped for cherry limeades after guitar lesson yesterday. So that's good?"

"Uh-huh. What's 'catatonic'?"

"I forget. I asked Dad what rhymes with Sonic. What else is good?"

"Well…in the fourth line, you've got three words that start with R. That's called alliteration."

"Cool!" Shelly beams. "I'm a poet and don't know it! What else?"

"Um. It rhymes."

"Yeah." Shelly bites a corner off her fingernail, which doesn't really have a corner left. "In other words, it sucks."

"I didn't say that—"

"It does, though." She flicks Miranda's paper with her finger. "Yours sounds—smart. Mine sounds stupid."

"Well…" Miranda can't deny it. "Mrs. Evangeline says you should write about your own experience. Since you don't have any boyfriends yet, you could write about some of the stuff you go through. Like with your Uncle Mike."

"Write about stuff that makes me barf? No thanks. Let's just say I can't be good at everything. If you could make it a little better, at least I can turn something in and get a participation ribbon. Okay?"

"But Shelly—they're due *today*."

"What? What about if I get an extension?"

Miranda shook her head. "Mrs. Evangeline said that's the absolute deadline, no exceptions, so she can get them printed up by December."

"Oh yeah." Shelly slams her head back against the seat as the bus stops to pick up Harley and Stella. Revving up again, the back wheel hits a bump. "Wait, I've got a better idea!"

Something tells Miranda she's not going to like this idea.

"What if I put my name on your poem?" Shelly rushes on before Miranda can protest. "See, you've already got your story and your description in the language arts fair and both of those are going to get ones. So you could share a teensy little poem with me and I could get a one too, because it's that good, and it would look great on my scholarship application!"

She looks so sparkly Miranda is wondering why she can't catch a spark. "But…"

"And wouldn't it be cool to share something like this? It would be like sharing clothes, only better because it's a secret, and you'd *really* be helping me out, and I could find some way to help you out too."

But it would be wrong! Miranda wants to say. *It would be lying because you didn't write it, I did, and besides I really like it and it's mine and I don't want to give it up forever which I would be doing because if you got a one beside your name for this poem nobody would be able to change it except you and I'm pretty sure you never would.*

She doesn't say any of this, of course. She just feels it, like water swelling up behind a big concrete dam, threatening to spill over. It's how she felt when Penelope asked her to pull the plug—a solid lump of feeling, blocking the words *yes* and *no*. Except *no* is on top. *No* would get over the dam first. And not just a polite little *en oh*, but a big honking *NO! NEVER! ABSOLUTELY NOT!*

The words seem bigger than she is. Maybe that's why they won't come out.

"Come on, Mir," Shelly begs. "We'll be BFFs. Please?" The bus slows down at the big curve outside of town to pick up the four Kalispell boys, whom Mrs. B calls the Brothers Calamity.

Best Friends Forever. Miranda feels the pressure of *NO!* shrinking a little. Does she mean it? Does she mean hanging out at the mall and doing each other's hair and sleeping over and maybe even vacations? That kind of friend? Or just the sit-together-on-the-bus friend? "Could we do something on Saturday?"

Shelly's eyebrows nudge together then spring apart. "Sure! You can come over in the morning and help me work out a dance routine for my camp audition DVD."

The four Kalispell boys, Todd, Taylor, Shawn, and Shane, tumble onto the bus like a pack of wildcats, making it harder to hold Shelly's attention. "What about the afternoon?" Miranda persists.

"Uh…" The eyebrows creep together again. "I think my mom wants to take me shopping for shoes."

"Can I go?" Miranda can't believe she said this, even after she says it.

"I don't think so. Mom doesn't like to have fun shopping. Just one store after another, bang, bang, bang, until you find what you're looking for. I think Evan's coming too. Yuck."

Miranda finds herself doubting this. If she watched their house on Saturday afternoon, would she observe Shelly and Mrs. Alvarez leaving without Evan? And if she were still watching a few hours later, would she see them return without shoes? Shelly has friends all over the place—friends from dance school, all-city glee club, and talent camp, friends Miranda will never meet because she's not in their league. She's a bus friend, and sometimes a come-over-for-a-morning friend. And a take-advantage-of friend?

They're almost to school. "So how about it? Can I use your poem or not?"

Miranda looks out the bus window a long time before her answer breaks free and trickles down the face of the dam.

* * *

Her mother has taken a personal day off work in order to clean house. Getting off work just to do more work makes Miranda sad, and when she comes home that afternoon, the sight of boxes piled up on the dining room table makes her even sadder, because obviously she'll be helping to finish the job.

"Hey, Pumpkin!" Mom calls over the twang of a steel guitar on the radio. "Glad you're home—we can get this job done in no time!"

Just like I thought, Miranda thinks.

Her mother pops out of the kitchen, wiping her face with a paper towel that leaves swipes of dusty sweat. "This all came from the attic. I've been sortin' and sneezin' all afternoon, but finally settled on what's keepable." She sneezes again, an explosion that seems to rocket around the walls. "I'll haul it back up, and if you can dust and vacuum while I take a shower, we'll splurge for dinner at Italian Garden, okay?"

"Okay." Italian Garden's triple-treat pasta sampler sounds pretty good right now.

"You look a little mopey. Is anything wrong?"

Miranda shakes her head.

"Look what I found up there." Mom picks up a large brown envelope and slides a stack of papers out of it. "My entire journalism career! Did you know I was a writer too? Started back in middle school, went all the way through senior year. I was editor that year. Since you're getting into writing, I thought you might be interested."

She seems…excited. Like she's been waiting all afternoon to spring this surprise. And that feels sad too, but Miranda musters a smile while reaching out for the envelope. "Sure. Thanks, Mom."

While waiting for her mother to move boxes, she reads the first two articles, each carefully cut from newsprint and taped to a sheet of white paper, all *by Linda Tucker, eighth grade*. The first reported on the remodeled school cafeteria, and the second complained about students throwing food in the remodeled cafeteria.

Miranda sighs. Mrs. Evangeline suggested that she write an article for the school newspaper about the language arts fair: "Not in general but specific. Give your thoughts about your favorite pieces, like a book review." Um, don't think so. No way. In fact, she's done with creative writing for this year. Maybe for next year too.

A headline catches her eye as she shuffles papers back in the envelope: *Dear Class of '85: That Wasn't Funny!* Unlike the rest, it sounds interesting. She's about to glance over it when her mother yells, "I'm hitting the shower now!"

Miranda puts the envelope aside, intending to give it another look. But she doesn't, or not for a long time.

***

During Thanksgiving break, she calls the Alvarez house twice but Shelly's busy: leaving early to catch the Black Friday sales, got an audition for a commercial on Saturday, going to spend all day Sunday at Grandma's—bo-ring! Those two syllables would describe Miranda's whole long weekend: Thanksgiving dinner at her Aunt Marcia's, with teenage cousins who split after the main event; the rest of the time, just hanging around. Her dad calls Friday night, but as usual, they don't have much to talk about and the conversation dries up after a few minutes. His wife probably had to remind him to call.

Shelly is sweet as coconut-cream pie on the bus Monday morning, but that's her way of showing gratitude. She never exactly says thank you for the poem. What she does say: "So, I made a list of my scholarship credits last night, with my volunteer gigs and the campaign and the language arts fair and two auditions, and Dad said it wasn't bad at all for two months. The language arts thing really helped. I have to work on the grades, though."

"That's great," Miranda says. And maybe it is, in a way. Maybe that language arts credit will shine like a star on Shelly's résumé, and she'll see how much it helped, and how much she owes Miranda, and how Miranda is a sweet girl and they ought to be doing more stuff together.

And maybe tomorrow, the popularity fairy will swoop down and crown her Miss BFF.

* * *

All the fair entries that got a one or two rating are published in a booklet and distributed to each participant. Miranda's copy goes into the drawer under the telephone book and quickly fades to a sore spot in her memory, along with Penelope and the Youth Court campaign. Except for one little thing. One little, very strange thing.

It comes in a Christmas card. The card shows a fireplace with stockings hanging over it and looks recycled—the envelope is too big, and a signature on the inside is scratched out. The address on the envelope is written in pencil, in careful block letters that try to look grown up. Inside the card is a folded page with a fringy edge, torn out of a booklet with a plastic comb binding.

Unfolded, the paper reveals the poem about the shed—*her* poem, over Shelly's name.

In the white space left by the slope of the diamante shape, more block lettering: *I lik this. Thank yu.*

December

Kaitlynn knows she will be famous but isn't sure what for.

On different days, she's a famous lawyer, senator, screenwriter, explorer…"Talk show host," her dad says. "No, wait—talk show hosts have to let somebody else do the talking sometimes."

Okay, so she does talk a lot. But that's only because she thinks a lot, and her ideas don't stick around unless she talks about them.

Ideas are like puffs of wind until she dresses them up in words. Or like a garden spider spinning away, around and around until the web is done and it signs a zigzaggy thread just below the middle. Once, after watching a spider at work in a corner of the front porch, she decided to give it super-powers and call it—her!—ZZZorinda. The idea popped into her head, just popped! Like a flashing fish out of a pond: Zip-Zap Zorinda!

ZZZorinda could fly, of course, and read minds and pick

up distress calls from hundreds of miles away. She could defeat any bad guy with the tools in a utility belt cinched around her tiny, tiny waist and always finished by wrapping him up in a neat web and signing it with a ZZZ.

There were tons of adventures waiting to be had by a super-hero spider. Kaitlynn wrote her first ZZZorinda story the very next day: Chapter One. She hasn't got to Chapter Two yet, but not for lack of thinking about it. Or talking about it.

Her mom says, "Not now, Katy. I'm trying to balance the checkbook."

Her dad says, "Very interesting. Did you happen to see where I left my hammer?"

Her brother Simon (age seven) says, "But how does she fly without any wings?" (She just does.) "But *how*? Why don't you make her an insect? Insects have wings; spiders don't. How about a ladybug?" (A ladybug can't wear a utility belt around her waist!) "Why not?" (A ladybug doesn't have a waist!!) "You could give her a utility jacket then. Or apron." (Whoever heard of a superhero with an *apron*?!) "I like it. Lots of pockets. You can put all kinds of stuff in an apron." (Just forget it, okay?)

Her brother Steven (age two and a half) says, "Coo!" mean-ing cool. At least he doesn't argue over details. Her dog Flicker says "Arf!" because Flicker always likes her ideas.

The problem is, Kaitlynn is having ideas so thick and fast that it's hard to stick with just one. And it's impossible to write them all down. Zip-Zap Zorinda shares space in her head with Flicker the Wonder Beagle, Dolly the philo-sophical goldfish, Kaitlynn the first female president of the

United States, Kaitlynn the on-the-spot reporter for the nightly news, and Kaitlynn the first human on Mars (using a fuel formula she invented herself). (Even though Kaitlynn the eleven-year-old fifth-grader doesn't know anything about chemistry. Or physics.)

And here's a new one: Kaitlynn the angel of the slums. Ever since she had to do a project about Mother Teresa of Calcutta for social studies, she's been inspired to make the world a better place. She begged her dad to take her to the nearest slum so she could pass out sandwiches and blankets, but he says they don't have slums in Centerview. Bummer! (As her dad likes to say.) She may just have to wait until she's old enough to move out on her own, and then she'll definitely find a slum.

Because Kaitlynn is not just a thinker. She's a doer. Like organizing the Hidden Acres Lightning Bug Festival in June or the Secret Society of Flower Bombers last winter, when she and her friends sneaked around the school and left flower stickers on the light switch covers and window frames. She thought of it as a way of brightening up the institution, and besides, it was fun to figure out ways to plant the stickers without getting caught. But "defacing property" was the way Mrs. Lewenhaus, the principal, put it when she announced over the PA system that whoever was doing it had better quit, now. The SSFB (there were four of them at the time, Misty, Andie, Sophie, and Kaitlynn) decided to suspend operations.

Their next idea (also Kaitlynn's!) was selling homemade Mother's Day cards at school. But they made the mistake of selling the cards before they made them, didn't get them all finished, and had to give some of the money back but couldn't remember who they'd taken it from. The other girls decided this was Kaitlynn's fault (even though she's an idea person, not a keep-tracker-of!), and they ended up paying out more than they took in, especially when people like Bender insisted he'd ordered a card from one of the girls but he wasn't sure which one. People like Bender you didn't argue with. So even though it wasn't all her fault that the Mother's Day idea didn't work out, Kaitlynn lost some friends over it, namely Misty and Andie.

Now that December's here, she's getting winter ideas. It's too bad the language arts fair is over because she has another inspiration for a story that might be even better than ZZZorinda. She got a one on ZZZorinda for the Language Arts Fair, but the evaluator had some suggestions Kaitlynn didn't get. Like, "This story could be even better with more description: give the reader an idea how ZZZorinda flies." That's a Simon kind of suggestion!

But she still got a one, and so did Shelly, and so did Miranda (two ones, in fact). "Congratulations!" she tells her fellow ones after boarding the bus on Friday afternoon the day the booklets got passed out.

"For what?" Shelly says. She's a little snotty with Kaitlynn as always, being a whole year older and a shooting star. But not so popping with ideas.

Kaitlynn holds up her copy of the booklet. "We all three got ones."

"Oh sure. I forgot." Shelly kind of rolls her eyes. "What'll you do with yours, Mir?"

Miranda's face seems headed for one expression before it settles on another. "We got one extra copy for my Aunt Marcia."

"Good idea. *Definitely* an Aunt Marcia thing."

Miranda changes the subject. "Did you see *Let's Dance* last night?"

"Are you kidding? With Becci Greenbaum and that football guy from the Eagles? He looked like he was about to pick her up and run for a touchdown."

They laugh, and Miranda says she thought Becci was going to trip over her own shoes, and Shelly says it wouldn't be the first time, and Kaitlynn would have changed seats, except afternoon seats are assigned. She was going to tell Shelly that her poem about the bus shed had inspired another story: "The Mystery of the Empty Shelter." It's only a bare sketch, though. She needs some material to fill it out. And just like that, an idea pops!

* * *

On the Monday morning ride, she waits until Mrs. B has turned around at the mysterious shelter and rumbled back up the gravel road and is looking both ways on the highway. Then she quickly moves back to the seat in front of Bender. "I have an idea."

"Sit down, Kaitlynn!" Mrs. B calls back, even though she already has.

"About what?" Bender growls. He sure has been a sour-puss lately.

"About how you can find out who lives back there."

That gets his attention. She's pretty sure the stop still bothers him, even though he pretends not to know what she's talking about. "Back where?"

"You know. The mystery stop. Here's my idea: you send them a letter. We know the address: 508 Farm Road 152. The number's on the mailbox."

"But there are three mailboxes," he objects. "How do you know that's the right one?"

"Because the other two have names on them. The middle box used to have a name, but it's been scraped off. I think whoever lives there just moved in over the summer and they haven't put the new name up yet." This strikes her as out-standing detective work. "*Or* they don't want anybody to know who they are."

His head is on the back of the seat and his butt hangs over the edge with his legs stretched out. Slowly, he pulls them in. "What's this letter supposed to say?"

"I haven't got that far yet."

Bender snorts.

"What about this: 'I know you're there. You can run but you can't hide.'" He stares at her, eyes narrowed. "Then sign it, 'a friend.'"

"What kind of 'friend' would write a note like that?"

"Well, think about it: if the note just said, 'Hi, my name's Bender, what's yours?' they'd probably throw it in the trash."

"Yeah, well…if *I* got a note that says 'You can run but you can't hide,' I'd call the cops.

"What about…" Ideas were still popping! "What about a p.s. that says…uh…'If you want to talk, tie a red ribbon on the bus shelter.'"

"And then what?"

"I don't know! You expect me to come up with the whole story right from the start? Wait till you see a red ribbon, and then decide what to do."

Brakes squeal as the bus stops for Pat and Pat. "What's in this for you?" he asks.

"I just got the idea when I was looking through the language arts fair book—I have a story in there, you know? It got a one—and I saw Shelly's poem about the bus stop. I thought it was really neat because only a few people would know what she was writing about, and they're all on this bus. So that gave me the idea about writing a story about the mystery and call it—"

"Okay, okay. Why don't *you* write the letter? Wouldn't that be 'really neat'?"

"But *you're* the one who wants to know. I'm just a little curious. And if I can't find the truth, I'll make something up. But you really want to know."

Bingo! She can tell he's thinking, even while he sticks his hands in his pockets and hunches back into the corner. "It's a stupid idea. Get outta here."

Kaitlynn turns around happily. It's one of her best ideas yet. She can't wait to see what comes of it.

* * *

Meanwhile, Christmas is coming! The goose is getting fat; please put a penny in the old man's hat. She tries to put a quarter in the Salvation Army hat—that is, kettle—every time they go to Walmart, but usually she can't get her coin purse out in time or her mother is in a hurry or she ends up with no change because there are so many other things to do with the money. For instance, she had to get one of the cute little teddy bear ornaments Shelly and Miranda made out of pompoms to sell for Shelly's camp fund. Mrs. B shuts down the operation when Shelly tries to peddle them on the bus. "No solicitation!" she says.

But back to the Salvation Army: it's too bad people have to make up their minds about whether to give to the needy while walking in and out of a store. People need time to think about those less fortunate and what their pitiful Christmas might be like with only a few cheap presents around the tree—if there even is a tree!—and a pot of beans on the table with maybe a bratwurst and a two-liter bottle of 7 Up. Hungry little children going to bed on Christmas Eve asking if Santa would come that night or were they too poor, and their sorrowful mom weeping into her pillow while their dad searches the Dumpster behind Toys"R"Us for any broken toys he might be able to fix… It's enough to bring tears to Kaitlynn's eyes just thinking about it.

And then, she has an idea!

On the second Wednesday in December, she steps in front

of the littles to be first on the bus, a plastic kettle in hand. Actually it's a witch's cauldron left over from Halloween, disguised with a wreath of holly around the lip. She takes a seat at the front of the bus directly behind Mrs. B, who says, "You can't sit there, Kait—"

But Kaitlynn quickly pulls a Santa cap out of one coat pocket and a string of jingle bells out of the other, crams the cap on her head, and grabs the bells by the knot in the string. Mrs. B opens her mouth again then closes it, as though deciding to hold off until she knows what's going on.

As the littles file by, Kaitlynn holds the kettle in one hand and bounces the string of bells with the other. The littles don't say much, just look puzzled, even her brother Simon.

The bigs are another story. Spencer stops in the narrow aisle. "I thought there was no solicitation."

She doesn't say anything, just keeps ringing.

"Logjam! Move on, there!" Mrs. B. calls.

Shelly rolls her eyes, Miranda shakes her head, Matthew passes by without expression. Alice glances at her and shyly smiles, Bender growls, Jay grins and drops in a gum wrapper, Igor swerves and pretends to throw up in the cauldron—that is, kettle.

Kaitlynn expects this. She just keeps ringing her bells, not saying a word—which in its way is even more remarkable than the steady jing-jing-a-ling that soon gets on everyone's nerves.

"Knock it off, already!" Bender yells from the back.

"That's enough, Kaitlynn," Mrs. B agrees as she turns left on the highway.

Kaitlynn smiles, stops ringing, and continues to hold the kettle on her knees. And doesn't say *anything*. At every stop, for Pat and Pat, Alison and Payton and Stella and Harley and the Bittmans and the Brothers Calamity, she holds out the kettle, and even jingles a little bit before the yells from the back drown her out. No big confrontations or questions, though—probably because everybody thinks this is just one of her ideas and tomorrow she'll have another.

Only, when tomorrow comes, it's the same idea.

Same kettle, same front seat, same no-talking and bell-ringing until Mrs. B tells her to stop. And no money.

This time, though, Mrs. B asks her to wait a minute while everybody else gets off at Harrison Elementary. "I'm not sure we're allowed to do this, Kaitlynn."

Kaitlynn guesses her meaning. "You mean ask for money? Like Shelly?"

"Right, but Shelly is raising money for herself. Is that what you're doing, or is it for your church or for Girl Scouts?"

"No! I got this idea because it's hard for me to give to the Salvation Army at Walmart because my mom's always in a hurry so we walk by too fast and I was thinking it would be good to have our own kettle and if it's on the bus we'd have plenty of time to think about what we could put in, like the quarter we were going to use to buy ice cream at lunch but—"

"Okay." Mrs. B holds up one hand—like most grown-ups do sooner or later when Kaitlynn gets going. "So this is for the Salvation Army?"

"Maybe, but—Well, last night, I was thinking we could

decide on our own needy family to help. Like..." She's getting an idea, even as she speaks! "Like, you know how the newspaper has two needy families of the week at Christmastime? I could cut those out and put them on a poster, and we can put the poster in the bus and"—this was so *cool!*—"just before Winter Break, we could vote on which family gets the money!"

She can't read Mrs. B's expression but thinks the lady is impressed. Kaitlynn sure is.

The driver in the bus behind them taps his horn, meaning, "Move it!"

Mrs. B shifts the gear lever. "I'll let you know this afternoon."

She might have checked the official Bus Driver's Rule Book or asked the boss—or maybe not. On her bus, Mrs. B pretty much *is* the boss. Anyway, that afternoon, making the last stop at Hidden Acres, she tells Kaitlynn to go for it. "But you need a way of accounting for money so everybody knows you're honest."

"I know." Kaitlynn holds out her kettle, still empty except for one gum wrapper. "Could you keep this?"

Next morning, she finds the kettle under the front seat—with money in it! One five, four ones and four quarters make a nice little pile. A Post-it note is stuck to the side with tape. In very clear print, the note reads: *Total to date: $10*

Joyfully, Kaitlynn crams on her Santa hat. But before pulling out her bells, she fishes around in her backpack for change. "Ten dollars and *thirty-five cents!*" she announces. Then she shuts her mouth and rings.

"I still don't think you're allowed to do this," says Spencer, the champion of law and order. But she just smiles.

"Move along, Spencer," says Mrs. B.

"I know a good cause," says Shelly. "My scholarship fund. No, really!" she protests as Miranda laughs her Shelly-you're-so-funny laugh.

Matthew doesn't appear to notice again, and Jay peers over his glasses to read the little sign. But Bender, last on as usual, says, "If I give you this, will you stop with the bells?" and drops in two quarters! Kaitlynn would have stopped ringing from surprise if he hadn't asked her to.

On the way to school, Pat (the girl one) says she might have some change that afternoon. The rambunctious Brothers Calamity nearly knock the kettle out of her hand while getting on, but one of them (no telling who) puts in a nickel.

Bringing the total up to ten dollars and ninety cents!

That afternoon, she gets a more little change but a lot more questions. "What's it for?" "Why're you doing this?" "Who gets the money?" "Who keeps the money overnight?"

"I do," says Mrs. B. "See you tomorrow."

If Mrs. B is in on it, it must be okay. She's barky and impatient and moody sometimes, but she's not wanted by the FBI, so far as anybody knows.

That night, Kaitlynn makes a poster. She finds the last two newspapers and cuts out the pictures of the families of the week: Mr. Pressley, whose wife ran off and left him with three little kids under seven years old, and the Burtons, an older couple who took in their two grandchildren even though Mr. Burton has Parkinson's disease.

She tapes the pictures to the poster, leaving room for four more families: two for each of the next two weeks. Across the top, she prints VOTE ON DEC. 20. That was the last day the newspaper would accept contributions.

With some holly stickers and a red ribbon at the top, the poster looks bright and Christmassy. It's under her arm when she climbs the bus steps next morning, but she's not sure what to do with it after that. And still nobody knows exactly what to do with her or the kettle. She props the poster behind her, but it keeps curling over and you can't see much except the word VOTE, which makes it look like Kaitlynn is running for office. She doesn't collect anything—not a penny!—on the whole trip to school, making her wonder if ten dollars and ninety cents is going to be her grand total. Enough for a very small turkey (or a very large chicken) for a needy-family Christmas feast, but not much more.

But that afternoon, Mrs. B has the poster up on an easel directly behind the driver's seat. It's high enough so kids can easily see the whole layout while edging past Kaitlynn and her jingling bells. And when she gets off the bus, the afternoon total is eleven dollars and sixty cents!

"Thanks, Mrs. B," she says before getting off the bus.

"You're welcome, Kaitlynn. I like what you're doing, especially since you got the idea on your own—right?"

Kaitlynn nods happily, her glasses bouncing up and down on her nose. "Ever since I read those two books on

Mother Teresa, I've been wanting to make a difference. But my dad says we don't have any slums here, so—"

"Do you mind if I keep the poster overnight? And add some kind of gauge to show how much money you've collected toward your goal?"

"Okay!" Kaitlynn isn't sure what Mrs. B means by a "gauge," but she doesn't especially want to haul a bulky piece of cardboard back and forth. She hops down one step, then turns around. "But what's my goal?"

"Oh…" Mrs. B reaches for the door lever. "One hundred dollars is realistic. That's about one-fifty per rider, and it'll give some family a start on a nice Christmas."

Kaitlynn's head is spinning as she steps off the bus. "One hundred dollars!" she says out loud to her own amazed brain. And Mrs. B had called it only a "start," so if her bus raises one hundred dollars, maybe some bank in town would match it, and she's no super shopper, but it seems to her you could buy a pretty good Christmas for two hundred bucks.

And she started it all with her great idea!

The gauge Mrs. B creates is a stack of bricks in five layers that looks like a chimney. Two boots stick out of the top, as if Santa had fallen in. This is probably because boots are easier to draw than Santa, but it's cute. The bricks are white except for the bottom row, where two whole bricks and half of another are colored red. The rows are labeled *20, 40, 60, 80, 100*—each brick representing five dollars. It looks great!

That afternoon, while the bus is waiting in the pickup lane to pull out on the street, Mrs. B lets Kaitlynn give a very short talk about each of the families on the poster and how the riders would get to vote on the one they'd like to give the money to. "And," she adds, "let's keep it a secret! No grown-ups will know, except Mrs. B. This will be something we do all by ourselves. Just us."

On the ride home that day, she collects another dollar and sixty cents!

On Thursday, she adds another family from the paper and speaks about them that afternoon: Tommy and Brenda Carpesian with their new baby and their seven-year-old boy who went to the primary school and just found out he had MD. "That stands for…um…what is it again, Mrs. B? Oh yeah, muscular dystrophy, which means in a few years, he won't be able to walk. Will they be our adopted family? Vote on December 20, and in the meantime, please give generously."

By the end of the week, the bottom row of bricks is all filled in plus a sliver of the second: twenty-one dollars and fifteen cents!

But they have less than two weeks to fill in the rest of the chimney. Can they do it? Kaitlynn lies awake thinking about it on Friday night and decides that real life can be as exciting as a story about ZZZorinda.

But then it gets even better.

On Monday morning, the bus is strung with silver tinsel from one end to the other—a sparkly line draped over each window and held there with duct tape. The low winter sun strikes glints from the garland and dances on the tired old beige ceiling.

"Is this allowed?" asks Spencer after climbing on board.

"Move on back, please," says Mrs. B.

"I like it," Kaitlynn chirps before shutting up for the ride.

Shelly stops halfway down the aisle. "Could we, like, bring an ornament from home to hang up?"

"Please find a seat, Shelly," says Mrs. B, and everybody notices she didn't say no.

Bender is the last on. The sparkle doesn't seem to create any answering sparkliness in him—he stomps up the steps and knocks the jingle bells aside, pulls the cap off Evan's head, and jerks the hood of Simon's sweatshirt over his eyes. Kaitlynn thinks of making a comment, but that would sort of break her vow of silence and won't do any good anyway. She hears Mrs. B sigh deeply and mutter something about incorrigibles before putting the bus in gear.

Another day, another dollar—or actually eighty cents from Igor and Jay, but lately she's been collecting more in the afternoon, especially if nobody bought dessert at lunch because it was dog-barfy apple crisp. Kaitlynn is feeling upbeat when the bus turns down Farm Road 152, but her mood shoots up like a Roman candle when the mystery shed rolls into view.

"Hey, they decorated too," says one of the littles.

The familiar scene scrolls by on the opposite windows: mossy roof, smudgy smoke, wispy trees with their bare branches. Under the cloudy sky, everything is some shade of gray or brown—except for the big plastic ribbon mounted around the near wall of the shed, just under the roof, tied in a wide bow with a sprig of pine.

And it's bright red.

The bus pauses a second longer than usual as Mrs. B's eyes rest on the bow, looking thoughtful. Kaitlynn is trying to remember what was special about red ribbons, when the memory springs like a jack-in-the-box: Bender's letter!

She twists around on the seat and looks toward the rear. Bender is staring out the window at the red bow, his jaw dropped like the bucket on Mike Mulligan's steam shovel.

* * *

That afternoon, after a trip that drags even more than usual, Kaitlynn jumps off the bus and catches up with Bender at the gazebo.

"What do you want?" he snaps at her.

"You sent a letter, didn't you?" His look tells her yes. "What did you say in it?"

"Nothing much." He steps up into the gazebo, drops on a bench, and gazes up at the ceiling. "Just, 'I know what you did last summer. The FBI has you under twenty-four-hour surveillance. If you want to talk, tie a red ribbon,' et cetera."

She gasps and swoops down beside him. "Bender!"

"I'm kidding, okay?"

"But there was something in it about a red ribbon, wasn't there? Or else they wouldn't have tied one."

"Yeah. I just asked if anybody there drove a black or dark blue pickup." He's looking down, picking crud out of the brass plaque that's mounted on the railing behind them. Kaitlynn knows what it says: *In Honor of Troy Lawrence Pasternak, Class of 1985.* Troy Lawrence was Jay's uncle, who was hurt in an accident right after graduating from high school. Or killed?— though Kaitlynn thinks *In Honor of* instead of *In Memory of* means the person is still alive. But still hurt—that's why the Pasternak Seniors built this nice gazebo for the neighborhood.

"A blue or black pickup? Why?"

"No special reason." Bender glares, meaning there darn well is a special reason but she'd better shut up about it.

"Did you sign your name?"

"'Course not. I just wrote 'From somebody on this bus.'"

"Okay." That seemed like a good signoff—mysterious but not threatening. "So if they have a black pickup, they were supposed to tie the ribbon." Bender nods shortly. "And they did! Now what?"

"Don't ask me." Bender is trying to look like his usual mean self, but there's a lot going on underneath. "They might just be decorating for Christmas."

"They're not just decorating for Christmas, and you know it!" Suddenly Kaitlynn is talking to an empty space because Bender has bolted. He's stomping down the gazebo steps. "Hey! You can't give up now, just when it gets interesting!"

He totally ignores that, striding across the commons on a direct line to his house. She races to catch up with him. "I think you should send another letter to 508 Farm Road 152 and tell them you're just a kid and don't mean any harm, but if they'd like to meet, they could hang a candy cane on the—"

That's as far as she gets before he throws an arm behind

him and almost smacks her in the jaw. But she still thinks it's a great idea.

That's Thursday. By Friday, the bus looks like an explosion in the Christmas factory, with decorations swaying from every dip of the sparkly tinsel garland. Igor asks if he can bring his family's fake fireplace with the fake light-up logs and set it up at the front of the bus, but Mrs. B tells him to sit down. The kettle collects a handful of change, even a couple of dollar bills...

On Monday, the second row of bricks is all filled in and the third is over halfway. Sixty-three dollars and thirty cents! Kaitlynn can't hold it in; a shout jumps out of her like a puppy let out of a carry-on cage after it's been cooped up for a flight to Florida. Then she collapses on the seat and starts ringing vigorously. Everybody who files by has to turn and look at the poster. Simon gives her a nod and a thumbs-up, Shelly says, "Way to go!" Miranda gasps in surprise, Matthew gives a quick sideways glance, Alice likewise but she also drops a quarter. Jay says, "Awesome!" Spencer says, "Munificent!" and Igor forgets to do anything goofy.

Bender, last on again, takes something from his pocket and slaps it on the poster. As he stomps down the aisle, Kaitlynn turns her head to see what he put there: a color photo of the shed, dressed in its Christmas best, from such an angle that a corner of roof from the house beyond juts into the frame. There is a patch of light in the upper corner, meaning Bender had taken it from the bus window. And printed it from his computer, because there was a border left at the bottom, cut a little crooked, and labeled *Mystery Stop*.

Kaitlynn frowns, wondering if this should be allowed. Maybe they need some rules.

But that afternoon, the picture is gone. She secretly sighs with relief because now she won't have to make a decision.

Except next morning, Bender does the exact same thing, with another copy of the same picture. And in the afternoon, it's gone.

Wednesday: picture up in the morning, down again in the afternoon. Total contributions for three days: four dollars and seventy-two cents, meaning one more brick filled. Everybody wondering what's up with Bender and Mrs. B (the only one who could be taking the picture down). Kaitlynn so excited she can hardly stand it. She cuts the last needy family out of the paper that night: Claudio and Virginia Esterbrook, whose baby was born with a hole in his heart and needs all kinds of surgery. She brings her double-sided tape so she can stick them on the poster while the others are boarding.

She's just finished when Mrs. B stops Bender in the aisle. "If you have another picture, don't bother. We already decided who gets voted on, and if everybody wants to add to the list, this project gets out of hand."

"Who decided?" Bender asks. "I didn't." He lifts his head and raises his voice. "Anybody here decide who to vote on?"

As everyone shakes their heads, Kaitlynn finally breaks her silence. "It was my idea! We wouldn't be taking money at all if I hadn't thought of it!"

"Yeah, but nobody would be giving if they didn't want to. And what's going to get out of hand if I add one more family?"

"They don't need this kind of help," Mrs. B says. "And how do you even know it's a family?"

"How do you know they don't need help?" Bender demands, his eyes narrowing suspiciously.

It's a good question, but Kaitlynn sees that Mrs. B is getting angry—not the quick toaster-pop kind of anger, like when she is telling them to pipe down or she'll stop this bus, but the slow kind that takes a while to build and almost as long to die. "Don't use that tone of voice with me, young man! Take your seat right now or I'll be having a talk with your parents this afternoon."

"Good luck with that," Bender mutters, starting down the aisle as Mrs. B bangs the door lever. Then he stops and raises his voice. "Who wants to add one more family to vote on?"

After a very short pause, Alice's hand shoots up. "Alice, you—" Mrs. B begins, but then she shuts herself up as though she'd almost said something ugly. Slowly, Miranda's hand goes up. Then Igor, Spencer, Jay, Shelly, and finally Matthew. In the front section, Simon is the first to raise his hand, which Kaitlynn thinks is kind of disloyal.

Bender turns around, grinning. "I love democracy."

Mrs. B's expression hasn't changed. "*Sit down*, Bender."

But that afternoon, when Kaitlynn takes her seat at the front of the bus, the picture is still there! All Mrs. B says is, "No speeches about these people. You know nothing about them."

For a half-second, Bender looks honestly grateful. "Thanks," he says.

Kaitlynn herself feels a little tippy, as if her project has come to a point and could either slide back or forward and she isn't sure which.

"Bender!" she hollers that afternoon, leaping off the bus so dramatically heads are turning as she catches up with him. "What's going on? Did you write another letter? Did you hear back?"

"Shhh!" He glances around as though hidden surveillance cameras might be monitoring his every move. "No, I didn't write another letter. I couldn't figure out what to write."

"But did you get something from them?"

He pauses before making a very brief, slight nod.

Kaitlynn gulps. It's like her stories have started coming true outside her head! "*Awesome!* What did they say?"

Again, he hesitates. Then he pulls an envelope out of the inside pocket of his jacket and hands it over.

The envelope has Bender's correct address but no name, just *To A Friend*. Inside is a Christmas card that's been cut to fit the envelope: a picture of a star with wise men on camels looking up at it. Inside is something about Wise Men Still Seeking Him, and she notices that the signature has been erased and written over. The writing says, *I know where you live.*

"Wow! How'd they figure out it was you? You didn't give them a return address, did you?"

He shakes his head irritably. "I'm not that stupid."

"So," she says eagerly, "it looks like somebody's stalking you, and you'd better watch your back."

He snatches the envelope. "A stalking message in a

Christmas card? And besides, it's obviously written by a kid, who's playing…some kind of game. And I don't want to play anymore."

"You don't know that! It might be a grown-up who's had a head injury like Troy Lawrence Pasternak so he writes big letters like that and now he's mad at the world and he thinks you're out to get him so he's going to get you first." She can't stop the giddy grin that stretches across her face.

"Shut *up*." Bender stuffs the envelope in his pocket. "And don't tell anybody, okay? The whole idea was really stupid."

"Then why are you trying to raise money for them? Is it to buy them off, so they'll leave you alone?"

He doesn't answer, just stalks across the common toward his house. Another mystery—Kaitlynn hugs herself and jumps up and down with excitement.

The next day, contributions total over five dollars, the most ever in a single afternoon. And on Monday morning, the grand total is ninety-three dollars—just seven short of their goal! As Hidden Acres kids pile on the bus, every one of them gazes in wonder at the almost-totally-red chimney. Spencer and Jay slap high fives, and Shelly says, "We did it!"

"Almost," Miranda corrects her, then adds, "Nice job, Kaitlynn."

Kaitlynn feels her smile glowing like a sixty-watt bulb. "Thanks."

Bender is one exception to the Good-Will-Toward-Men. He barely glances at the poster, stomping on—and later off— the bus without a word to anybody.

On the afternoon ride, Kaitlynn collects five dollars and

seventeen cents. Less than two dollars to go! She's the last off the bus at Hidden Acres, and as she leaps the two steps onto the ground, she's so pumped with success Bender has to yell twice to get her attention. He's standing at the entrance to the gazebo and not alone. Three of the littles have already started for home, but everybody else (except Shelly who stayed in town for a guitar lesson) lingers in a rough circle around Bender. He's speaking as she joins them.

"...vote on Wednesday. But we all know the family I put up won't win."

"You didn't put up a family," Spencer says. "You put up a *house*. Or technically, a shed."

"And we're the only ones who even know about it," Jay adds. "The guys who get on after us don't have a clue."

"I know who does have a clue," Bender says. "Mrs. B."

All eyes shift to the back of the school bus, just disappearing over the rise. "What do you mean?" asks Igor.

"She knows who lives there. The school superintendent doesn't make her stop every day at a place where nobody gets on. If there was some kind of screwup at the beginning of the year, they would've worked it out a long time before now."

Igor frowns, like this had never occurred to him. "So why does Mrs. B keep stopping there?"

Jay asks, "Is that any of our business?"

"Number one," Bender says, "I don't know. And number two...maybe."

"Could we cut this short?" Spencer complains. "It's cold out here."

119

"Okay." Bender takes a deep breath. "I was wondering if we—just us in the neighborhood—could raise a little more money for those people at the, uh, mystery stop."

Everybody is stunned. Is this Bender the bully speaking?

He stares back with a bullying expression. "Well, could we?"

Kaitlynn's feelings are mixed. So much that she's speechless, which is pretty unusual.

Miranda says, "I have about five dollars left over from Christmas shopping."

"I do too," Bender says. "Five dollars, I mean. Anybody else?"

He looks around expectantly. But the spirit of generosity isn't working overtime. *Unlike for her idea*, Kaitlynn can't help but think. It might have helped if Bender wore a Santa hat and rang jingle bells.

Matthew, on the edge of the group, drifts away and starts toward home. "I don't know," Jay says. "I'm maxed out right now, and we did just raise a hundred bucks."

"Besides," Spencer says, "how do we know the money will get to them?"

Bender's face goes a little redder than the weather can account for. "Because I say so."

"Don't get mad at me. You're the one with the history."

Spencer, who is smaller than Bender, might not have said such a thing if he hadn't been standing close to Jay, who's bigger. But what he said is true, as Kaitlynn knows from her Mother's-Day-card extortion incident last year.

Simon pipes up, "You can have my milk money for this week—two-fifty."

Simon hoards his milk money and has saved up almost forty dollars since school started. So it's not as generous as it sounds. And nobody makes a similar offer.

Jay shifts his backpack to one shoulder. "Nice thought and all, but not this time. See ya." He starts across the common with Spencer.

Miranda hesitates. "Well…let me know," she says at last. Bender just nods without looking at her, and she turns away, taking the opposite direction from Spencer and Jay. Evan tugs at Simon's jacket and they start toward the Killebrew house.

That leaves Kaitlynn, who finally finds her voice. "If you're going to do a community project, it should be different from the one that other people have already thought of."

"It's not a 'community project,'" he snaps. "Unlike some people, I don't do stuff just to get gold stars on a Sunday school chart."

As it happens, Kaitlynn does have a lot of gold stars on her Sunday school chart—except for the one about keeping quiet and paying attention—but so what? "I'm doing this because I feel sorry for families that won't have a good Christmas this year because—"

"Well, I don't feel sorry for people," he interrupts her, "and I don't want anybody feeling sorry for me."

Who does? she wonders. "Then why do you want to collect more money? So you'll have an excuse to take it to them and find out who they are?"

"No!" he says so fiercely she has to wonder if maybe the answer is really yes.

"Then why?"

"Do you want to cough up some cash?"

"No, because—"

"Then I'm not telling." He turns around, takes two running steps across the gazebo, and vaults over the opposite rail, which kids are always being told not to do because the gazebo is getting a little rickety. Mr. and Mrs. Pasternak Senior gave it to the community, but so far the community hasn't picked up a hammer to make the repairs everybody agrees need making.

Kaitlynn realizes she should still be glowing with success, but her bulb must have been hooked up to a dimmer switch because Bender sure turned it down. What's wrong with him? Can't he be happy with one Christmas good deed, instead of feeling he has to go one better? Even while wondering this, Kaitlynn somehow knows that Bender is not just playing a game of one-upmanship. And he's probably not buying off a stalker either, as cool as that would be. It may be a sneaky way to solve the mystery of the empty bus shed—but she doubts that too.

So what kind of game is it? She has no idea. And for an idea person, that feels about as comfortable as burrs under your socks.

Winter Break

On the Monday before New Year's, Mrs. B drives over to Hidden Acres for a newspaper interview and picture with Kaitlynn Killebrew. She doesn't drive the school bus, of course, just her trusty dark blue pickup. Maribeth Grand, the reporter/photographer, already has most of the story from Kaitlynn (probably more than she bargained for) by the time Mrs. B arrives to give a grown-up's perspective.

"I'm proud of what Kaitlynn and these kids accomplished," Mrs. B tells Maribeth. "It's an inspiration to everyone in the community."

Kaitlynn beams and is still beaming when Maribeth snaps the picture of her with the bus driver's arm across her shoulders and the chimney poster propped up between them with all its bricks colored in. They had exceeded their goal, raising $107.53 for Mr. Pressley with the runaway wife and three little kids.

Kaitlynn's little brother Simon speaks up from the floor, where he's sulking because they didn't let him in the picture.

"It would have been more. Bender wanted to raise extra for the mystery stop but—"

"What do you mean, Bender wanted to give money to them?" Mrs. B asks Simon in a tone that comes out rather sharp.

"Well, you know he *wanted* to," Kaitlynn reminds her, "or he wouldn't have put that picture up."

Simon pipes up again. "Bender said—"

"Why don't you get lost?" Kaitlynn interrupts. "Go play with your Cobra Force Space Station you've been begging for since Halloween."

"It's an *underground bunker*, not a space station." Sighing, Simon pushes himself off the floor and stomps out of the room. Maribeth Grand leaves shortly after, promising that the article will appear in Wednesday's paper.

Mrs. B leaves also. After climbing into the pickup, she decides to go the long way around Hidden Acres, which will take her past the Thompson house.

It's a dreary day with clouds hanging low as hammocks. Mrs. B drives slowly past the long driveway going up to the Truman house, where Alice lives. Even though she knows Mary Ellen Truman well—too well—Mrs. B doesn't even think of dropping in for a visit. Mainly because they haven't spoken to each other since August.

The next house on the loop is Pasternak Junior's, then someone she doesn't know because they don't have kids, then the Thompsons'. Mrs. B is wondering if she should try to get to the bottom of Bender's involvement with the mystery house. Does he know more than he should?

The first thing she notices is a for sale sign in the yard.

The pickup skids a little as she stomps the brake pedal. When did that happen? And why?

Job transfer? Downsizing? Or maybe a divorce?

A banging on her tailgate jerks her out of her reverie: *Clang! Clang! Clang!*

It's Pasternak Senior, one hand holding a leash and the other holding a cane, which must be made of steel for all the noise it's making. He's yelling too, but the noise of the cane is so loud she can't make out any words.

She rolls down the window: "Hey!"

The banging stops for a moment. "You've got a lotta nerve coming back here!" Then it starts again: *Clang! Clang!*

"Hey!" she yells, jumping out of the cab. "Stop that!"

He stops with the cane but not with the glare. "I'd be ashamed, if I were you."

Mrs. B glances around helplessly. She barely knows the old man, only enough to nod when he happens to be walking his dog past the gazebo while the kids are boarding. Fortunately Mrs. Pasternak Junior, Jay's mom, is hurrying out of their house nearby, tugging a jacket over her sweat suit, and calling, "Poppy! What's the matter?"

Pasternak Senior waves his cane and almost catches Mrs. B on the chin. "Back to the scene of the crime! Some nerve, I'd say."

"What crime?" Mrs. B asks.

"My stolen wheelchair!" he yells.

"But Poppy," Jay's mom says, "this is—you're the bus driver, aren't you?" she quickly asks Mrs. B. "Right. It's the bus driver, Poppy. She picks Jay up for school every morning."

The old man wrinkles up his forehead, which is already pretty wrinkled. "But it's a black pickup, like I saw that morning."

"You're not the one who saw it, Poppy, remember? Dave Killebrew saw it when he was loading his van, and he wasn't sure about the color—just dark, is all he said. And besides, this one's blue."

After a moment, Mr. Pasternak Senior lowers the cane and extends his other hand. "Forgive me, young lady. A case of mistaken identity."

Mrs. B shakes the hand. Anybody who calls her young lady obviously has some redeeming qualities. "Not a problem, sir. Happy New Year."

"Same to you." He tosses up the cane and touches it to his hat, like the hero of an old-fashioned movie musical in top hat and tails.

"Come on, Poppy," says his daughter-in-law. "I just put a pot of coffee on. Come in and warm up." They turn toward Pasternak Junior's house.

For the first time, Mrs. B notices that the leash Mr. Pasternak is holding has no dog on the other end of it.

January

Spencer's mom expects him to win the Nobel Prize in physics or chemistry someday. Spencer himself has begun to have his doubts.

He's a genius, according to his mother. According to his father too, sort of. When his father says so, it's in the context of, "Okay, genius, knock off the dissertation and go cut the grass!" Or, "Get your genius apparatus off the kitchen table so I can figure out what's wrong with my amplifier."

His mom, Maureen Maguire Haggerty, admits to being a little pushy sometimes but insists she isn't that way by nature. She was just a happy-go-lucky teenager when she dropped out of college to marry a struggling young musician who happened to be drop-dead gorgeous, and for years they lived large together, gig-to-gig and hand-to-mouth, until Spencer came along. If Spencer had been a normal baby who just slept and pooped all the time, Maureen Maguire Haggerty would have settled down to being a normal mother, whatever that was. Maybe even have more kids.

But from the first week, if not the first hour, Spencer was no ordinary baby. Everybody remarked on how attentive he was. "The nurses all said it looked exactly like you were *thinking* about them, the way you looked at things with your big blue eyes," his mom likes to say. And of course, he talked early and walked early, knew all the letters of the alphabet by the time he was two, and could read (not recite) *The Cat in the Hat* before kindergarten.

Raising a genius became a full-time job for Maureen Maguire Haggerty, who bought classical music for him to listen to and *Baby Einstein* DVDs to watch and flashcards to look at. As soon as he was old enough, she started enrolling him in science clubs and summer enrichment programs. Now that he's on the list for Space Camp, she is quietly checking out universities and scholarships.

Meanwhile his dad, Chuck Haggerty, the struggling musician, bought a house and half a music store. Running the store and teaching guitar and playing local gigs with his band, Whiplash, keeps him so busy he doesn't have much to say about Spencer's educational opportunities—except for the occasional, "Where we gonna get the money for that?" But in spite of his (sometimes) sarcastic comments, he agrees that Spencer is unusually bright and should be encouraged. "As long as we're not too pushy. Let him enjoy being a kid."

Spencer enjoys being a kid, but he mostly enjoys being a genius. Except lately, not so much.

"What are you doing for the science fair?" Igor asks him as they gather at the gazebo on the first day after winter break.

Igor is not what you'd call the academic type; normally he'd be asking everybody what they got for Christmas (Spencer got a NASA-rated telescope and an Ultra-Tetris game pack). So it's funny, and a little disturbing, that the first thing out of Igor's mouth this morning would be the very thing Spencer is starting to worry about. "Why?"

"'Cause I'm going to have the coolest project this year! I got the idea right after Christmas. I gotta scoop out the competition." Igor is talking so fast his words pile up on the cold air in little puffs of steam.

"You mean 'scope out.' What's your project?"

"It's a secret. And I'm gonna do it all by myself with no help. So what's yours?"

Igor's as eager as a squirmy little puppy, so Spencer decides to tell him. Not that it's a big secret: "Mouse maze."

"Awesome! You mean, with real mice?"

"Duh. What's the alternative—windup mice?"

"What are they supposed to do?"

"Run around in the maze—what else?" These questions are beginning to irritate him.

"Cool! I asked you first because you're sure to have the best project. But it won't beat mine."

The bus arrives, a blob of yellow on the gray landscape, rolling to a stop in a cloud of exhaust. The Thompsons' SUV pulls up at the same moment and ejects Bender from the backseat, but just as Mrs. Thompson steps on the accelerator, the STOP sign swings out from the side of the bus. She's so frustrated she almost lays on her horn but taps it instead, making a peevish little toot. Bender moseys over to the bus, taking his time to join the end of the line.

Spencer observes the drama while waiting to board.

"They're splitting up," says Shelly to Miranda, directly behind him.

"What? Who?"

"Bender's folks. Didn't you notice the for sale sign in their yard? His dad moved out when they got back from Colorado."

"How do you know?"

"Mrs. Thompson asked my mom to review her sales contracts, like Mr. Thompson used to do. It'll be a little extra money since Mom quit her job. But not enough." As he steps up into the bus, Spencer glances back to see Shelly make a face and nibble a fingernail.

Igor grabs a seat in front of Kaitlynn and immediately turns around to "scoop out" her science project. Jay boards last after dashing across the common. "Slept late," he explains, settling in next to Spencer. "Winter break ought to last a month, like they do in college."

The STOP sign snaps, and immediately Mrs. Thompson dodges around the bus, gunning the motor. "Did you hear about Bender?" Spencer asks Jay.

"Hear what?"

"His mom and dad are splitting up."

"Oh. Too bad. That must be why he's been such a jerk lately."

"What do you mean, *lately*?"

"Yeah." Jay yawns again. "Good point. Hey, me and Poppy made our play-offs chart last night. You want to hear my picks?"

"Sure," Spencer says, knowing he doesn't have much choice. Every January, Jay and his grandfather draw up their projected Super Bowl play-off teams, with winners and point spreads. That means football talk for a whole month, or actually from mid-December to mid-February. Spencer puts up with it. Jay is in the middle of a long-winded comparison between the Patriots and the Giants when Bender yells from the back of the bus.

"HEY!" Heads turn to the back where he sits straight as a pencil. "We didn't stop!"

It's true—instead of slowing and turning on Farm Road 152, the bus barreled right by.

"What's going on?" Bender demands.

"It's not on the route anymore," Mrs. B calls back.

"How come?"

"Is that any of your business?" The driver is keeping her eyes forward.

Bender slumps back in his seat, arms crossed and brow furrowed, as though thinking through one of his math problems. Meanwhile, a scuffling in the seat in front of Spencer earns a roar from Mrs. B.

"Sit DOWN, Igor!"

"Dang," Igor mutters, shrinking back to his place in front of Kaitlynn. "Jay!" he hisses across the aisle. "Catch you later!"

"What's he all excited about?" Jay asks Spencer.

"Science fair."

"Dude." Jay's jaw creaks with another yawn. "Science fair's not for *weeks*. Who's thinking about it now?"

* * *

Spencer, that's who. Science fair is a very big deal around his house, since he's supposed to win the Nobel Prize someday. Ever since third grade, when his mom came down hard on his desire to build a plaster volcano ("*No* volcanoes. If you can't do something original, don't do anything."), he'd come up with a bigger and better project every year. This year especially, because sixth-graders are eligible to go to the regional science fair in March and state in May. Then on to nationals in June. He's aiming for state, though nationals would be fine with him too.

His project had sounded promising at first. "I'm going to build a mouse maze," he told his mom early in October.

"Great. And what will you investigate with the maze?"

He hadn't thought far beyond the basic idea, mostly because he just wanted to build a maze. Mazes were cool. "Um…test their memory."

"Sounds good. How?"

He did some online research and discovered several nutritional supplements that were supposed to feed the frontal lobe—the section of the brain mostly responsible for memory. The most extravagant claims were for milk thistle, a substance he'd never heard of. But it was available at the local health food store.

So there was his plan: buy the mice, build the maze, run the trials, and keep careful records to determine if herbal supplements really had any effect on the critters' memories. He should have started in November, but his mom signed him up for an interactive "Live Cam in Space" project that required a lot of prep, and his Youth Court duties took up way more time than he expected.

In December, his "normal kid" regulator kicked in: with Christmas and winter break, who wanted to worry about the science fair? After a little prodding from his mom, he purchased three pairs of mice in various colors, which he named Lucy and Linus, Albert and Marie, and George and Martha. He kept the sexes apart, or at least tried to, until he discovered George building a nest. So Georgina went into the ladies' cage and Spencer kept the babies as alternates, even though two of them died tragically young.

The mice are the raw material for his experiment but don't actually get down to business until the first weekend in January. "It'll be awesome," he tells Jay, who's helping build the maze.

"I guess," Jay says as he lets Lucy crawl over his hand. He's supposed to be cutting corrugated cardboard strips. "These things feel creepy with their itty bitty paws."

"Put it back. They shouldn't be handled too much—it might interfere with the data."

"'Interfere with the data'? That's so *scientific*, dude. Hey, what if you breed a superior race of mice that remember where you put your gym shoes? You could teach 'em to communicate and sell 'em in little cages so they could be carried right along with us and—argh! It pooped on me!"

"They do that a lot. Put it back, okay? No, not in the boys' cage—the other one!"

"Stupid mice." Jay returns Lucy to her cage, a converted aquarium with a screen wire top. "For little things, they sure do stink."

"They eat all the time. So they poop all the time. That's what my research has uncovered so far."

"Cool. I didn't know science could be so…"

"Interesting? Useful?"

"No…poopy."

Spencer hadn't realized how science could be so frustrating. Earlier projects from third, fourth, and fifth grade involved bread mold, sunflowers, and earthworms. They had also involved help from his mother, but both agreed he was going to do it on his own this year. That might have been the kind of resolution made to be broken, except that last fall, Chuck Haggerty bought out his partner to become sole owner of the music store, and Maureen Maguire Haggerty is really busy with bookkeeping and taxes. So whenever Spencer starts to ask her a project-related question, she shakes her head. "Uh-uh. It's strictly hands-off this year, remember? Look it up or ask Mr. Betts."

Mr. Betts is his science teacher but not much better than his mom when it comes to questions. He seldom gives a straight answer but makes suggestions about how you can find it out on your own, which is really helpful. Not.

So Spencer is on his own, even when Georgina croaks and Martha escapes and Lucy and Albert nibble holes in his cardboard maze because he left them in there too long. Or, worst of all, show no improvement in memory whatsoever, even when he ups the dosage or combines memory-boosting supplements. He keeps careful records on his laptop—except for the three days' worth that he accidentally deleted and couldn't get back. And that week he was sick with the flu. But no matter how he views the data, it still says the same thing. Which is nothing.

"Well, then," his mother says after three weeks. "That's your result. 'Commonly marketed herbal supplements promoted as memory enhancers are shown to have no discernible effect on laboratory mice.'" She's slicing beef for sukiyaki and can't help looking disappointed because his project isn't sexy enough to go to state.

"That's not very interesting," Spencer mutters.

"Except now you know what *doesn't* work—"

"You know what?" his dad chimes in while crossing the kitchen from the garage. "I'll bet most scientific research is boring as a box of rocks. Ninety percent, at least."

"Don't discourage him, Chuck—"

"I'm not. That's just a fact. I'll write a song about it; that'll be interesting."

What makes it worse is that his peers in the neighborhood—well, some of them…okay, two of them—are really getting into the fair this year. Igor still refuses to say what his project is, only that it'll be the best ever. Hard to believe, because Igor went the volcano route in fourth grade and nothing before. This year, he's not only entering, but he continues to be very interested in the competition.

"What are you doing?" he asks everybody on the bus,

even the Brothers Calamity (who just laugh at him). When asked, Matthew shrugs, Kaitlynn cheerfully admits to making a volcano, Miranda's has something to do with plants, and whatever Alice says is soon forgotten. Shelly gasps, "Science project?! My camp application is due in *four weeks*! I have to finish my demo CD!"

Jay is studying the salt-replacing effects of Gatorade, and Bender is making a shrunken head.

"Wow!" gasps Igor. "A real one?"

Bender snorts. "Why bother if it's not real? I've been reading up on how they do it in South America."

Igor is so excited he's halfway over the seat. "So how do they do it in South America?"

"Sit down, Igor!" Mrs. B yells from the front.

"First," says Bender, "you take off the head of the victim."

Jay, who is sitting with Spencer across the aisle, joins the conversation. "But don't you have to ask them if you can borrow it?"

"Whatever. Then you peel the skin from the skull and throw the skull away."

Spencer is intrigued in spite of himself. "Why don't you keep it?"

"Okay, you keep it if you want a nice pencil holder for your desk. But for the skin, first you boil it till it shrinks to about half-size, then turn it inside out and scrape all the flesh off and let it dry for at least a day. Then you sew the mouth and eyes closed and stuff it with hot rocks to make it shrink even more. After about three days—"

"Okay, okay," Igor interrupts. "It's not for real, right?"

"Of course it's for real. That's how they did it—do it."

"But you're not going to get a real head and—"

"I think beheading is against the law," Spencer points out.

"Definitely," Jay agrees.

"Uh-huh," Bender says. "Ever hear of medical schools? And morgues?"

Of course, everybody hears about Bender's project from Igor, and at least it steals interest from Spencer's pathetic little mouse maze. He wishes he'd never even thought of the idea now—it's totally lame. Or maybe if he'd started it sooner…but how could he, with track and extra credit reading in social studies and the glee club Christmas show? And by the way, how smart was that, to let the music teacher talk him into glee club as a way of "branching out"? During the second session of Youth Court this month, he got in a shouting match with one of the defendants and had to be suspended ("recused") from the case by Mr. Pearsall, who later asked him if he was feeling stressed.

He'll probably get a good grade on the science project, as well as encouraging remarks and reminders—lots of them—that research is one part inspiration and nine parts perspiration. Also that Thomas Edison tried, like, three thousand six hundred seventy-two different filaments before he came up with the one for his incandescent lightbulb. But still, boring as a box of rocks, as his dad says, even though some girls will think the mice are cute.

"There's always next year!" his mom says brightly.

But actually, science fair is only a symptom of the real problem.

The real problem is Spencer is starting to think he's not genius material after all. Only smart enough to get into the gifted and talented program where, instead of math drills and spelling tests, you do group projects and enrichment circles (which are really easier but that's a secret nobody tells).

His doubts began with the physics camp in St. Louis last summer. It was a little over his head, but that was only to be expected since most of the participants were one or two grades above him. One of the speakers was an astronomer from McDonald Observatory who took them to the Science Center Planetarium and talked about supernovas and black holes. To tell the truth, Spencer couldn't follow a lot of it, but the parts he did understand sounded really cool. The guy kept mentioning this book: *A Brief History of Time*.

So when Spencer got back from camp, he checked out the book from the library. It's by this guy Stephen Hawking, a physicist with ALS. That's a disease that twisted his body so he looks like a pretzel. But ALS didn't affect his brain.

Chapter One was okay, but Spencer read Chapter Two twice and felt even dumber the second time. Of course, he was only twelve and lacked a few basic concepts (as his mom said) so he returned the book to the library and forgot about it...

Until the morning he passes Matthew on the bus and happens to notice he's reading a book and immediately recognizes the cover because Stephen Hawking is hard to mistake: *A Brief History of Time*.

He stops so abruptly Jay runs into him. "Hey!"

Spencer is staring, which he knows is rude but he can't help it. "Do you get that book?" he blurts out.

Matthew looks up, startled. "Huh?"

"That book. Do you understand it?"

"Yeah…mostly."

"Move it, dude," Jay says behind him. Spencer moves, but it's like he's sleepwalking.

Matthew understands! Matthew and Stephen Hawking are homies! Matthew the weird, the silent, is just possibly a genius. Don't they say Einstein was kind of a weird kid too?

"What's up with you?" Jay asks. "You mad at somebody?"

"No." But actually, yes.

It bothers him so much that that afternoon, after the bus has emptied and its passengers are scattering, Spencer catches up to Matthew at the bend of Courtney Circle, where Meadow Lane runs to a cul-de-sac.

"So," Spencer says, panting, "are you doing a science project on that book or what?"

Matthew glances around like he's looking for an escape. "Why?"

"I just want to know. Because…because I read it last summer." *Stupid*, he thinks. If Matthew asks him anything about it, he's dead in the water.

"I'm interested," Matthew says, and after a pause, "Is that okay?"

"Sure it is. I just wondered if you were doing anything with it."

Matthew's expression changes from irritated to cornered again. "What if I am?"

"Nothing! I just—" Spencer has to stop. What does he *just*, after all? "Well, are you?"

"Only if my mother makes me," says Matthew. "Bye." He stalks away toward his house on the south side of the cul-de-sac. Spencer lingers a moment, telling himself to chill.

But Rude Shock Number Two awaits him at home: Marie, one of the mice in his control group, has expired. In other words, croaked. She's lying in a corner of the cage with her tiny claws curled up while Lucy sniffs around interestedly, like she might take a nibble. "I can't believe this! Do real scientists go through mice this fast?"

"I'm sure they do." His mother, drawn from her desk by his cry of dismay, shakes her head in sympathy. "Dozens of them. Maybe you should have started a month earlier and set up a breeding operation in the garage so you'd have all the mice you needed. But hindsight's 20/20."

"It was a stupid idea. I wish I'd never even thought of it."

"It was a good idea, Spencer. It just needed a little more setup time."

"I was busy."

"You were too busy. I was afraid you'd get overcommitted with Youth Court and glee club, and it looks like you did. Next year, you'll have to set some priorities and—"

"I don't want to do this next year. I don't want to do anything!"

"Come on, sweetie. Every scientist has setbacks. Genius is one part inspiration and—"

"I'm *not* a genius!" Spencer throws his jacket, which catches the mouse cage by one corner and knocks the lid askew. Then he picks up the maze and slams it on the table top, jarring some of the walls loose.

"Spencer! What's gotten into you?" his mother yells. "Stop that right now! It's not like you have all the time in the world to put it back together."

"Who says I'm putting it back together?"

"What do you mean?"

"I mean, I am not entering this inane project!"

"Yes, you are!" She throws herself between him and his maze, her red hair blazing. Along with the rest of her. Though he's tall enough now for them to see eye to eye, she more than matches his determination. "I did not raise a quitter!" She's practically screaming. "This was your idea, and what you start, you finish!"

This is more excitement than the mice have seen in all their short, experimental lives and much more than Spencer wants. After realizing he can't punch his mom, he unclenches his fists. "Okay. *Okay*. I'll finish the stupid project, but I'll probably get a C on it, and I don't even care."

"Don't use that snarky tone with me, young man. Go to your room!"

She hasn't sent him to his room since he was ten. He rolls his eyes as he goes, and an hour later, he refuses to come out for dinner. "Fine!" snaps his mom, flouncing away from the door. The soles of her Nikes, which must have picked up something sticky in the kitchen, squelch angrily down the hall. Spencer tunes them out as he lies on his bed, staring up at the phosphorescent stars he and his mom stuck on the ceiling years ago.

Reputations are hard to lose once you have one. For instance, everybody labels Bender as a bully, not without reason. But Bender also has an amazing number sense that people don't see because they're not looking for it. Or Igor is supposed to be dumb because his grades are poor as dirt. But he can strategize with the best, as Spencer knows from playing *World at War* with (and losing to) him. And Jay's the typical average student, but since his grandfather taught him to play chess, he's won two school tournaments and beats Spencer three times out of four.

"Everybody is smart in their own way," his mom likes to say, even though she obviously thinks his way is the best: letter-, number-, book-smart. Straight-A-smart. But not genius-smart. In fact, genius probably has nothing to do with the kind of smart Spencer is. How much longer can he get away with it?

A knock comes about seven o'clock. "*What?*" Spencer says.

"What yourself?" says the voice outside.

Spencer sighs, sitting up on the bed. "Come in, Dad."

The doorknob turns and his father glides in, one hand gripping the neck of an acoustic guitar—a Martin, not top of the line, but close. He closes the door behind him. "So what's the drama queen scene around here?"

"Didn't Mom tell you?"

"Well, yeah—if you want to call it 'telling.' With all the dashes and exclamation marks and hah!—hah!—" Here his dad imitates perfectly the sharp, angry sighs Mom uses for punctuation when she's upset. "With all that, I'm not sure I got the whole story."

Spencer has to smile, a little. "You probably got most of it."

His dad ambles across the carpet and sinks down on the bed. Chuck Haggerty is still good-looking, as dads go—Shelly, who takes guitar lessons from him, once told Spencer his dad was *hot*. Which is not a word that should apply to a parent, but that's just Shelly. Chuck tosses a lock of wavy brown hair out of his eyes with a sideways jerk. "Mind if I tune while we talk?" Spencer shrugs, and his dad plays a soft chord, frowning at the sour tone. Tightening one of the keys, he asks, "So what's the deal, genius?"

"Don't call me that!"

"Whoa, man." (*Twannnng!* goes a string.) "What's the matter, pushed your hot button? You find somebody smarter than you?"

Spencer is so startled he answers honestly. "Uh, yeah. Maybe."

His father nods, plucking the opening bass riff from "Heartbreak Hotel." "Right. Word of wisdom from your old man: get over it."

Spencer swallows. "That's three words."

"Who's counting? Listen, I was just a few years older than you when I decided I was going to play the greatest guitar since Jimi Hendrix."

"Who?"

Chuck shakes his head. "Kids today. You're talkin' guitar hero?" He hunches over the Martin, and his right hand swoops down on the strings, ripping out a series of chords. "That was Jimi. My one ambition: good as him. Or better, that would be okay too."

"Is there some kind of…Jimmy Henderson Guitar Olympics you could compete in?"

"*Hendrix.* As a matter of fact, there is. The annual Hendrix Last Man Standing Play-offs in Seattle. Jimi's hometown."

Sometimes Spencer suspects his dad is making stuff up. "Let me guess. You were not the last man standing."

"Buddy, I didn't even get to Seattle." Absently, Chuck strums a series of bluesy chords. "Bunch of us got together in Des Moines to put a purse together for the winner to go to the big show. All-night jam in the Rough House Club, winner by acclamation. I came in third. In *Des Moines.*" His fingers still strumming, his eyes go somewhere else.

"That's tough," Spencer says after a minute.

The faraway eyes return. "That's life, buddy. Win some, lose some." (*Ta da!* sing the strings.) "And there's always compensation. Like you." Chuck Haggerty reaches forward, claps a hand on Spencer's head, and tousles his red hair, something he hasn't done since Spencer was maybe nine. "Hey, now I've got her tuned, you want to take her for a ride?" He means the guitar.

"I don't think so. Not now—"

"Yes, now. Music hath charms, y'know. To soothe the savage beast."

Chuck hands over the instrument, and Spencer has to take it. Sighing, he plays a G chord. Then plays it again, note by note. "The C string sounds a little off."

"Good ear." His dad nods. "See if you can get it back on." Spencer tightens the key, plucking the string continuously until it sounds right to him. "That's it. Now wing off."

Spencer plays a succession of C, G, and D—all the chords he knows. He plays them again in a different order, then allows his dad to show him an easy fingering pattern for stepping between the chords. It's kind of fun, actually.

"Cool!" says Chuck. "Let me grab the Gib, and we'll jam." The Gib is his prize Gibson that only he is allowed to play.

Spencer quickly hands over the guitar. "Not now, Dad. I've got a big algebra test tomorrow, and I'm so behind I'll probably have to study for it."

"Yeah…okay." Chuck takes the instrument reluctantly, remembering what he came in for. "And this science fair thing? Think you ought to finish what you start 'n' all that?"

"Yeah. I'll finish it."

"Rockin'." His dad socks him gently on the shoulder before standing up. "Next year? Do something without mice. They stink, man. And remember we still love ya, even if you don't turn out to be a boy wonder."

Spencer kind of smiles as his dad shuts the door behind him, but he doesn't feel much better. It isn't his mother's standards he's trying to meet, not anymore. It's his own.

* * *

"There!" exclaims his mom. "I don't know about you, but I think it looks very professional!"

Once they've set it up in the junior high gym, his project looks better than he thought it would. His display board catches the eye in a way that distracts from how boring the results are. He's also made a little booklet with biographies of all the mice—some details invented—including epitaphs for the ones who had died in the line of duty. ("Cute!" his mother says. "Imaginative—the judges'll like that.") The maze occupies the space in front of the display board, with a fresh coat of spray paint to disguise the patched holes. Tomorrow he'll bring his two best-performing mice and run them through as part of his presentation.

This might not be so bad after all.

The other exhibits are mostly run-of-the-mill. Bender has not come through with a shrunken head—no surprise. Igor's supersecret project turns out to be a display board about snakes. Spencer doesn't take time to read it; though neat enough, he doesn't expect it to win more than a participation ribbon. Alice's project makes him pause—it's about spinal cord injuries and how they affect the motor skills of victims, especially with walking. She used a naked Ken doll, its back discreetly turned to the passersby, to show the connection of nerves and muscles in the lower spine. She also made a booklet of rehab exercises. He takes a minute to thumb through the booklet with its carefully drawn pictures and handwriting that slopes downward on the page. Behind him, passing kids snigger at Ken's plastic butt.

Spencer sees a few more projects likely to win first and second-place ribbons, but his chances of winning best of show, and maybe going on to regionals, are looking pretty good.

On the way out, they meet Matthew and his mother coming in. With a box and a display board. Instantly, Spencer feels his confidence take a dive from a thirty-foot tower without a bungee cord.

"Hi, Camille," says his mom. "So Matthew has a project this year?"

"Just barely," replies Ms. Tupper. "He finished it less than an hour ago. And if it weren't for my being an obnoxious nag about it, we wouldn't be here at all."

"I know the feeling," Maureen Maguire Haggerty says, and Spencer grimaces. It's the first time he's felt any kinship with Matthew—mother trouble—though Matthew's face doesn't show anything.

"What's your project on?" he asks.

Matthew looks up in that quick, defensive way he has, as though startled anyone would notice him. "Physics."

"Better go," his mom says. "We'll barely have time to set up as it is."

With a round of "see you's," they part company. "Well," says Mom, once they're out of earshot, "I didn't notice any competition, did you?"

Spencer shakes his head, but now he's not too sure.

* * *

Loading the bus next morning takes longer than usual because of extra baggage—all the bits and pieces of projects that didn't get set up the night before, especially among the littles. Also, it's stuffed animal day for the kindergartners, meaning an argument between Mrs. B and Igor's little brother Al over whether his giant gorilla should be allowed to take up a whole seat. "Okay," she finally allows. "But if the bus is full on the way home, the gorilla stays behind. *Comprende?*"

Spencer brings Lucy and Linus, his best runners, in a small plastic cage. Kaitlynn thinks they're adorable. "Please, can I hold them?"

"Sure." He doesn't care if she takes them home, once they've done their run for the judges. He never wants to see another mouse. "Just don't open the cage."

"Of *course* not!"

"Did you see my project last night?" Igor asks eagerly. "What do you think?"

"Um, looks nice."

"Wait'll the judging comes up." Igor hugs his backpack. "Just wait."

"O-kaay."

"Everybody sit down!" Mrs. B yells. "Bender, are you staying there?"

Bender, who is three seats from the back instead of his usual rear-most position, just nods. While taking a seat beside Jay, Spencer notices a little smile on Bender's face and wonders what he's up to. Shelly and Miranda are two seats in front of him and Jay, Igor just behind Bender, Kaitlynn in the middle of the bus, Matthew in the second seat from the back, as usual. Spencer eyes Matthew before sitting down: no apparent extra equipment for his project. *Get a grip*, he tells himself. Just because Matthew was reading that book one time doesn't mean squat. He could have lied about understanding it. And a project about "physics" could be anything, like a solar system model made of Styrofoam balls.

Alice boards last and takes a seat by herself, just in front of Kaitlynn. "Want to see some adorable mice?" Kaitlynn asks her.

"Don't open that cage!" Mrs. B calls back.

"I'm *not!*"

The bus pulls away from the subdivision, rolls down Farm Road 216, pauses at the corner, and pulls out on the highway.

"Attention, people! I have another service project," Shelly announces.

"You're moving to Alaska?" Bender asks. "As a public service?"

Shelly ignores him. "It's a canned food drive. Tomorrow I'm going—"

"*We're* going," Miranda corrects her.

"Miranda and I are going around the neighborhood with a bag for each house. Put any canned goods you can spare in the bag, and we'll be back to pick them up on—"

Bender takes something out of his backpack—something a little smaller than a baseball. "Here, catch!" he calls, throwing it in Shelly's direction.

At that point, all heck breaks loose.

She catches the object, turns it, and screams, throwing it back without aiming. It lands on Igor's lap.

Igor jumps up, spilling his backpack to the floor. "A shrunken head!" he yells. "Bender made a SHRUNKEN HEAD!" He kicks the object behind him, where it rolls in front of Matthew, who jumps up with a strangled cry and kicks the head down the aisle.

"WHAT THE SAM HILL IS GOING ON BACK THERE?!" yells Mrs. B. Except she doesn't exactly say *Sam Hill*.

"Bender did it!" Shelly screams. "He threw that thing at me!"

"It's a shrunken head!" Igor yells over her.

"No, it's not!" Bender shouted. "It's just a—"

"Bender! You are in big trouble—"

Kaitlynn lets loose with an absolutely every-hair-on-your-arm-raising scream: "SNAKE! There's a snake on the floor! I saw it!"

It should be illegal to yell such a thing on a school bus. But it's apparently true—little kids are now screaming, "Snake! Snake!" and climbing up on their seats. And Igor is shouting, "Don't hurt her! She's mine—don't stomp her, *please*!"

Spencer seems to be the only one sitting still. Jay is on his feet, peering ahead, shouting "Where? *Where?*" Almost everybody is shouting by now, except Mrs. B. Spencer notices the bus turning right and bumping down the familiar half-mile of Farm Road 152. Just like old times, the bus pulls even with the shed then backs into the crossroads. Mrs. B jerks the gearshift, swings the door lever, and charges down the aisle. She grabs Alice by the upper arm and pulls her back toward the front, yelling, "Everybody off! Now! Except you, Igor. *And* Bender. You two stay and catch the snake."

"Can I stay too?" Jay asks.

"*Everybody!* Don't argue with me!" Mrs. B has pushed Alice through the door—Spencer is wondering why start with her, unless Mrs. B thought the girl was too quiet and inconspicuous to even move on her own—and now the driver is practically shoving the hysterical littles after Alice, one by one. Snakes are cold-blooded, Spencer remembers, and would head for the heat, like somebody's pant leg. That thought makes him want to get someplace cold, really quick.

Jay is grumbling behind him, "I'll bet I'm the best snake catcher on this bus."

Meanwhile Igor moans, "She's harmless! Don't step on her, *please.*" The girls are pale as marshmallows but at least they're quiet, even Kaitlynn.

Evacuating a bus on a January morning, with shreds of gray cloud spitting snow, turns out not to be fun. The littles huddle together in the bus shed, guarded by Mrs. B, who keeps yelling at them to "Stay right here! Don't wander off! Right here!" Spencer, Jay, and the girls are closer to the bus door, where Jay keeps trying to see in.

"Don't even think about it, Jay!" Mrs. B calls.

"Think about *what?* Dude," he mutters, "I just want to know what's going on." They can hear the thump of feet inside and the muffled voices of the two boys shouting at each other: "I see her!" "Get over by the emergency window—no, the other one!"

"Hey, Shelly," says Jay, "you want to see what Bender threw at you?" He takes it out of his jacket, a roundish object on a string. One side of it is covered with coarse black hair that turns out to be a patch of fake fur. The other side looks somewhat like a face, with a piggish nose and black beans for eyes, one of which has fallen out.

"It's just a dried-up apple," Jay says.

"That is *so* lame," Shelly sniffs.

"Bender might get expelled for this," says Miranda.

"Igor should too," says Shelly. "Who's *insane* enough to bring a live snake on a bus?"

Kaitlynn still hasn't said a thing. When Alice asks her, "What kind of snake is it?" she just stares.

"Where's Matthew?" shouts Mrs. B.

"I'll look," Spencer volunteers. Earlier he noticed Matthew wandering to the back of the shed, so he follows. Coming around the corner, he sees the other boy bending to pick up something from the ground. Spencer notices lines that look like bike tracks in the sandy soil. Or like two bikes running parallel. Or like a wheelchair? Curious.

"What's that?" he asks as Matthew studies the object he picked up.

Matthew jerks in surprise. "I don't know. Some kind of belt buckle or…I don't know." Reluctantly, he holds it out: a rectangular piece of pewter-colored metal with an eagle on it, wings spread as though ready to take flight.

"Might be valuable," Spencer says.

"Maybe." Matthew sticks it in his jacket pocket.

"You might be stealing," Spencer says, more pointedly.

"Finders keepers. I guess."

"So…" Spencer awkwardly gets around to what he really wants to know. "Did you set up your project in time?" Matthew nods in reply, his eyes on the ground. "What's it about? Besides 'physics'?"

"Black holes."

"Really?" Spencer feels his stomach tightening. "What about them?"

Matthew glances around, like he hopes for an alternate universe to open up nearby. Why can't he ever just look *at* anybody? "Like…equations based on general relativity and a computer model of what it would take to turn our sun into a black hole."

Spencer opens his mouth to say something totally fake like, "Sounds cool," when a shout from the bus breaks off the conversation.

They run around the shed. Two boys are standing in the open doorway of the bus. Igor holds a rippling orange-and-gold corn snake by the neck. If a snake can be said to have a neck. "See? She's *nice*. Her name's Cornelia, and my stepdad got her for Christmas. She's the best part of my science project, and I was going to show and tell about her during the judging today. Only my backpack fell over when Shelly threw that head at me and—"

"I didn't throw it at *you*!" Shelly sputters.

"Hey, Spence," Bender says. "Sorry about the little rodent." He holds out a clenched fist, from which something is swinging by the tail: Lucy, who appears to be deceased, stiff little legs splayed like a tick's. "At least we rescued it before Cornelia got her jaws on it. The other one got away."

All at once, Kaitlynn starts talking again. "I just opened the cage to pet them, one time, then I closed it again, only I guess it wasn't closed all the way, because when I saw that snake, I jumped and the mouse cage hit the floor and I'm really sorry because now your project is ruined and…."

Spencer's reaction surprises everybody, most of all himself. He laughs. In fact, he laughs so hard his legs can't hold him up anymore, and he collapses on the rough gravel road.

February

Matthew Tupper never expected to be famous. But after the science fair, he was, a little. Because he had to go and win it.

"Black Holes and White Dwarfs" was just something he got interested in, right about the time his mother decided he had to do a science fair project. "It's time you started participating in school, not just dreaming your life away. Dreams have to meet reality sooner or later."

His grandmother disagreed. "Participate in what, I'd like to know? The system? The system that kept our people oppressed for my-lennia?"

"Not millennia, Mama. Centuries, maybe."

"Makes no difference. If Matthew participates in the system, it oughta be 'cause he wants to, not 'cause you make him. Stop aggravatin' the boy."

"I don't call it 'aggravating' to insist he do his best and get off that planet he lives on…"

And there they'd go. One good thing about a mama and a granny who are at odds all the time is that once they start arguing, they forget about him.

Though, to be fair, they don't mess with him much, being busy with their own stuff. His mother teaches English at the community college while working on her PhD in African American literature. His grandmother leads a double life: Granny at home and "Uthisha the Zulu Storyteller" at folk festivals, schools, and book fairs all over the Midwest. She had traced her ancestry, near as she could tell, to South Africa—so the Zulu thing isn't all the way bogus. But she was born Gloria Potts in Kansas City. They moved here two years ago, mostly so Matthew could go to a nice small-town school and not be tempted to join a gang. Which is okay with him, but shows you how clueless his mother is sometimes: they don't have gangs on that planet he lives on.

Some of his teachers worry about him. "Are you feeling all right, Matthew?" "Are things okay at home?" "Have you been getting enough sleep?" Yeah, yeah, yeah to all that. He knows what they're thinking, though. It was the same in Kansas City. Every time some kid goes berserk and shoots up his school, all the teachers and neighbors and relatives are shocked. "He was such a quiet young man, never bothered anybody." "He was so polite." "He always followed directions and colored inside the lines." That's Matthew.

Except it isn't.

Sure he colors inside the lines, but that's because he figured out a long time ago that if you just do what they want, they'll leave you alone. Mostly. Doing what they want doesn't take a lot of brainpower, and that's good, because whatever he happens to be interested in, he thinks about *all the time*. He used to assume this was normal but has begun to see it's not.

Like when Calvin moved away. Calvin was his best friend— duh, only friend—in third and fourth grade, probably because he was brainy and bookish and his dad, a professor at the University of Missouri–Kansas City, was dating Matthew's mother. That threw them together a lot, like on picnics and trips to the zoo. But they'd already used up their common interests when Calvin came over to say that his father had just accepted an offer from the University of Wyoming.

He wasn't happy. Matthew got that, but not much else. He was lying on his stomach by his grandmother's rose garden, studying an anthill and wondering if ants ever got tired.

They didn't seem to, running around like machines. But even machines had to get their energy from somewhere, like batteries. If ants wore down, how did they get recharged? Or maybe they didn't; maybe they just wore out and dried up and new ants took their place, again and again and again. How could you tell? It wasn't like they had any distinguishing marks.

Maybe he could borrow a bottle of his mother's nail polish and mark each one with a tiny dot and then change color the next day, and the next, and see how long the original colors stuck around, and keep records—

"Hey, man? You hear anything I said?"

Calvin was interrupting some interesting questions. "Uh…
you're moving."

"Way to go, Sherlock! Do you remember why?"

"Did you tell me?"

Calvin stood up and kicked the anthill into oblivion.
"That's it! Bet you won't even notice when I'm gone."

He was right about that. Matthew didn't notice too much,
though they parted on good enough terms and Calvin said
he would email but only did once. Which was okay, because
Matthew didn't even once.

By the end of that same summer, his mother earned her
master's degree and accepted a teaching job at a community
college eighty miles away. The family moved to Hidden
Acres—White Breadville, Granny called it. The neighbors
thought she was priceless. Matthew's obsessions migrated
from insects to perpetual motion to time travel to relativity to
astrophysics, leading to this year's science fair project he was
glad was over. Except he had to go and win it.

* * *

"You're famous!" Kaitlynn hollers as she jumps on the bus and
waves her copy of a newspaper in his face. It's February, and
those are her first words to him all year.

Jay leans over the seat to have a look. "That's you all right.
Didn't know you won. Way to go, dude." That's the most Jay
has ever said to him too.

"Thanks," Matthew says uncertainly.

"Did you see it, Spencer?" Kaitlynn pokes the newspaper at him, but Spencer just shakes his head, pushes past her, and plops down in the next-to-last seat.

"Everybody sit down!" Mrs. B shouts, putting the bus in gear.

"Let me see." Bender reaches over the backs of two seats. This is his first day back on the bus after a week of suspension for causing a disturbance with his shrunken head. (Igor's been suspended for two weeks.)

Kaitlynn hands the newspaper back, meanwhile chattering away, "It's a really long article. Maribeth Grand wrote it— she's the same one who came over and interviewed me! To tell the truth, I didn't understand all the science stuff…"

To tell the truth, Matthew is thinking, the reporter didn't seem to understand it either—he'd bet anything she hashed up the explanation.

"…and if you read the whole article, it says at the end that the project is going to the regional science fair…"

Unfortunately so, and he may have to ride the thing all the way to state.

"…or even nationals! I didn't even know there was such a thing as a National Science Fair, but it's in Washington, DC, every summer and—"

"Cool," Bender says, scanning the article. "Local African American boy makes good."

"Bender!"

"What? He's not African American?"

"Ice it, dude," Jay mutters.

"What'd I say?"

Miranda and Shelly send disapproving looks to the rear. But Matthew feels himself smiling, almost. Personally, he thinks this tippy-toeing around race is stupid. His mother would have gone cold and rigid at Bender's remark, like she did when Coach Beall wanted him to try out for basketball ("Is *that* all he thinks you're good for?"). His granny would pop and sputter, like she does when telling how her husband, Tom Tupper, got beat up when he tried to vote in Cass County, Missouri, in 1956. But Matthew himself feels nothing whatsoever. Yep, he's African American. In the whole big cosmic scheme, so what?

He glances sideways at Bender, who has unfolded the newspaper and is staring at the bottom of the page. Suddenly, he tears off the corner.

"Hey!" Kaitlynn protests. "That's my newspaper."

"Sorry," Bender says, quickly handing it back. Except for the part he keeps. "Saw this thing I have to… It's not important. Just have to…show my dad. I mean, my mom."

* * *

Matthew's mother brings a newspaper home that evening. "Well, what do you think? Was it worth the trouble to turn in a science project?" He's supposed to say yes.

He shrugs instead.

"Just suckin' up to the Man," his grandmother sniffs. She's putting together a feathered headdress for a Chicago book festival weekend after next. The dinette table is covered with feathers that make him sneeze. "Go 'long wit' choo!" she says irritably to the flying down.

"The Man pays my salary, mama," his mother replies mildly. "Hey, bro," she says as Matthew passes her on the way to his room. "At least look at the article, okay?"

He takes the newspaper to his room and flops on his bed. He'll look at the article so he can say he did and then forget about the whole thing until regionals comes around. Propped on his elbows, he turns to page two—

And there he is! Accepting the certificate of merit for top-rated science fair project. He can't quite look at himself in the picture. Mr. Barnes, the junior high principal, is grinning at the camera, and the chairman of the judging committee (whose name Matthew can't remember even though the man teaches at the same college as his mother) is presenting the certificate with one hand and shaking Matthew's hand with the other. That was right after he congratulated Matthew on originality and execution but suggested he work on the math before regionals.

"Now smile," he remembers the reporter saying. Matthew smiled, though in the picture it's more of a smirk, and now he remembers why. When the shutter snapped, he was recalling how Bender held Spencer's dead mouse by the tail and imagining a similar dead mouse hanging from the judge's hand as it shakes his.

Below the fold are letters to the editor, where readers have a chance to complain about misplaced stop signs or price gouging at the gasoline pump. Something catches his eye: a little drawing about two by three inches, just above a notice in the lower right corner. He frowns at it. After a few seconds, he shifts his right hip to pull something out of the pocket and lay it down beside the drawing. It's a perfect match, except for size: two eagles, wings lifted to launch, one in ink and one in pewter. The ink image is sharper, enough that he can read the words on the banner streaming from the eagle's beak: *Class of '85.* The artist's initials are in the corner, though they're too small to make out.

Ever since picking up the clamp-on buckle at the bus shed, he's carried it in his pocket. No particular reason—he just likes the weight and coolness of it. Sometimes when his thoughts go sailing off past Polaris, he feels his fingers curling around it, as though to anchor himself to a little chunk of here and now. His fingers are grasping now, as he reads:

Eagles Soar Again!

It's almost twenty years! To all you class of '85-ers who skipped our tenth reunion: it's time to come out of the woodwork! Local Centerview Eagles can make the reunion committee's job easier if you make your presence known. Also, if you can pass along any contact info regarding our fellow alumni who have moved out of state—except perhaps He Who Shall Remain Nameless— please, please, please send it to the P.O. Box below. Let's make our twentieth-year milestone the best ever!

Reunion committee co-chairs,
Tricia Evertts Knox
Anne (Annie) Myra Bender Thompson

Matthew reads the notice at least three times. Apparently, something happened to the class of '85 that a lot of them would like to forget. And apparently, one particular person in the class had a lot to do with it. *He Who Shall Remain Nameless* reminds him briefly of Calvin, a Harry Potter fan, whose face he can barely recall and whose presence he doesn't miss.

There's only one person he misses, even though (or maybe because) he's never met him.

Years ago, his father was one of those things he thought about all the time. Thinking being all he could do, because his mother wouldn't tell him squat: "He was a very important person in my life at the time, Matthew. An intelligent man who'd made something of himself. But he did not want to be a father. He said he would help me in any possible material way, and when you got older and needed such help, you could call on him. But he couldn't give much of himself, you see? That bucket's done emptied out long ago."

Except it hasn't. There are ways Matthew doesn't look like, talk like, or act like his mama. There are times he catches her looking at him as though she's seeing someone else. As though he's haunted by a ghost—by *He Who Shall Remain Nameless*.

It's kind of creepy.

Matthew stares at the paper eagle in the newspaper while tracing the raised contours of the pewter eagle with his fingers.

The reunion committee for the class of '85 is looking for lost classmates. What if Matthew's father (whose name his mother promises to tell him when he's older) is also looking for him? What if he's roaming up and down the corridors of

Matthew's brain, looking for an opening in time and space to touch him? Matthew's heart speeds up, imagining that touch, but he doesn't know if he longs for it or fears it.

Abruptly he remembers Bender tearing out this corner of the newspaper and feels curiosity nudging him in the side.

* * *

Where he comes from, February is Black History Month and Valentine's Day is a white holiday started by some dead white saint. The schools he went to in Kansas City never had any use for it, and he himself can't see the point of spending an hour on February 14 frantically trading little cards with hearts and cartoon characters on them and making sure you had one for everybody in class. At least by seventh grade, Valentine's Day isn't something he has to participate in.

Hardly anybody does. Shelly announces she'll serenade your sweetheart for five dollars per song (Matthew doesn't think she got many takers), and Kaitlynn is telling everybody she was up until ten-thirty last night making special cards for all her teachers, former and present. The littles' little backpacks are bulging with cards as they clamber on board. One of those backpacks ends up in the aisle, and Matthew accidentally kicks it while heading for his seat.

"Hey!" squeaks a voice behind him. Matthew bends down to pick up the backpack and return it. But the next minute, he's surprised to find himself flat on his stomach, his head ringing from an encounter with the floor.

He didn't just fall. He was pushed.

He hauls himself up and turns around, expecting Bender. But Bender has already claimed the back seat. Instead, it's Spencer: the wiry, jumpy redhead who seemed unusually interested in his science fair project.

Matthew doesn't think in terms of race very much; "live and let live" is working okay for him. But he's the child of his mama and granny and the kind of schools he went to before moving here and probably something in his DNA too—because the minute he turns around and sees Spencer smirking at him, he thinks, *White Boy*. And then he punches.

Spencer boings back like a spring. He's smaller than Matthew but faster, and in about two seconds, Matthew is on the floor again with Spencer on top of him, getting in two hits for every one of Matthew's. A ruckus breaks out all around them, but Matthew feels like he's in a pod by himself, punching back at the unknown force that has been trying to get to him for a long, long time.

Then all of a sudden, he's punching air. A ring of white faces is hanging over him, roughly heart-shaped (is it still Valentine's Day?) with Spencer at the point, flushed and panting, held back by Jay. Then both of them are pushed aside by Mrs. B, whose face is as red as Spencer's.

"What's this about? I'm surprised at you, Spencer. You too, Matthew. The quietest, nicest boys on this bus—what have you two got to fight about?"

* * *

Thinking about that question takes up most of the morning: what has he got to fight about? And where did the fight come from? Not until after lunch does Matthew realize something. His belt buckle with the eagle on it, whose weight felt so solid and reassuring in his pocket, is gone.

It must have slipped out while Spencer was pounding him. And then…two possibilities—it got kicked to one side or somebody picked it up. Some boy, probably. Some white boy.

He isn't the kind to resort to violence, but he might have a few punches left if that's what it took. First, he'd search the bus—after asking permission, like a nice quiet boy. Then, if the search turned up zero, he'd go house to house in Hidden Acres and quietly ask who has his eagle. That's how much he wants it back.

The junior high kids are last off in the morning and first on in the afternoon, so only a handful of them have to wait while Matthew searches the bus and finds nothing but candy wrappers. He feels Bender's eyes on him as Bender heads for his assigned seat but returns no one's gaze until Mrs. B stops at the elementary school. Then he stares Spencer down, packing a message in his eyes: *You'd better not have my eagle, or I'll hurt you bad.*

First a tour of the neighborhood. He'll start with Bender, whose house is closest.

But in one of those surprises Steven Hawking might call a singularity, Bender starts with him. After Matthew has walked home from the bus and said hello to his grandmother and stuck a couple of frozen eggrolls into the microwave, his doorbell rings.

"Who that?" hollers Granny from the family room where she's watching TV. Doorbells ringing are pretty rare around here, unless it's a package delivery.

But instead of a package, it's Bender, with a book in one hand. In the other is a pewter belt buckle with an eagle on it. Holding it up like a police badge, Bender asks, "Is this yours?"

Matthew tries to speak and swallow at the same time and ends up nodding.

"Where'd you get it?" is Bender's next question.

"I—um—found it?"

"Where?"

"Why?"

"You first."

"No, you."

Bender, who has been leaning in like a bulldog, leans back. "It's cold out here. How about I come in?"

Matthew can't think of any reason why not. Passing the family room on the way to the kitchen, he says, "That's my grandmother." All the intro he means to make, but Bender stops, makes eye contact, and says, "Pleased to meet you, ma'am. I'm Bender Thompson."

Granny clearly doesn't expect such politeness from a neighborhood boy, and Matthew doesn't expect it of *this* boy. "Bender," the old lady repeats. "What kind of name is that?"

"It's my mother's maiden name, ma'am," Bender says. "My real full name is Charles Bender Thompson. Like my brother's is John Thornton Thompson, after my dad's grandfather."

"They's some fancy-sounding names," Granny says. "Nice

to make yo' acquaintance. Now get along. I got things to do."
She returns her attention to the TV.

In the kitchen, Matthew nods toward his plate with one
and a half eggrolls on it. "You, uh, hungry?"

"Enough with the hospitality." Bender hikes himself up on
one of the bar stools and slaps the book on the counter, laying
the buckle on top. "Where did you find this?"

Matthew is still trying to catch up to the last three minutes.
"Remember…when we all had to get off the bus so you could
catch Igor's snake?"

"Sure I remember! That was only two weeks ago!"

Time is relative, Matthew thinks of saying. But doesn't. "I
found it then."

Bender straightens up like a dog on the scent. "You mean
by the bus shed?"

"Yeah. Behind it."

"Anybody see you pick it up?"

"Spencer. He followed me."

"Spencer? Baby Einstein? Does this have anything to do
with why he knocked you down on the bus?"

Matthew shakes his head. Picking up the pewter eagle and
tucking it in his pocket, he says, "Your turn."

Bender hesitates before pulling a piece of newspaper from
between the pages of the book. Matthew knows what it is
before it's unfolded, of course.

"Last fall," Bender begins, "I met this guy. Never mind how.
I was sort of lost, and he gave me a ride home in a pickup
truck." He stops, as though Matthew should say something

here. But Matthew can't think of what to say. "One of the first things I noticed about him was that thing, with the eagle? It was on his belt. I'm sure of it."

"Where were you?"

"It was so foggy I couldn't tell where I was when he picked me up, and I was too, uh, disoriented to clock the distance on the truck's odometer when he dropped me off at home. But now I'd bet anything I met him on Farm Road 152. I even think I know who he is."

Matthew has never thought much about Farm Road 152 one way or another, so Bender's words don't have the effect he obviously means them to have. But there's a curious energy radiating from an unknown source, like when virtual particles can only be observed by what's happening around them. The index finger of Bender's right hand is tapping one corner of the book. One word will release the energy, and after a pause, Matthew decides to say it. "Who?"

The cover springs open; pages rattle by. It's a high school yearbook: flashing faces, black-and-white snapshots, club photos of teens in rows. Suddenly the pages stop—at a white space headed by the word SENIORS, and under the heading, an enlarged reproduction of the same eagle in the newspaper and on the belt buckle.

"Oh," says Matthew.

"Right," says Bender. "Look at the initials." He turns the book around and points to three letters on the lower right. JSH. The artist?

"Whose yearbook is this?" Matthew asks.

"My mom's. You may have noticed—she graduated in 1985."

"Why would I notice that?"

Bender sighs, picks up the newspaper clipping, and points to a name. "That's my mom. Myra Bender Thompson. Only Myra is her middle name. In high school, she went by her first name, Anne, and I guess her friends called her Annie. I never knew that. After seeing that letter in the newspaper, I hunted all over the house for this yearbook. It was in a box in the garage."

He's turning pages again. The class of '85 scrolls by, three or four to a page, each in a setting or pose that was supposed to indicate how they saw themselves or wanted others to see them. "There's my mom." Bender pauses briefly at a studio shot of a girl lying on her stomach, arms crossed and chin propped on a football. Beside the picture is a long list of her activities and clubs, followed by a quote that he has no time to read. "Cheerleader," Bender remarks, already moving on. "It figures. But look." He stops, flattens the pages, and swivels the book around again so Matthew can get the full effect.

The picture shows a young man in a button-down shirt and hands straight at his sides and heavy horn-rimmed glasses—exactly like the class nerd. Except that he's standing on his head. The picture is slightly blurry, as though a friend snapped it just before he fell over. Matthew's eyes go to the name beside the picture: Jason Stanley Hall. "JSH?" Matthew asks.

"The only one," Bender replies. "The only one of the seniors with those initials."

The boy had no credits by his name, only a quote: *A legend in his own time.* "What does that mean?"

"Some stupid thing they do every year. The class of '85 was supposed to write their own epitaphs."

"Epitaphs?"

"What they'd put on their tombstones. My mom's is *Crashed and burned*. Creepy, huh? Typical overachiever. But here's the thing…"

Bender hesitates so long that Matthew steals a look at him. He's gazing at the upside-down boy (who would be right-side-up for him) as though he'd found his long-lost dad. Finally he says, "This is the guy who picked me up on Farm Road 152. I'm sure of it."

"Why? Did he stand on his head?"

"Good one. No, I just got a close look at him. Older now, but this is the guy."

Matthew leans closer to the picture, and something clicks. "You mean, 'he who shall remain nameless'?"

"That's what I think too!"

"Why?"

"Why do you think so?"

"I asked you first."

"Okay." Eagerly Bender starts turning pages again, stopping at points of interest like a tour guide. "He doesn't show up in any more of the pictures, just the stuff he did. Crazy stuff. Like here—principal's car covered with saran wrap. Everybody knows who did it. And here—counselor's office packed full of balloons. Must have taken all night to do that. Oh yeah, and Murray High's track studded with toothpicks, and live turtles in the wastebaskets. This guy was *awesome*."

"But…he went too far?" Matthew guessed.

"Yeah." Bender paused. "That's the missing piece, and I think it had something to do with graduation. Because there aren't any graduation pictures—not a single one. Every yearbook I've ever seen has graduation pictures—that's what it's all about. *Getting out.* But not here. And look at this."

Bender turns to the personalities section and flattens the page at *Most likely to succeed.* "Here's my mom, of course. But look who the guy is."

Matthew stares at the grinning couple under the south portico of the high school. The girl is standing on the boy's shoulders with her arms raised, as though holding up the roof. He reads: *Anne Bender. Troy Pasternak.* That name sounds familiar.

"Yeah," Bender is saying. "That Troy Pasternak."

"Which Troy Pasternak?"

"His name is on the gazebo, remember?"

"He died?"

"No. I asked my mom—who doesn't know I found her yearbook. She said he was hurt in an accident that messed him up. For life. He's in a nursing home somewhere."

"What kind of accident?"

"She didn't want to talk about it. And if I asked a bunch of questions, she'd get suspicious. She's been…real hard to live with lately. But I'm thinking it still hurts, because from the yearbook, it looks like they were an *item.*"

After a moment, Matthew says, "Weird."

"Totally." Bender feathers the pages back to the beginning,

like years in reverse, and slams the book shut. "Like, if she married him, I wouldn't be here. And she didn't. And I've got a real strong hunch it's because of JSH."

"A hunch is not evidence," Matthew corrected.

"I know, but things are adding up. I asked Jay what happened to his uncle, and all he knows is that he fell down some steps at graduation. Says his grandmother cries every time Troy's name comes up, so it doesn't come up much. And when I met the guy on the road, he was edgy. Like he didn't want anybody to know he was there. Like he had a *past*." Bender flips back to the boy standing on his head and stares intently at him. "I've got to know."

A long silence draws out, making Matthew feel he ought to say something. "What about newspaper archives? Did you look online?"

Bender shakes his head. "I've been grounded from the computer. Two weeks, just for tossing a shrunken head on the bus. Can't anybody take a joke?"

Matthew can't help but grin. Not at Bender, but at a spot on the wall behind him, where there's an imaginary door he decides to open. Nodding toward the house computer set up in the dining room, he says, "You can use mine."

They say you can find anything on the Internet, but that's only partially true. Newspaper archives going back twenty years are available only for a price, and that price would include somebody's mother killing them once she found out they'd used her credit card. They search for Jason Stanley Hall and Troy Lawrence Pasternak but turn up only genealogical records, a college basketball player in New Hampshire, and a theater director in Spokane. They've about run out of ideas when Matthew's mother comes home.

She covers her surprise at Matthew having company. But surprise is harder to conceal when she invites Bender to dinner, and Bender accepts. Since it's Granny's night to cook, they have black-eyed peas and cornbread, which Bender scarfs down like a brother, with perfect manners. Granny takes a liking to him. Even insists he stay while she tries out one of her new stories.

Matthew is used to sitting on the floor in a darkened room while Uthisha the Zulu Storyteller, in native dress, moans and wails through a tale of how the zebra got its stripes or why the Zulu people are so tall and strong. Her stories are based on real African folktales, but she juices them up with a little jive talk or hip-hop rhythm. To Bender, it's all new, though; sitting beside him, Matthew feels the rock-solid attention, the chuckle at a joke, the gasp of surprise. He is drawn into his grandmother's act like never before and has to wonder why he can hear it better through someone who's still pretty much a stranger to him.

"What was that all about?" his mother demands when the front door finally closes behind their visitor, a little after eight.

"What was what all about?"

"Is this kid your new best friend?"

Matthew feels for the eagle in his pocket and gazes at the door. "Don't you want me to have friends?"

She sighs. "I want you to have the kind of friend who knows when it's time to go home."

"But you invited him to dinner. And Granny invited—"

"Never mind. Let's go wash up."

But while rinsing dishes for Matthew to stack in the dishwasher, she can't let it alone. "I wish I could figure out his game."

"What game?" Matthew asks, studying a smudge of butter on a plate.

"He's sly. I don't believe his Mr. Manners act for a minute. And what's with all that yammering on about his brother?"

Matthew shrugs. Then he realizes they knew a lot about Thorn now and very little about Bender.

Mama wipes her hands and hangs up the dishtowel. "I'd watch that one if I were you."

* * *

Next morning, the temperature gauge reads fifteen; the littles are huddled with their parents in steamy cars by the gazebo, and the big kids wait until the last minute to dash across the crunchy grass and get in line. Bender boards last, stopping beside Spencer. "Did you do it yet?"

Spencer squints up at him. "Do what?"

"Apologize to Matthew for knocking him down."

Spencer's shifty eyes glance out the window. "It was an accident. And he punched me first."

"Any time, Bender," Mrs. B calls from the front.

"I'm not done," Bender says to Spencer and unhurriedly takes his seat.

Spencer whirls around, his glance raking Matthew before settling on Bender. "Not done with *what?*"

"Are you messing with him?" Matthew asks later—much later, when Bender is over at his house and they're trying to dig up more online information on J. S. Hall and the class of '85.

"Messing with little Spencer?" Bender's eyes widen innocently. "*Me?*"

"Might've been an accident, like he said. And I did hit him first."

"No way it was an accident. His flinty eyes've been digging holes in you for weeks."

"Guess I never noticed."

"Well, you ought to start noticing things, dude, before you get run over by a truck." Bender points to the screen. "Try typing in 'high school graduation pranks.'"

"That would give us a million hits. And it would be everybody else's tricks, not the one we're looking for."

"So what? Might give us some good ideas."

Matthew sighs, already a little bored with the project. In his opinion, people are not as interesting as astral bodies. His fingers tap restlessly over the keys before clicking the drop-down menu on the browser bar. "Okay, but first—this is my favorite website right now: Oxford University's astrophysics page. Outstanding animations." He clicks a link.

Bender leans forward reluctantly and stares at the flaming star on the screen as it burns from white to yellow to deep orange, finally collapsing to a lump of matter so dense that nothing can escape from it, not even light. Little by little, Bender's attention is captured; first he looks, then reads, then rereads, then looks again with growing comprehension. Matthew doesn't see this, since he's also staring at the screen. But somehow he feels it.

"So that's what a black hole is," Bender says at last.

"Uh-huh."

"Weird. That's my family."

"Your what?"

"My brother. Thorn's always been squat in the middle of everything, like a big fat sun, sucking up all the oxygen. Even when he went away to college. But…"

After a brief silence, Matthew clicks the replay button, and the star bursts to brilliant white again. "But what?"

Bender's voice sounds dry and crinkly. "We went on this family ski trip over Christmas? First vacation in four years. It was a big deal because Thorn hasn't been home since June—he did this hotshot political internship in DC over the summer. So the folks were all excited and happy—Dad didn't build anything all month, and Mom hardly picked any fights with him—and Thorn met us at Breckinridge just like they'd planned, except…when he got off the plane, we didn't recognize him."

The dying star on the screen pulses through its orange phase. "Why not?"

"He looked like a homeless guy. He'd let his hair grow and he hadn't shaved in a week and his beard was coming in all stubbly. My mom walked right by him before he called to her. We went to dinner right after that, and he told us he'd dropped out of Dartmouth. Just dropped out—in the middle of his junior year. Said he didn't know what he wanted anymore but he had to get away, go find himself. He actually said that."

Go find myself, Matthew thought. What would that be like? How would you know where to start looking?

"The folks didn't take it very well," Bender went on. "At all. And you want to know what's funny? It's exactly what I'd wished for since I was six—to see them beat up on *him* for a change. But now that they were actually doing it, it wasn't fun. They both think he's on something—drugs, I mean—and Mom believes he's gonna go up to Alaska and starve to death, like that dude who camped out in the bus. Or fall in a freezing river or something. They yelled at each other for three days. Thorn and my mom, that is. Dad just clammed up, and one day, he disappeared and we didn't see him until dinner. The last night, they told us they were splitting up and Thorn's, uh, news had nothing to do with it; it was already decided. Real sweet family vacation, all in all. I did learn to ski, though. It's fun. Wait a minute."

The red star on the screen crumples and shrinks into nothingness. Bender touches the screen, at the cold dark center. "It's like *that*. Like Thorn just turned the light out. But he's still there, and we're still circling around him like always, but we can't see him anymore. Can't talk about him, but his gravity is dragging worse than ever. It's dead center at our house— this freaky quietness, even though my mom has the TV on all the time. I feel like we should, you know, talk sometimes, but we've never learned how."

That might explain why Bender is always slow to go home.

Matthew frowns at the thought of his own black hole: his invisible dad, thick and silent with a gravitational pull so strong it could warp him. If he let it.

"Theoretically," Matthew says, "if you were a virtual particle with an antimatter twin, the mass of the black hole would pull you in but your antiparticle could escape."

"That's nice. This was your science fair project, right? You going to regionals?"

Matthew blinks, like he's been under some kind of spell. "I have to. Probably won't get beyond that, though. The judges say it's weak on math."

For the first time, Bender looks at him. Matthew, still gazing at the screen (after clicking the replay button one more time), feels the intensity of an idea forming in someone else's head. "Weak on math?" A pause and then, "You want some help with that? By the way, what's for dinner?"

✳ ✳ ✳

On Monday morning, Bender does not head for the back seat but slides in beside Matthew so suddenly the latter backs up against the windows. "Guess what I learned last night?"

"Uh…"

"My mom says anybody can find out who owns property around here. You just take the address in to the county assessor's office and they'll tell you."

"So?" Matthew is still backed up, wondering who wants to know who owns what.

"*So?* She's going to find out who owns that house on Farm Road 152!"

"Oh." Since they've been working on his black hole project all weekend, Matthew has forgotten Bender's interest in the Mystery Stop.

"Yeah, go figure. Here all our high-tech Internet research turns up nada and the answer might be right under our nose. Or in the courthouse."

"Hey Bender! I'm in your seat!" a voice comes from behind them: Igor's. It's his first day back on the bus. "Bender? Aren't you going to do anything?"

"Take it," he calls back idly. "By the way—" to Matthew again, who has relaxed somewhat. "We'll have to refigure that gravity equation. I was reading up on Planck's constant last night…"

Spencer sprawls into a forward seat, spilling his backpack so Jay has to sit somewhere else.

"What's going on?" Igor pipes up as Mrs. B puts the bus in gear. "I'm gone two weeks and everybody reshuffles like a card deck?"

Ignoring him, Bender stretches forward and taps Spencer on the shoulder. "How about that apology, whiz kid?"

"Bug off." Only Spencer doesn't exactly say *bug*.

"Oooooo. Bad attitude, dude. I could file a complaint with Youth Court. What if you had to come up before yourself?"

Spencer doesn't answer, just hikes his shoulders. From across the aisle, Jay says, "He quit Youth Court."

"What? After that hard-fought campaign for truth and justice? All for naught?"

"Yeah, well," Jay explains, "he's been throwing himself this pity party ever since he didn't win the science fair."

Spencer whirls around. "Screw you, jock!"

"Get over yourself, nerd!"

"Boys!" Mrs. B, pausing at the highway stop sign, turns all the way around with a disbelieving expression. "What's got into you two? I thought you were best friends."

"What about you?" Spencer hisses at Jay. "You've been pissed ever since your Super Bowl team lost."

Jay's face turns rocky. "My. Super Bowl team. *Didn't*. Lose."

"Are you sure? Maybe you couldn't see to read the score. Or maybe your grandfather got confused."

Jay seems to curl up on his seat—then he springs at Spencer.

"That's it!" yells Mrs. B, who's been watching closely. "Come up to the front, Jay."

It's the first time Jay has occupied that seat since fourth grade. He shifts his backpack to one shoulder and marches forward defiantly.

From the back, Igor's voice creeps out like a baby duck after a thunderstorm. "What's going on?"

Bender turns to Matthew with a lopsided grin. "Sad, really. Death of a beautiful friendship."

As for Matthew, he feels like he's being dragged by the heels into the real world. And he's not sure he likes it.

Around eight o'clock that night, the phone rings; turns out it's for him. "Why, Charles Bender Thompson!" he hears his granny answering. "Haven't seen you in a fly's age! How you be, honey?" The two of them have quite a little conversation,

Mama sighing and shaking her head at the computer, before Granny gives up the phone.

"Guess what?" is Bender's greeting.

Matthew is trying to guess the last time somebody called him. "What?"

"Remember I told you my mom was checking property records at the assessor's office?"

"Uh-huh."

"Well, she did, and she even made a copy of the map. Actually, they're called plats. I'm looking at it right now: five acres, one house, one barn, a pump house, *and* a bus shed. Guess who owns it?"

Matthew feels a yawn coming on. "Who?"

"Teresa Birch."

Matthew is about to say, "Who?" again when his jaw closes with a snap. Because he remembers, from some overheard conversation, that Teresa Birch is better known as Mrs. B.

March

Jay Thomas Pasternak III doesn't care about fame. He just wants to play running back for an NFL team (first choice Cowboys, second choice Steelers) and have one magic season and go to the Super Bowl. Maybe more than one magic season. "Jay Pasternak: MVP"; "Pasternak Smashes Records"; "Pasternak Scores Upset of the Year." Those were the kinds of headlines he imagines, but that doesn't mean he wants to be famous. All it means is he wants to be the best running back ever. Though he'd settle for top ten if he has to.

His father likes to say Jay got a running start by popping up in a family of four older sisters who liked to chase him. If he didn't feel like getting caught and tickled or dunked in the pool or dressed up as a baby to play house, he ran. Fast. Sneaky too—he figured out all kinds of ducks and dodges and how to fake one direction and go another. He developed a trick of slowing down a little until they were right on top of him before turning a quick one-eighty that put him face-to-face with four screaming demons who were always taken by surprise. Then he'd do an end run or plow right through. When they tried to surround him, he ducked and wove so fast their grabbing hands grabbed only air.

"He's a running back," said his grandfather, Jay Pasternak Senior. "Sure as shootin'."

"Maybe," admitted his dad, Jay Pasternak Junior.

Senior had played quarterback at the University of Kansas during a championship season, which was a very big deal. Junior, Jay's father, wasn't interested in football, which was also a big deal because Senior made it one. When Uncle Troy was in high school, he made up for Junior's lack of interest: captain of the team in his senior year and headed for the University of Missouri on an athletic scholarship. But then the accident happened. It's a good thing Jay III came along, with not only a talent for the game but a passion for it too. Poppy could finally forgive Dad for not loving football, because Dad had had a kid who did.

Starting right after New Year's, Jay and Poppy have their own little betting pool for the NFL play-offs; each contributes a bag of Skittles to the pot and writes their predictions on a chart. Poppy always ends up with more Skittles as the season progresses.

Except for this season, which sees Jay ahead of Poppy by mid-January. That might have been an early warning, but it's not until they're watching the quarterfinals that Jay begins to wonder if something might be wrong. For one thing, even though Poppy follows the action just fine, he has a hard time keeping the teams straight, continually matching Arizona against Dallas and New England to Tennessee, when it's the other way around.

By Super Bowl time, Poppy's pick is Arizona and Jay's is New England. Poppy seems sharp as a tack during the pregame show and stays one step ahead of the announcers during the first half. But during halftime, he gets up for a beer and comes back with a carton of orange juice, which he carefully pours into an empty Coors can and sips while making angry faces at the blond girl prancing around the stage. "Who's that broad?"

"It's Claire. She's hot right now."

"She's got to be cold in a skimpy outfit like that. Whoo-hoo, sister! Put it on! Put it on! Look at the way that top jiggles. Any minute now, she's going to pop right out of—"

"Jay!" Geemaw seems to materialize outside her craft room door. "Watch what you're saying to the boy."

"What do you mean? Come look at this chick, and tell me how long until—"

Geemaw plows into the room like an oil tanker; for a small woman, she can throw her weight around when she wants to. "Jay, I think you'd better watch the rest of the game at home."

"But—but they won't even have it on at home! Dad'll be watching some World War II junk on the History Channel!"

"I'll give him a call. I'm sure he'll make an exception." She picks up Jay's coat and starts helping him on with it, as though he were five years old. Meanwhile, Poppy is making the kind of comments about Claire that Jay has only heard from guys at school and in the movies he's not supposed to watch. Which surprises him: isn't Poppy too old to know words like that?

"We'll see you tomorrow," Geemaw promises while hustling him toward the back door. "Come over after school and you two can talk about the game."

She must have called Dad as soon as Jay was out the door, for once he's crossed his grandparents' backyard and taken the shortcut through the woods, Dad's watching a Super Bowl SUV commercial. Jay wipes the fog off his glasses and sits down as the third quarter begins, even though his sister Julie complains she's missing *The Vampire Chronicles*. Dad watches with him, though having no interest whatsoever, he can't say anything intelligent about the plays. So he doesn't say anything, and neither does Jay, and the whole house seems so quiet and strange it's like watching in solitary confinement at some prison.

When the game is finally over (New England wins), Mom makes hot chocolate, and the three of them sit down at the kitchen table for a talk. None of his sisters participate: Joanna and Jessica are in college now, Jaynell is working on a science project at her lab partner's house, and Julie is gabbing on her phone. Once the talk starts, Jay realizes he's being told things his sisters already know.

"Poppy's…had some issues lately," Dad begins.

"Is he going nuts?"

"No, no. It's just that…well, he's in his eighties, Jay. At that age, some people lose a little…they start to lose…"

"Their marbles," Jay finishes. No point beating around the bush.

"I wouldn't say that," his mother protests. "But he is losing some memory, some sense of where he is." *Marbles*, Jay corrects her silently. "It's called dementia."

In other words, nuts. "Are they going to lock him up?" His voice sounds thin and strange to his ears.

Both parents jump on that phrase. "Oh no no no," Mom says, while Dad begins, "Well, I wouldn't put it that way, but…"

The *but* is left hanging, like one of those cartoon characters that runs off a cliff before realizing there's gravity down there.

"What we mean," continues Mom, "is that's not the plan *now*. But he's become pretty challenging for Geemaw. She deals with a lot of things we don't see. Haven't you noticed how she does all the driving now?"

Jay recalls the trip he took with his grandparents last summer. Geemaw did most of the driving, but he thought that was because Poppy wanted to sit sideways in the front seat and chat with Jay in the back. When he wasn't making comments on Geemaw's driving, that is.

Dad goes on, "Last Thanksgiving, he decided to go out for a beer at two in the morning and drove the car into a ditch. If it had have been a tree or a utility pole, he might be dead now. Geemaw called me, and I found him asleep behind the steering wheel with only a sweater over his pajamas and the temperature around thirty degrees. So—"

"Maybe he was sleepwalking," Jay interrupts. "Did you think about that?"

His dad sighs. "Hey, bud. I know how you feel, but—"

"No, you don't!" Jay jumps up so fast he knocks over his

chair. He's shouting, he's so mad. "You *don't* know how I feel." They didn't know how it felt being the only one in the family to go nearsighted, and they don't understand now. It's complicated—the weight of his grandfather's hand on his head, from five years old to ten, and how his grandfather knew when to stop putting a hand on his head. The gleam in his eye when anticipating a brilliant play. Or the way the setting sun makes a little halo of silver hairs on his balding head as Jay runs long to catch a pass, snapped from that quarterback arm that never forgot how to throw. That's all part of how he feels, along with the chalky taste in the back of his throat.

"Now, sweetheart," his mom begins.

"Settle down, Jay," his dad says. "Nobody's decided anything yet."

Not *yet*. If not yet, then when?

Jay's already faced one crisis this year, and Poppy's the one who got him through it. Sure there are nearsighted NFL players, he said; lots of 'em. Ever heard of contact lenses? By the time Jay graduates high school (with a football scholarship), he'll be dazzling the coaches and recruiters so much nobody will even ask about his vision.

But how will Poppy get him through this crisis, if Poppy is the crisis?

* * *

March blows in from the south this year, with a string of sunny warm days that send the sweaters, jackets, and hoodies to the back of the closet. "Don't lose them," everybody's mother says. "You'll need them again."

But while boarding the bus in Windbreakers, they know they'll be walking home in T-shirts. Bender even climbs on in wearing a T-shirt, followed by Matthew. Bender pauses to tie Marilu Wong's pigtails together ("Hey!" she squeaks), and Matthew says, "Back of the bus, white boy."

They laugh, and Jay follows, shaking his head. He takes a middle seat, trying to remember if he finished his homework last night or just dreamed he did.

Shelly is asking everybody if they'd like to buy a luscious milk chocolate candy bar for her Star Camp fund. "They're just Hershey Bars!" Bender calls from the back. "For four times what you'd pay at Dollar General."

"They are not!" Shelly protests. "Look at this elegant gold wrapper."

"My mom and I bought four," Miranda says loyally.

"Hey, Jay!" Igor says. "What'll you pay for my cheese sandwich so I can buy cigarettes and hang out on the street this summer?"

"Sit down, Igor!" shouts Mrs. B, who hasn't yet forgiven him for the snake incident.

Spencer boards last, dragging down the aisle and dropping on the seat opposite Jay like a used dishrag. They haven't spoken to each other in a couple of weeks, but Jay's forgotten why. "What's up?"

Spencer glances at him quickly, suspiciously. "Last night, I told my mom I don't want to go to Space Camp. She still wants to fight about it."

"What? She's been trying to get you in for two years! And you were all excited last fall."

"I *thought* I was excited. Back when I *thought* I was smart."

Jay sighs and shakes his head. "Get over it, dude. You can't—"

"Shhh!" says Spencer.

An argument is going on up front. Mrs. B, her hand on the door lever, is telling somebody they can't get on. "Sir, this is a school bus," she's insisting. "We're not going to Union Station."

A voice comes from outside, a voice Jay immediately recognizes, with a plunging heart. "I have to catch the 9:30 express!" Poppy exclaims. "It'll take thirty minutes to get there! What's the matter with you, woman?"

Jay starts to stand up but doesn't know what he will do after that, so he kind of hangs in between standing and sitting.

"Sir, please step back. I have to—I'm closing—No!" Mrs. B slams the door on Poppy's fist. As he bangs the door, she shifts down and revs the accelerator, pulling away so fast the old man staggers back. He raises his fist as the bus rolls by— Jay can see him and faintly hear him, shouting words he's not supposed to around the children. Panzer barks indignantly.

Jay slowly sits down. Spencer is staring at him. So are Shelly, Miranda, Kaitlynn, Igor, Matthew, and Bender. "Sorry, man," Spencer mutters, and from the back comes a snicker from Bender, followed by a "Shhh!" from somebody else.

In all his days, Jay can't remember a ride that quiet.

* * *

"Jay," his mother tells him that afternoon, "Terry Birch called this morning and told me what happened on the bus."

"It was just a mistake," he says defensively. "Poppy thought the school bus looked like that senior citizens van that takes old people to town to shop…"

She isn't buying. "The school bus looks nothing like the OATS bus, Jay. A few days ago, he forgot he gave up driving and pitched a fit when he couldn't find his car keys. Geemaw called me, and it was all we could do to—"

"All *right*, I get it. You're gonna lock him up in an old folks home."

"Nobody's made any decisions yet."

"But you're getting there. He's just a little confused, that's all."

His mother is looking at him with pity in her eyes, and he hates that. "I'm really sorry, Jay. This is always a sad thing to watch."

He grabs an apple from the basket on the countertop and takes a bite out of it. "I'm watching, all right. Don't try anything sneaky." He storms off to his room before she can ask him to explain what he means.

Two days later, March blows cold again. There's even a 60 percent chance of late-afternoon snow in the forecast: possible accumulation three to six inches. Everybody's hopeful that it will be the first good snow of the winter. "Maybe I won't see you tomorrow," is Mrs. B's touching farewell.

Spencer catches up with Jay as they start toward home. "You still got your sled?" he asks, as though their little spat had never happened.

"If my sister didn't wreck it when she had her slumber party." Julie told him, after the fact, how five girls had piled on his sled and rode it downhill in a heavy frost.

"We could try it on that hill behind the Ellisons' house. It's nice and steep."

"Cool." Jay holds out a fist, and they bump knuckles.

"By the way," Spencer goes on, "I changed my mind about Space Camp. You're right, I just need to—"

"Hold on a minute." Jay has spotted his grandmother striding toward them, dressed like a bag lady with polyester slacks stuffed into rubber boots, her good dress coat flapping about her knees and gray hair springing wildly from a crocheted cap. Fear clutches him—is she going crazy too?

Her voice sounds thin and screechy in the cold air. "Have any of you kids seen Panzer?"

Out of breath, she tells them how Poppy had taken the dog for a walk after lunch, as usual, and returned without him. Geemaw hadn't noticed at first because she was busy with a scrapbook project, but when she emerged from her craft room and found Poppy snoring in the recliner in front of the TV, Panzer was not on the doggie bed beside him. Nor was he in the house or backyard. Geemaw woke Poppy: *Where's Panzer?*

Poppy just looked at her: *Panzer who?*

At this point in the story, Geemaw breaks down. Jay lifts an awkward hand to her shoulder but finds his mouth too dry to speak.

Spencer says, "Don't worry, Mrs. Pasternak. We'll find

him. Everybody knows Panzer, right?" A group of kids gather around. Heads nod.

"We should organize!" Kaitlynn says. "We need a—a command central, and send people off in different directions to search behind all the houses and in the woods—"

"Okay," Shelly says. "We're organizing a Hidden Acres Dogquest right now. I'm chairman, Mir is co-chair, Kaitlynn's field captain…"

Jay can see this going on Shelly's scholarship résumé. But he's sort of grateful to her for taking over, and she comes up with a good plan. The littles search house-to-house while Spencer takes the north side of the loop, Jay the west, Kaitlynn the southeast field where the picnic tables are, and Igor and Miranda the woods. Shelly stays in the gazebo with her phone and a whistle, contributed by Jay, to signal whenever Panzer is found.

It's the shyest, quietest kid on the bus who actually finds the dog: Alice. Jay didn't even know Alice was looking. But when he hears two shrill blasts on his whistle, he stops beating the brush in the west field and runs back to the gazebo where all the other kids are waiting. Alice holds the whimpering dachshund in her arms while Kaitlynn and the littles try to pet him. Panzer is tucked into her jacket, but he's still shivering, maybe from fear as well as cold. "I found him in the culvert by Meadow Lane," Alice explains, her own voice a little shaky. Her lips are a little blue too. "He was tied to a tree, so he couldn't get home."

"Poor puppy!" cries Kaitlynn, stroking Panzer's head while he tries to lick her.

"Thanks," says Jay. "I'll take him." He hates what her story implies: that Poppy was the one who tied Panzer up and left him and forgot about him. The dog could have frozen to death or been lunch for a hungry fox or bobcat. "How did you see him in the culvert?"

"I didn't," Alice says shyly. "I just know holes are good places to hide."

Jay kind of wonders how she knows that, but he only says thanks again. The little dachshund gets the cuddle of his life, and then they all go home feeling good, except Jay.

Poppy doesn't remember anything about it—though he does recall Panzer now. Geemaw decides she's had enough.

Turns out she and Jay's dad have been looking into residential care (a nice way of saying nursing home), and there's an opening at one of the places on their short list: Sunset Hills. Miranda's mother has already brought over the paperwork and helped Geemaw get everything in order, and on Friday afternoon, Jay's father drives Poppy to town to help him "settle in."

All this happens while Jay's not watching. "You *what*?!" he yells when his parents tell him on Friday afternoon. He hurls his backpack across the kitchen for punctuation.

His mom begins, "Please, sweetheart—"

"It was getting bad, son," says his dad. "He's really gone downhill fast. It's shocking, almost, to see how—"

"Enough with how bad he is!" Jay is still shouting. "You didn't even think about asking me, right, to see if I had any other solution?"

His mom says, "Well no, but—"

"What solution, Jay?" replies his dad. "We'll ask you now. And if you can answer in a calm, respectful manner, we'll listen."

"I've been thinking," Jay says, as respectfully as he can manage. "He could move in with us. I'll help take care of him. He could have Jessica's old room, and if Julie doesn't like it, she can move over to Geemaw's…" His mom moans and his dad is shaking his head. "All right, I'll move in with him! I'll help Geemaw with him—I'll even quit track and soccer so I can be home in the afternoons. Poppy and me, we have this thing between us—" Now both parents are shaking their heads. "See? You're not even listening!"

"It's a lot more complicated than that, Jay. All kind of issues, from health to emotional—"

"I don't care about *issues*, okay? Poppy's not an *issue*, he's—he's—"

"Fair enough," admits his dad. "He's not an issue, he's a human being, and a husband and a father and a grandfather, and he's losing touch with all those things. We can't help him anymore. We have to get him to a place where he can be helped."

"You mean 'kept,'" Jay mutters. "Like Uncle Troy."

His father sighs. With a *Let's-be-careful* look at him, Mom says, "What we mean is, Poppy's condition can't be cured but there may be ways that'll help him deal with it better, like… therapies and drugs and—"

"Drugs? Just keep him doped up and out of it?"

"No, but... Look, this is hard on all of us, not just you. We're all going to have to readjust and accept the inevitable. After church this Sunday, we're going over to visit as a family, and you can see for yourself how—"

"You can visit," Jay says firmly. "I'm not."

"Now, Jay..." begins his mother.

"Come on, son," says his father. "You can't just pretend this isn't happening. Or that he doesn't exist anymore."

"I know he exists. Better than you do. I just want to go by myself. After school some day next week, like Tuesday when I don't have soccer."

Neither parent likes the idea, but there's no good reason to object. So they finally agree: instead of getting on the bus next Tuesday afternoon, Jay will walk to Sunset Hills. Julie will pick him up there after cheerleader tryouts. If Jay has to wait for her, he can start on his homework in the lobby.

That's the plan. But Jay has his own plan.

He's figured out that nobody is reaching Poppy where he lives. Out of the whole family, his wife of fifty-two years included, only Jay can do that. Because Jay lives in the same place. So when he loads up his backpack for school on Tuesday, his football goes at the bottom—the one Poppy gave him two years ago, signed by Brett Favre. It's the one they toss around the backyard together. Unlike Poppy's championship ball from the University of Kansas, which holds a place of honor over the fireplace, Jay's has their sweat on it, their memories in it. Even bumping along in his backpack on a chilly morning, it feels warm.

While boarding the bus, he's so focused on his mission that it's hard to pay attention when Miranda says, "Shelly has an announcement!" Shelly's announcements are pretty common, but this time she's not selling anything.

"My mom went to the hospital last night. I have a new baby sister, Eve Marie, eight pounds, two ounces." She bows to the applause and whistles.

As the noise dies down, Bender's voice comes from the back: "And next week, she'll be selling cute little baby toes for fifty bucks apiece!"

The boys laugh; Miranda says, "*Gross*, Bender!"; Shelly licks her finger and makes an invisible tick mark in the air; and Mrs. B shouts, "Congratulations and sit down!"

Jay cradles his backpack as though it had a baby in it. If someone can be born, chances are someone else can be reborn.

✳ ✳ ✳

After the last bell that afternoon, he shoulders his backpack for the jog over to Sunset Hills—just over a mile, which he can do without breaking a sweat. When he arrives, the receptionist tells him where Poppy's room is. South wing, Alzheimer's unit—*even though he doesn't have Alzheimer's*, Jay silently corrects her. *Just dementia.*

As he walks down the hall, counting up numbers on the doors, his mind strays in the other direction, toward Uncle Troy's room. Since he's here, maybe he should stop by to say hello. But Jay has never just "stopped by" his uncle's room;

only at Christmas and birthdays when his parents make him. It's tough, seeing a grown man with the mind of a five-year-old. Geemaw visits him almost every day, but usually without Poppy. Uncle Troy is probably the only thing Poppy won't talk about—hurts too much, Jay figures. Shoot, it hurts Jay, who never even knew the promising young wide receiver headed to Mizzou. Uncle Troy doesn't even go by his first name here; everybody calls him Larry, which is short for his middle—

"Sonny, sonny. I need to tell you something I need to tell you…"

An old lady in a saggy dress has him by the elbow. She only comes to his shoulder, but he's terrified. He tries not to grip too hard as he pries her clawlike fingers off his arm, jumping as a shout comes from the room behind him, or at least it begins as a shout, but the voice gets higher and higher until it becomes a scream. "Sonny…"

The nurse's aide taking a man's blood pressure across the hall raises her eyebrows. "Who're you looking for, sweetie?"

Jay tries to speak, can't, coughs to clear his throat. "Um, Jay Pasternak Senior?"

"Two doors down, left side. He might be asleep." Jay nods and passes by, breathing shallowly through his mouth because the place doesn't smell too good.

Poppy isn't asleep; he's sitting up in a wheelchair—a *wheelchair?!*—staring at some documentary on TV. Something about World War II. On the History Channel.

Jay lets out his breath in a rush; this is worse than he

thought. Past time for an intervention. He reaches into his backpack and plants himself in front of the television, bouncing the football lightly in one hand. "Hey Poppy, what's up?"

His grandfather looks at him with no change in expression, as though Jay were a World War II documentary. Keeping his voice deliberately bright, like he'd just run over to his grandparents' house after school to toss the old pigskin around, Jay says, "Why did they put you in a wheelchair, man? Are you razzing the nurses?"

The word *nurses* ticks the old man off. "Bunch of—" he says, calling them a not very nice name.

Jay tries a knowing laugh. "I just ran over after school to shoot the breeze. Not much is going on. We have our first soccer game this week, so—"

"Soccer's a stupid game," Poppy interrupts. "Sissy, European…"

"…runaround," Jay finishes with him. He laughs again, for real this time. "I know; I'm just doing it for the moves. So I can try out for junior varsity next fall, remember? You're coming to see me play." Jay comes closer. "Listen, Poppy. Are you listening? We have to talk, okay?"

The old man is looking at him, and his eyes seem more focused. "Okay."

Jay places his football on the old man's lap and lays the bony hands upon it. Then he puts his own hands on top, as though the ball were a magic medium for communication. "Poppy? We've got to get you out of here, man. This place is no good for you. Mom was trying to feed me a load of crap, like you might get better here, but you can only get worse. Lookit, you're in a wheelchair already. Uh-uh, no way. *No way* are you ready for a wheelchair.

"So listen—are you listening? You've got to do what they say. Do whatever stupid therapy they give you and—and start paying attention and—" His grandfather has opened his mouth and is shaping his lips, like he's trying to catch the words for a reply. He's trying—Jay can feel it. All he needs is a little help, a little encouragement. *All these years, he's been here for me,* Jay is thinking. *Now I can be here for him.* "What, Poppy? What is it?"

The old man squints at him, really hard, concentrating. "Who...who are you?"

* * *

Jay takes his hands off the football. It rolls off the slope of the old man's lap and bounces clunkily on the tile floor. Then he slowly stands, turns, and walks out, leaving his backpack by the door.

Once in the hall, he just keeps walking, past the wheelchairs, the rising scream, that lady who suddenly steps out from her room saying *Sonny, sonny.* He pushes open a side door to an empty courtyard, a little garden, a sidewalk winding around to a gate. He follows the trail, opens the gate, and escapes.

His Nikes clang on the sidewalk. Where to? Where to? The hospital is just a few blocks north, and behind the hospital is a path where his track coach took the relay team for practice last fall. It's part of the old railroad bed, abandoned when the tracks were taken up; Coach says they're turning it into a bike trail. The high school cross-country team runs it for five miles every other day during the season.

He dashes across the hospital parking lot and finds the trailhead. After a few hundred yards, the asphalt bends into a loop, but Jay goes straight north on the old railroad bed.

His breath is good, his legs strong. They pump ("like a well-oiled machine!" Coach barks), his arms keeping pace, nose in, mouth out, four, five, six...

It's when he slows down that everything catches up to him.

Not fair. It's not fair! I just wanted him to see me play varsity, four more years maybe. We planned it, talked about it. Scouts, agents. High school to college, full scholarship. Good football school—Kansas? Oklahoma, maybe. The eyes of Texas are upon you! Scouts, agents, first-round draft pick for the Cowboys or Steelers. They had it planned. Poppy still knew people. He stayed in the loop, knew who to call. Go long, Jay—go long! Watch it— tackle on your right! Watch your left! Get mad at that durn block!

He's getting mad. The old man could have hung on just a little longer, couldn't he? He's held on for eighty-two years; what's four or five more? Didn't he have a lot to live for? *He had me.* "He—had—me!" Jay gasps out. All those years of disappointment—Dad a nerd, Uncle Troy a mental case— waiting for a son who could run. Jay's the one. He's the one who puts that spark in his grandpa's eye, everybody says so. "Thinks you hung the moon," Geemaw tells him.

But that spark is gone—disappeared—like Poppy scattered

it and stamped it and even peed on it to make sure it was totally, completely, 100 percent gone. And never, ever, ever to light again. Nothing left. It looked like Poppy, a little, but Poppy was gone. Ran off and left him when he could have held on for just a few more years. Jay hates it. Hates it, hates it, hates—

"I hate you, Poppy!"

Somehow, he finds himself on his hands and knees. The ground is still hard-packed and cold from winter. His fingers curl, gripping the earth, and next minute, he's sobbing like a girl. The earth tilts sideways, taking Jay with it.

Who are you?

Who am I? You knew me best of all—I need you to tell *me!*

Minutes pass, or maybe hours, while he's curled up like a grub worm, and the wind mutters *who are you who are you who...you....*

After a while, he sits up, dry as paper, recognizing that he's lost.

Should he go back, or forward?

The sun is slipping, and a cold breeze rattles the leaves on the oak trees. Rattles his teeth too—he's been shivering for a while now. The path has gradually become narrower and bushier, but it's still a path. He figures he's covered at least four miles from town, over halfway home. Forward it is. He pulls himself up and starts out at a trot, trying to guess his direction by the position of the sun. If this is the old railroad bed, it can't get too far from the highway, can it? A faint, occasional hum of tires on his right seems to bear out that guess.

But as he jogs on, and a half-mile slowly stretches to a whole mile and even more slowly becomes two, he's beginning to wonder. Especially now that the sun is gone and the air has turned cold and he has only a hoodie over his T-shirt and maybe ten minutes of twilight left. The days have been pretty warm but the nights are cold, especially clear nights that crumple the grass with frost. Like this. Listening hard, he can no longer hear the highway.

They'll be looking for him. Should he stop? That's what you're supposed to do when lost in the woods—hole up somewhere and wait to be found. But his legs feel so heavy. If he stopped, he might never get started again. He'd freeze. As long as he's moving, he can't freeze…

The wind shifts, carrying a scent of wood smoke to his nose. Smoke = fire = warmth = house! There must be a house nearby, and they'd probably have a phone, and he could make a call and bring this little story to an end. *Sorry, Mom, sorry, Dad, I'll never do it again; okay if you ground me since I don't really want to go anywhere.*

He follows his nose along some kind of path…opening up to some kind of…

Camp: a pile of coals raked in a pile to hold their warmth, a shack or else just a lean-to knocked together with scrap lumber, a rolled-up sleeping bag, a knife in a scabbard resting on a sawed-off tree stump—

Something touches his shoulder.

He jerks to one side and barely sees the claw of a skinned animal hanging in a tree. The animal, in spite of being very dead, growls at him.

He jumps back, and another claw rakes his cheek, knocking off his glasses. He doesn't stick around.

A burst of adrenaline propels him down the old roadbed. He forgets about pacing himself or in-through-the-nose-out-through-the-mouth; he just flat-out runs and very shortly runs smack into the very thing he'd been looking for all this time: a real road.

A gravel road, anyway. It's not the highway, but the hum of asphalt is coming to him a little clearer now. Maybe he's close. His legs keep moving, even though his lungs are begging them to stop and every breath seems to rip a new one in his chest.

Then he comes to a crossroads, and there it is.

It looks familiar yet strange. That's because he's never seen it from this angle, in near-darkness.

It's the bus shed on Farm Road 152. So now he knows where he is.

The sight of one familiar object crowds out all his other senses; it's not only all he sees but all he hears, smells, touches, and tastes as he crosses the narrow road and collapses on the bench. Then he pulls his feet up and leans against the wall and does nothing but breathe. Blood is drying on his cheek where something scratched him—a tree branch, he knows now, not an animal. It snatched off his glasses, and maybe he should be glad it didn't poke out an eye.

The voices come to him slowly. It's a still night, so clear he can feel the stars. Sounds carry like taps on a crystal glass. He remembers there's a house nearby; it sounds as though the people might be standing outside on the porch or in the driveway. Both are women's voices, one louder than the other. "…can't go on like this forever" are the first words he hears.

It sounds angry. It also sounds familiar.

Then shouting, back and forth.

"How long has he been here?"

"He's not here!"

"Who do you think you're kidding?"

"He's *not here*! Now leave us alone!"

"If I leave now, I'm not coming back!"

"Fine!" A door slams, a motor roars, an old pickup truck zooms past in a spray of gravel. His brain is quivering from exhaustion or else he'd know who it was. He's sure he would know, but for now…

It would have been simple to knock on the door and ask to use the phone. But he doesn't. A haze of strong feeling seems to hover around the house, and he's too tired to deal with it. So before his knees freeze in place, he hauls himself to his feet and trudges uphill toward the highway.

They're looking for him. Maybe the first car that passes will be driven by somebody who's keeping an eye out. And sure enough, he's been walking the shoulder for only a couple of minutes when a vehicle slows down, stops, backs up.

It's his sister Julie, who was supposed to pick him up at Sunset Hills hours ago. Better her, he thinks, than his mother, who would probably have burst into hysterical tears at the sight of him. Even though it wouldn't be long before she tore into him for losing another pair of glasses and those things don't grow on trees.

But what does Julie do—Julie, who's chased him, tripped him, yelled at him, and sat on him? Burst into hysterical tears.

April

Igor doesn't want to be famous. He just wants to be noticed. And that's not as simple as it seems, because he has a lot to hide.

Fame means your picture on the cover of a magazine or showing up on *Hollywood Nights* more than once. Or being the subject of a manhunt on one of those twenty-four-hour news channels his mother is always watching, which doesn't help her peace of mind.

Igor just wants to be able to go anywhere and have people notice him: *Who's that new guy? That's Igor. Started hanging out here a couple of weeks ago. Funny guy. Everybody likes him. Hey, Igor! Somebody wants to meet you.*

He'd been to four different schools by the time he got through first grade—which isn't quite as bad as it sounds because it took him two years to finish first grade. That's one of his secrets: nobody knows he is really twelve years old instead of eleven. His mother changed his birth year at the second kindergarten he went to and never changed it back. She had her reasons—still does. And Igor can get away with it because he looks younger than his real age. But another advantage is he would have seemed even dumber in sixth grade than he does in fifth.

His grades still suck, though. "There're a lot more important things than getting good grades," his mother says in between report cards. "Like you being a good person. If you turn out to be good, Jamie, I don't care if you're smart."

That didn't come out quite right, but he thinks he knows what she means.

She calls him Jamie, not Igor, because Robert James Price Sanderson is his real name. That's the second thing about him that most people don't know or soon forget. When he was in his first kindergarten, one of the teacher assistants thought he looked like he belonged in an old vampire movie because of his pale skin and dark hair that comes to a point in the middle of his forehead. So she called him Igor—who is actually a character in *Frankenstein*, not *Dracula*—and soon everybody else did too. And somehow the name traveled with him. At the beginning of every school year, all his teachers know his real name. By the end, they've forgotten it. When he graduates from high school, if he ever does, they'll probably announce him as Igor Sanderson, and there it would be on his diploma, in fancy letters.

But to graduate from high school, he'll have to get through fifth grade, and it isn't looking too good right now. Achievement tests are coming up in April, and just the thought of it makes his bones feel like Jell-O. "It doesn't mean you're stupid, Jamie," his mother said after he brought home his last report card. "It just means you don't take tests so good. And I never did either. There's nothing wrong with your brain."

"Are you sure?" All those Cs and Ds (and one B, for P.E.) stacked up like kids' blocks in a tower he couldn't knock down.

"Sure I'm sure. Your brain's better than mine."

"Better than Dad's?"

"I don't know about that. There's nothing your dad can't do."

"I mean my real dad."

Her hand shot out and slapped him—*whack!*

One second, that hand was holding up the bottom of his baby sister Jade, and the next it was stinging his cheek. Then it snaked around his neck and pulled him against her soft trembling shoulder. "I'm sorry, honey. But listen, you've got to stop saying those things, you hear? I can't tolerate it."

He knows that, and he also knows he'll say one of those things again sometime. Something about his dad, that is. It's like he can't help it, and that thought bothers him even more than the thought of three days of achievement tests.

That's the third thing people don't know about him: his father is nuts.

Not his stepdad, Al Sanderson. But his real father, Bobby Price. Igor doesn't remember Bobby Price, or maybe he does. Thousands of people do, because for a little while, nine years ago, Bobby Price was very famous. And so was Igor.

His mom, Vickie Price, had split up with Bobby because he was abusive and unpredictable. They had one little boy, two and a half years old. All three lived in Fresno, California. One day, when Vickie was at work, Bobby Price walked into Wee Treasures Day Care Center with a handgun, pointed it at the day care ladies and kids, threatened to shoot anybody who stopped him, grabbed his little boy, dashed out, and took off in a stolen car.

The little boy was Igor, of course. He sort of wishes he could remember it. But then, maybe it's a good thing he can't.

Is Igor dumber than his dad? Bobby Price had done something very stupid but was pretty smart in how he went about it. He drove the stolen car four blocks, allowing bystanders to get a good look at it, before darting into an abandoned garage where his own car, a 2004 Chevy Cavalier, was parked. Then he transferred Igor to the Cavalier, made him curl up on the floor, threw a blanket over him, and motored north for several miles before doubling back and taking a series of county roads headed toward Mexico. In this way, stopping only to dye Igor's hair blond and his own hair brown, he managed to elude the cops for two and a half days.

It was during that time he got famous—and Igor too, because those twenty-four-hour news channels were showing pictures of them several times a day, along with fuzzy footage from the Little Treasures Day Care security camera and tearful messages from his mother pleading with Bobby Price and anyone who might know their whereabouts to please please *please* return her little boy.

Tips poured in, and most of them weren't any good, but the police were finally able to track down the Cavalier, which

Bobby had purchased from a private individual the day before the kidnapping. The cops stopped him in Arizona, at a roadblock only sixty miles from the Mexican border.

Igor, aside from a bad dye job, appeared to be just fine. He was properly buckled into his car seat, with a very wet diaper, a dirty face, and a full tummy. There were no marks on him except for a bad case of diaper rash. Bobby Price had been driving day and night, getting by on short naps and pills, stopping frequently for Chinese fire drills. Igor was probably ready to stop—he still doesn't like road trips.

What Bobby planned to do in Mexico with a little boy to support remained a mystery. He never said, not even during his trial. The trial and conviction and sentencing took several months, during which Vickie Price met Al Sanderson: a veteran, ten years older, steady and boring. Once Bobby was safely locked up in Tanglewood Medium Security Prison, they got married, started having babies, and moved a lot.

Hidden Acres is the longest Igor has lived anywhere— almost eighteen months. He likes it, and so does his mom. She likes her big backyard with the garden and her one-and-a-half-story house surrounded by shade trees that make it hard to see from the road, maybe even from the air. She has met her nearest neighbors and likes the fact that they mind their own business. She loves her family: Big Al and Little Al (now almost six), Samantha (three and a half), baby Jade, and Igor. Staying home most of the time with the door locked and the curtains drawn suits her fine, because she's nervous by nature, and the kidnapping made her much worse.

This has been a rough year, with Big Al's construction business taking him away for weeks at a time. Vickie has locked Igor out of the house twice since school began. The week after Thanksgiving, she set up the Christmas tree and tore it right down again when Big Al called to say he was taking that job in Louisiana. Igor was sent to the principal's office twice during December, and Little Al once, which made their mom grab a handful of receipts out of the kitchen drawer and threaten to take their Christmas presents back. They pretty much lived on macaroni and cheese until Big Al returned the day before Christmas Eve (when they got their tree back, with presents underneath). Since work dried up after the holidays, the rest of winter was okay except for less money, meaning more macaroni and cheese.

Big Al started getting long-distance jobs again in the spring, but lately Vickie's mood has improved with the weather. At least Igor thinks so. So he's not expecting anything amiss on a lovely spring day, buzzing with bees and popping with apple blossoms, when he walks home from the bus and lets himself in to find the living room rearranged. Two armchairs are turned over on their sides to make a fort, and the couch cushions are piled up on top of them. The drapes are on the floor, and a trail of chocolate syrup leads to the kitchen, where Little Al perches on the countertop, shoveling dry beans down the garbage disposal. None of this, Igor knows from experience, is a good sign.

After pulling his brother out of the sink, he goes looking for their mom. She seems to be passed out in her bedroom with the heavy drapes closed. She looks like Sleeping Beauty in a nest of white pillows, her dark hair spread out and coming to a peak over a face that's still pretty when she's not yelling. "Just a migraine," she whispers to Igor, barely opening her eyes. "Are the girls still asleep? Can you see what Little Al's up to?"

Jade is awake, with a stinky diaper that Igor changes before returning to the kitchen, just in time to stop his brother from turning the disposal on with all those beans still in it. "You're not my boss!" Little Al cries when pulled off the counter for the second time. But he settles down with a Popsicle on the kitchen floor (Jade gets one too, but not red, because the food coloring makes her hyper), and Igor starts scooping beans out of the disposal with a spoon. Also slimy old celery tops and potato peels—and a wad of paper.

It's an envelope, mashed up as though a fist had clenched it and thrust it in the disposal with all its might. One end looks a little chewed, but the other is intact enough to read the return address: Tanglewood Medium Security Prison.

Igor stops breathing for a moment. Here, in his hand, right now, is a letter from his dad.

It's the first one he's ever held or even seen up close. He's heard of them, though. At least three times before. In fact, the only time his mother mentions Bobby Price, it's because of a letter: "Your father found us. We're moving to—" Nevada, Kansas, Oklahoma, here.

His father found him.

It's like an itch, the memory he can't quite remember: himself tucked like a football under an arm while a huge man yells

213

and waves a gun around a room full of little kids all peeing their pants. Followed by a fifty-hour road trip reported by all the major news networks. Sometimes Igor will hear a piece of a song that sounds very familiar, though he can't name it, and he wonders if his dad was playing it over and over on their cross-country run. Or he wonders why the smell of gasoline always hypes him up. Or why he often dreams about skidding sideways in a car.

Something different about this time, though. He's not dreaming, remembering, or guessing—he's got the actual letter in his actual hand.

The envelope looks like it was still sealed when his mom crammed it down the drain and turned the disposal on. He wonders why she stopped before it got all the way chewed up. Maybe because she had second thoughts, or maybe because Little Al put the cat in the dryer and pushed the "on" button, like he had once before.

Whatever—she's down for the count and Igor's holding some kind of communication from Tanglewood Prison, and nobody can stop him from opening it. His thumb hooks under the envelope flap...

And a scream breaks from the family room, where Samantha, just up from her nap, has swiped Jade's Popsicle. Sighing, Igor stuffs the envelope in his pocket and grabs the Popsicle, now crusted with dirt and cat hair picked up while Jade crawled from the kitchen with it. He dashes to the nearest bathroom to wash it off while both girls bawl. Meanwhile, Little Al turns the dishwasher on.

"Jamie! *Please* do something!" his mother calls forlornly from her bedroom.

Igor runs back to the kitchen and separates his brother from the dishwasher (after checking to make sure there's no cat inside). Then he collects Samantha and Jade and sits all three of them at the table for a snack of raisins and graham crackers. He'll probably be responsible for dinner too. That happens every time his mother gets an afternoon migraine. Little Al demands a drink, which makes Samantha want a drink, and after Igor has poured strawberry milk for them and is looking for Jade's sippy cup, Samantha knocks her cup over and freaks out when her graham crackers get soaked.

"Jamie! Please..." moans his mom.

He slams a dishrag on the table, picks up Jade, grabs Little Al by the hand, and dribbling Samantha between his feet like a soccer ball, herds all three of them outside. He puts the baby in her swing and runs for the back door before Little Al catches on. He reaches the door a second before his brother, latches it behind him, and lets Al holler and kick to his heart's content. Then he calls Miranda, whose number is stuck on the refrigerator door with a magnet.

She picks up on the second ring. "Are you busy?" he asks without saying hello.

"No..." She sounds uncertain. He's never called before.

"Could you come over and help me watch the kids? My mom's down with a headache and I've got...a lot of homework. Just for an hour?"

"Oh. Sure!" She sounds so eager he wonders why he never thought of calling her before.

He manages to stop Little Al from kicking all the sand out of Samantha's sandbox just about the time that Miranda arrives with a nylon rope. "Good idea," he says. "We can tie him to that tree."

She laughs. "Silly Igor! I want to try something with the rope. But that tree is perfect." She loops the rope over a low branch of the birch tree in the backyard. Then she dares Little Al to climb up the trunk and rappel down.

"That's cool," Igor says with real admiration. He kind of wants to try it himself.

Miranda smiles. "I saw it on TV. You know *Treehouse Family*, that reality show on cable?"

"Not really. Okay if I split so I can do a little reading before dinner? Since I'll probably have to cook it?"

"Sure—I'll watch the kids."

He escapes to his room, which Little Al shares, unlocks Cornelia's cage, and drapes the snake over his shoulders. She likes the warmth of his neck. Then he climbs to the top bunk and opens the envelope at last. He didn't lie to Miranda about "a little reading," since he doesn't think it will take long to read whatever was in the envelope. But he's wrong.

It's a letter, all right. Handwritten. Igor feels his head wobble, because he's never seen anything written by Bobby Price, not even a signature on a Christmas card.

But after the first glance, it's a big disappointment. The letter is almost impossible to read. For three reasons: 1) the ink has run; 2) at least a fourth of it got chewed up in the garbage disposal; and 3) his father's handwriting is terrible. Kind of like Igor's, in fact—now he can understand what his teachers are always griping about.

He can make out a few words—like his own name. Not Igor, or course, but Jim. Somehow that combination of letters jumps off the page, even if smudgy: *Jim.* Or *Jim…?* Or even *JIM!* It's like a whole lifetime of calls: calls to come in for dinner, or come and explain what happened to the bathroom mirror, or just come and say hello to the old man when he gets home from work. Calls he never heard, saved up in this letter to be spilled all at once. Big Al's probably the best stepfather a kid could have, but he calls him Igor like everybody else.

"Jim" is his other life, running with ghost-steps alongside the real one. It may even be who he really is on the inside.

And it's too much for now. Igor sits up in his bed, over-whelmed with too-muchness. Another reason why he can't read the letter so good; his eyes are all watery. So he just sits there as Cornelia's snaky heart beats against his neck and happy shouts ring from his half-siblings in the yard and a big gaping hole of silence fills the house.

After a while, he flattens the letter carefully and presses it between the pages of his math workbook.

Miranda's poking around in the pantry when he returns to the kitchen, while Jade sits on the floor banging a set of measuring cups. "I don't mean to be nosy," Miranda says. "But your mom still isn't feeling well, so I told her I'd see what we could do for dinner."

"No; that's great."

"Here's some tuna cans. How do the kids like tuna noodle casserole?"

"Not much."

"Macaroni and cheese?"

"Barf. Don't even think about it."

They settle on teriyaki meatballs found in the back of the freezer, with rice and glazed baby carrots. Miranda pulls out a couple of pans while Igor rolls a can of pork and beans toward Jade, who shrieks with joy. "How'd you learn to cook?" he asks.

"Oh, I usually do two or three meals a week because my mom works late on Wednesday and Thursday. And I did most of the baking for Shelly's bake sale last weekend."

"Right. I remember." Shelly was advertising the bake sale two weeks before and selling leftovers on the Monday after. "How'd that go?"

"Pretty good. We made sixty-seven dollars. And I gained three pounds," she added, self-consciously tugging at her jeans.

Igor retrieves the can that Jade kicked under the pantry door, then rolls it toward his baby sister again. She kicks her feet and claps her hands. He wonders if Bobby Price ever played this game with him.

"Are you ready for the tests next week?" Miranda asks.

He groans out loud. "Why'd you have to say that? I'm trying to forget."

"Sorry. But it might be better if you did just forget. Relax and let the answers come out of your subconscious."

"My subconscious doesn't have any answers. I don't know

why they do this every year. How does spending two days filling in little ovals with a pencil prepare us for adultery?"

Miranda pauses, staring at him. "You mean adulthood?"

"What'd I say?"

She laughs and shakes her head, and all of a sudden, he has
an idea.

It may be the kind of idea he should forget, but it's like
a booger that won't shake off his finger. Even after dinner,
and stacking the dishes in the dishwasher, and straightening
the overturned chairs and coffee table in the living room, and
checking on his mom (who is finally sound asleep), and bath-
ing Jade and Samantha (Miranda is really working overtime),
the idea sticks.

When the babies are in bed and Little Al is playing *Alien
Wars* (which he's not allowed on school nights, but Igor figures it's educational because you have to count the aliens you
vaporize), Miranda seems reluctant to go home. "Are you sure
you'll be okay?" she asks.

"Yeah, I'll set the alarm so I can get up early in case
Mom doesn't."

"But who'll take care of the babies when you leave for school?"

"She's usually awake by then. If not, I'll wake her up." Igor
is sharing more about his family than he probably should. "I've
done it before when she gets…nervous."

"Does she get…nervous a lot?"

"No…I mean, not really, but… Hold on a minute."

He's made a decision. He runs to his room, grabs his math
workbook, and runs back to the kitchen. After a glance at his

mom to make sure she's really out like a light, he sits down at the kitchen table and opens his notebook. "She got this in the mail today."

Mystified, Miranda sits next to him. "Who's it from?"

"From…my uncle. Her brother." (*Liar! Liar!* he thinks.) "He's in jail."

To his relief, she doesn't ask *For what?* He hasn't made that part up yet. "What's in the letter?"

"That's just it. I'm not sure." He opens his workbook to where the paper is, flattened but not quite dry, and smudgier than ever. "I think it upset Mom a little because she crumpled it and put it down the garbage disposal."

"Oh." Miranda carefully turns the letter toward her and squints at it. "Who's 'Jim'?"

"His, uh, little boy. I think."

"You mean your cousin?" Igor nods, because it doesn't seem as much like lying if you don't actually *say* anything. Miranda goes on, "Okay, this says, 'I'm taking a course in…psychology?…and reading about…' Hm. That word's totally gone. 'I'll be…something…parole.' Maybe, 'I'll be up for parole.'"

"What's parole?"

"It's when you serve part of your sentence and you've got a good record so they think about letting you out early."

"Really?" Igor's voice comes out squeaky. "Like, if you've served maybe half of a fifteen-year sentence? Like eight or nine years?"

"That sounds about right." Miranda is still studying the letter. "This says, 'Tell Jim I'll…' uh…'see him then'? 'See him there,' maybe."

Igor feels a little twinge on the back of his neck. "Are you sure it says *see* him?"

"Not really. Maybe *saw* him. Or *sew* him." She notices his face. "Are you okay?"

"Sure."

"Look—down here? This says 'Watch out.' The ink's run but it's clear enough to read. And look—" She turns the paper over. "It's marked so hard the impression's on the other side."

"Let me see." He leans closer, and sure enough, the pen marks have raised the paper on the back. Like the writer really wanted to emphasize that point. "Are there any more words like that?"

Miranda tilts the paper and sights down the slope. "Not that I can see. Wonder what she's supposed to watch out for?"

"I don't know." Igor can feel his face freezing, like all the blood was streaming out.

"It might be a joke."

"Yeah, but if he's up for parole, it might mean he's headed this way. Like, watch out for *me*."

"Maybe." She places the letter on the table and spreads out her fingers on top. "Is he…uh…violent?"

"No. No." Unless pointing a handgun at a bunch of little kids could be considered *violent*. "No…I don't really remember him."

Miranda keeps smoothing the paper with one hand. "Are you worried?"

"I don't know." Though in fact, he probably was a little worried, and a few other things too, like anxious, excited, afraid…

"Look, Igor, it's probably nothing to worry about—or be ashamed of either. Lots of families have a black sheep."

"Like yours?"

"Not really, but… Well, for instance. Shelly's Uncle Mike has been in all kinds of trouble with the law. It started in high school when he hung out with this wild kid who was, like, the prank king. Shelly's told me about her uncle's problems with bad checks and stuff, but I don't think she even knows about the worst—" She stops herself abruptly.

"The worst what?" Igor asks.

"Maybe I shouldn't tell you, because it's like gossip. My mother just happened to write an article about it for her school newspaper in seventh grade. That's how I know."

"If it was in the newspaper, it's not gossip," Igor points out. Makes sense to him.

"Well…just to help you feel better about your uncle. This guy Shelly's uncle used to hang out with—Jason somebody— wanted to do the ultimate graduation prank. So he got a bunch of guys to go along with the plan, which was to fill Ziploc bags with little balls—mostly bouncy rubber balls, but also marbles—and hide them under their gowns. Mike was a junior that year, so his job was to bring the bags in a box and hide them in a certain spot that the gang would know about. Nobody knows for sure how many were involved, but it was at least a dozen."

"How did it work?" Igor is very interested in earning the title of Prank King for himself someday, so he's always collecting ideas.

"Well. Back in the day, they had graduation in the stadium, and all the seniors were supposed to gather in the upper bleachers at the end zone. When 'Pomp and Circumstance' started playing, they all stood up and marched down to the seats in front of the speakers' platform.

"So the music starts and everybody stands, and while they're marching, all the seniors who were in on the plan opened their bags, and the balls and marbles fell out and bounced all over the place. They were supposed to wad up their plastic bags right after that and hide them in their pockets or clothes—which would be easy under a graduation gown—so nobody would ever know who actually did it."

"Cool!" says Igor.

"Except for one thing. The seniors who didn't know about it weren't prepared, so there was some slipping and falling, especially with the marbles. That was supposed to happen. Nobody was supposed to get really hurt. But somebody did: Troy Pasternak."

"Pasternak? Like the Pasternaks we know?"

"Yep. You've seen that plaque on the gazebo—'In Honor of Troy Lawrence Pasternak'? He was Jay's dad's little brother. Jay's uncle. He was senior class president and a football hero and all that. So he slipped as he was coming down those concrete stairs and couldn't get his balance back and fell all the way down the steps and landed on his head.

"They didn't know how bad it was at first—somebody called an ambulance, and as soon as he was off to the hospital, they went on with graduation. But Troy was in a coma for two months, and when he finally came out of it, his brain was totally messed up. He's been in a nursing home ever since."

"Oh." Igor makes a mental note to pass on the bouncy-ball trick.

"None of the seniors admitted to anything, but everybody knew who the ringleader was. And somebody saw Shelly's Uncle Mike with a box of Ziploc bags, so they searched his car and found extra bags with marbles—Shelly says he's not too smart. Mike blabbed about whose idea it was, but the Jason guy skipped town right after graduation and nobody's seen or heard of him since. That was all in my mom's article. She did a good job of reporting."

Miranda suddenly stands, and the letter flutters in the draft. "I'd better go! I told her I'd be home by nine, and it's five past."

Igor jumps to his feet. "Thanks again. For coming over and everything. Oh—and don't mention this letter to my mom, because she'll get all upset. Or anybody else, because…"

"Sure, I understand. Do you ever write to him?"

"Uh…no." He's never had the address.

But now he does.

"Sometimes it's easier to communicate in writing," Miranda says. "It is for me, anyway. Like, I've always had a hard time talking to my dad on the phone, but since Christmas, I've been trying to email once a week. I just write about what's going on and stuff—nothing big—but he's been writing back. Last Saturday when he called, we had a real conversation."

"That's good." For some reason, Igor feels an overwhelming urge to throw his arms around her and squeeze hard, even though she's two inches taller and not his mom. Also a grade ahead of him, even though they're really the same age.

Instead, he sticks out his hand. "I guess I'll...see you tomorrow."

She takes it, and it's funny, but he gets the feeling that she would have hugged him back. "Okay. I hope your mother's better soon."

* * *

His mother seems to be feeling okay in the morning. She's stirring oatmeal for Jade when Igor stumbles into the kitchen yawning, because he and Little Al stayed up past eleven playing *Alien Wars*. "Thanks for taking over last night," she says. "I'm sorry."

"'S okay." He takes a bowl from the cupboard and a box of raisin bran from the corner cabinet. "Miranda helped a lot."

"She's such a nice girl. I'm glad you thought of calling her."

"Uh-huh." Next, a gallon of milk from the fridge. "Mom, do you ever, like, write to anybody?"

"What do you mean?" A spoon stops halfway to Jade's mouth.

"Like letters. Or email."

"Sure I do. That's how I keep up with your Aunt Beth. I'd rather call, but she likes the emails. Or that crazy Facebook. I just can't get into that stuff." She shoves a spoonful of oatmeal in Jade's mouth and goes for another. "I mean, why stick yourself up on some website where *anybody* can find out all about you?"

Igor takes a breath. "Do you ever write to…my dad?"

His mother's hand stops again then glides on toward Jade's mouth. "Why should I? He calls almost every night when he's gone."

"You know who I mean."

The spoon dives into the oatmeal and sticks up like a flag. "Do I?"

"Come on, Mom. What if he gets out on parole?"

Her eyes shift to the disposal and back again—really quick, but he sees it. "I'm not going to talk about it."

"But, Mom—"

"I'm not talking about it!"

"Not even when he shows up?"

"What do you mean?"

"He will sometime, won't he? He's not dead!"

Jade winds up her I-want-my-breakfast siren, but the spoon is now flipping little chunks of oatmeal at Igor. "Keep your voice down!"

"Why? Afraid the neighbors will find out my dad's a jailbird?"

"Shut *up*! And listen, mister, I don't know what kind of game you're playing with all these questions, but don't think I haven't noticed!"

"Noticed what?"

"All these questions!"

"About what?"

"You know what!"

"I don't know what," says Little Al, now dragging himself into the kitchen. "What?"

"Out!" yells their mother, standing up and pointing to the door while Jade cranks the decibel level up to a ten.

"But I haven't had breakfast yet!" Little Al yells back.

Mom fumbles in the cabinet for a package of Pop-Tarts and throws it at them. "There's breakfast! You can share."

"But—"

"*Out!!*"

Igor is already on his way. He snatches their jackets off the hook by the back door. "Let's go, Ally."

"But my lunch! And I didn't brush my teeth!"

"That never bothered you before. Come on!"

They leave without lunches, snacks, or even backpacks; if anybody asks, Igor intends only to say that his mom threw him out of the house ten minutes early.

"What's the matter with her?" Little Al whines as they trudge across the common.

Igor shrugs, even though he knows. But he doesn't know enough! That's why the crazy thought that occurred to him last night, which seemed so far out it might have been Jupiter, is now speeding toward earth like a comet.

It's a soft spring morning, all pink and cream about the edges with a touch of lilac in the air. Bender and Matthew are already at the gazebo, arguing over some science thing. Jay arrives soon after, flinging his backpack on a bench and collapsing beside it. Spencer is close behind.

"What's the matter?" Bender asks Jay.

"Shut up."

"He lost the soccer game last night." Spencer climbs the

gazebo steps with his backpack over one shoulder and his guitar case in the other hand. Lately he's been taking the guitar to school on Tuesdays so he can jam with the junior high jazz band during lunch. "Had the ball lined up with the goal and kicked it with the side of his foot so it went out of bounds. Coach ripped him a new one, right there on the field."

"Soccer's a stupid game," Jay mutters, pushing his glasses up on his nose. "Sissy, European runaround."

"So stick to running," says Spencer. "You're a *great* runner." Jay makes a noise, something between a snort and a laugh. "No, seriously. You ran over seven miles that day, and it might have been farther if—"

"Dude," Jay says warningly.

"If what?" asks Bender.

Spencer says, "Remember that night he was late and everybody was looking for him?"

Jay rounds on him furiously. "*Dude!*"

"He found some kind of hermit's hideout on the old railroad bed. Hey, let go!" Spencer squirms out of the half nelson Jay locks on his neck. "Scared the crap out of him."

"I told you not to tell!"

"I didn't promise!" Spencer rubs his neck. "It's not the kind of secret you ought to keep. What if he's somebody wanted by the FBI?"

Bender is all over it: *Where? When? Who?* Igor, preoccupied with his own thoughts, can't muster much interest in some old hermit, whatever that is. Bender pulls a piece of newspaper out of his pocket. The other boys are gathering around it when Little Al tugs on Igor's shirt. "There's Mom."

A blue station wagon pulls up, hand frantically waving from the window. Sighing, Igor slouches over. "Here's your lunch," his mom sniffs. "And Little Al's." She hands over two paper bags, and Igor imagines the contents: a slapped-together PB&J, a bag of chips, and maybe an apple if she had one to throw in. "And here's your backpack. I couldn't find Little Al's. I'm sorry, honey, but I wish you wouldn't bring up...certain things. It makes me crazy."

"I know," Igor says simply, his arms loaded with stuff. He doesn't say *I'm sorry.*

"I've gotta go—Jade's in her playpen and Samantha's waking up."

"Okay." Igor steps back from the car, hands Little Al his lunch, and is all the way back to the gazebo before he hears the station wagon rev up and make a wide U-turn.

"Zip it," Bender is saying. "Here come the girls. If Kaitlynn gets hold of this, we'll have to have a neighborhood garage sale for the guy."

"Just forget I said anything," Jay says. "Or *he* said anything," he adds with a kick at Spencer. "My dad would have a cow if he finds out I didn't tell him first."

"My dad would think it's a hoot," Spencer says.

"My dad wouldn't hear even if I told him," Bender says. "Even if he still lived with us."

"My dad doesn't seem to exist," Matthew says.

And my dad, Igor is thinking, *is going to hear from me.* He's made up his mind; the comet has crashed.

* * *

Dear ~~Dad Bobby~~ Mr. Price,

*This is Jim. Even tho evrybody calls me Igor. I am in 5th
grade now. I dont do too good in scool but evrybody likes
me. Almost, ha. My step dad is cool. He got us a snake for
Cristmas. Its a corn snake. She belongs to both of us but I
get to keep her in my room. I want to know if you will get
out on peroll soon. Thats all for now.*

Love,
Igor (Jim)

p.s. Dont tell mom I wrote to you.

Rereading the letter, he realizes he should have started over
after the cross-outs on the first line rather than going on. His
teacher is always making the class turn in a sloppy copy, then
rewrite after corrections, so he was probably thinking he'd
make a neat copy after the first draft. But the joke is on him:
aside from the first line, the letter is almost painfully neat,
much better than his usual work. If he tried to copy the whole
thing, it would probably look worse than the original.

But how does it sound? Does he say too much about his
stepfather, like enough to make his real father jealous? Probably
okay—there's more about the snake than about Big Al. Is it
bragging to say that (almost) everybody likes him? Even if it's
(mostly) true? Should he include one of his wallet-size school

pictures from the kitchen drawer or wait to see if Bobby Price writes back?

But wait—what if his dad does write back? What would that do to Mom, to receive an envelope addressed to "Jim" from Tanglewood Medium Security Prison? After pondering for a minute, Igor adds one more postscript:

> *p.s.s. If you write back, dont send it to me. send it to Miranda Scott at 370 Courtney Circle ect.*

That raises the stakes. He'll have to admit the truth to Miranda: that the man in jail is a closer relative than he'd said. It would also mean breaking numerous promises to his mother that he wouldn't tell anybody—but the promise is half-broken already.

Igor decides to let the letter go, just as it is. He sneaks a stamp and an envelope from the desk drawer in the family room, copies the return address on the face of his envelope, slides his letter inside, and slaps a stamp on it. Tomorrow morning, he'll slip it into the Mulroonys' mailbox and raise their flag—they both leave for work early, so nobody will know.

It'll be easy. So why is his heart pounding like a jackhammer?

＊ ＊ ＊

On Wednesday, achievement tests start. For two days, he sits in strange classrooms filling in ovals in test booklets, pushing his brain like a wheelbarrow past rows of words and numbers.

It seems tougher this year than usual, and maybe that's because the letter is on its way west, taking his brain with it.

Friday is an early dismissal day. In the morning, he and the bus arrive at the gazebo at the same time. He lines up with the others, feeling perfectly still inside. So much so that Mrs. B remarks, "Are you okay, Igor?"

Bender, Matthew, Jay, and Spencer are holding a conference in the back. As Igor takes a seat by himself, Shelly climbs aboard with a pair of sparkly pompoms, which she pumps up and down while screeching, "I have an announcement!!"

From the back, Bender groans loudly.

"When I got home from school yesterday, there was a letter waiting for me. From Shooting Star Camp." She pauses. "I got a partial scholarship! And…I'm…IN!"

Shelly waves the pompoms again and leads three cheers. On her way down the aisle, she slaps high fives with the littles, Kaitlynn, even Alice, finally dropping down beside Miranda.

"Does this mean you can stop selling stuff?" asks Jay.

"And making announcements?" asks Bender.

"Congratulations," says Mrs. B. "Let's roll."

Sitting one seat behind her, Igor can feel the energy radiating from Shelly. But Miranda seems to wilt like yesterday's french fries. He hears her ask, "Why didn't you call and tell me last night?"

"Last night? I had a *ton* of people to call. My grandmas and Aunt Maria and Aunt Shonda and my dance teacher and voice coach and everybody on the Y-Team and this booking agent I've been talking to. Plus I had to write a letter of acceptance, and then Mom and I went through all my costumes to see if I should take any with me, and we made a list of the supplies we had to buy—the baby crying all the time—and listen to my dad wonder how we were going to find money for the airfare and…"

Shelly chatters happily all the way to school. At every single stop, she jumps up to wave her pompoms and make her announcement. Miranda barely says two words. Igor notices— funny how feeling quiet makes him notice stuff. Like the little sniffs Miranda is making and the way she flicks at her eyes with her index finger.

When they finally pull into the bus line at school, Shelly is first to pop up. While she's hurrying to gather her stuff, one of the pompoms flips to the floor under Miranda's feet. "Oops! Hand me that, would you, Mir?"

Miranda picks up the pompom. Then she stands and hurls it with all her might to the rear of the bus where it bounces off the seat Bender and Matthew just vacated.

Shelly looks more puzzled than angry. "Wha—What's with you?"

"Get your own stuff from now on!" Miranda clutches her backpack in both arms and pushes past Shelly, marching up the aisle like she'll plow right through the windshield if Mrs. B doesn't let her off. Mrs. B is not supposed to let anybody off before they're all the way in the bus lane, but she takes one look at Miranda's face and pushes the door lever without a word.

Igor's eye falls upon a lunch sack listing sadly on its side where Miranda's feet used to be. He squeezes past Shelly and scoops it up. Hurrying up the aisle, he waves the bag at Mrs. B and points out the window. "She left it. Can I—"

With a sigh, the driver opens the door again. Igor glances back; every face has the same stunned expression except Shelly, who throws up her hands in total cluelessness. "*What?*" she asks Igor. He shakes his head and leaps all three steps with a single bound.

Though she's moving right along, Miranda's not hard to catch up to. "You left this," he says, holding out her lunch bag.

She snatches it out of his hand, walking a little faster as their bus inches up beside them. Soon the doors will open and spill everybody out, and he knows she wants to get out of range. They turn the corner of the bus lane and head up the big curve of sidewalk leading to the main entrance. Two flags snap on the wind as they pass the flagpole.

Miranda says, "She could have called me." Her voice sounds weepy. "I helped her with all that. I managed her campaign, made most of the Christmas ornaments she sold, let her steal my poem, collected canned goods—"

"Steal your what?"

"My *poem.*" Miranda sniffs loudly. "My poem about the empty bus stop, that Shelly got me to turn in with her name, and she got a one on it and it was in the book. But somebody knew it was mine, because I got an anonymous Christmas card with a copy of the poem in it. *My* poem. And besides"—*sniff*—"I did almost all the baking for her bake sale—which was my idea too. She—she could have at least called me."

He recognizes the sounds of an oncoming meltdown from long experience with his mom and has already started feeling the side pockets of his backpack for a wad of Kleenex.

Miranda almost runs the last few steps, aiming at a spot under the porch roof where a shadow waits to hide her. Pressing her back against the concrete wall, she gulps out, "I'm not jealous or anything. I'd be happy for her if she'd let me be happy *with* her. I don't mind being the ugly boring friend, I just—just wanna be—I just—"

He found it! Digging out the scrunched-up package, he pulls a scrunched-up (but clean) tissue from it just in time. Her breath is chugging and her nose is running as she snatches it from him.

"You're not ugly," he says. And means it, even though, with her red eyes and wet nose, she has looked better.

The first bell rings. "Thanks," she sniffs then stuffs the tissue in her pocket and bolts for the door before she has to meet anyone from the bus.

Igor follows more slowly. If he's late, it won't be the first time.

✳ ✳ ✳

When school gets out at noon, Shelly tries to talk to Miranda but soon gives up and takes her assigned seat. She's still pumped but not so obnoxious about it. Igor is starting to pay more attention, and he notices that when Bender and Matthew board the bus, Bender stops for a quick message to Spencer and Jay. The four of them, now that he thinks about it, have been very chummy for the last week or so, and it's starting to bother him. What's up with that? Are they cooking up a plan? And why can't he be part of it?

It's a rowdier ride than usual and seems twice as long, but finally the bus reaches its final destination. As the last riders pile off, Igor falls in behind Spencer and Jay, who are heading in the same direction as Matthew and Bender. He lags back, watching the four of them meet at the gazebo.

Sometimes acting impulsively is a good thing—if he'd stopped to consider his next move, someone would have noticed him. He jogs across the grass as though taking a shortcut toward home, then angles back in a straight line that ends in the rose of Sharon bushes beside the gazebo entrance. From here, he can pick up almost every word.

A plan is being made. After a few seconds, it seems the plan has some glitches, and a few seconds more reveals the glitch is Spencer.

"Tell your mom you can't do it," Bender is saying. "So what if you miss one Space Camp orientation?"

"I can't tell her that," Spencer says. "She's already ticked off at my dad because I took up the guitar—says it distracts me from academic pursuits."

Bender makes a rude noise. "*This* is an academic pursuit. It's all about knowledge."

"But what are we supposed to do with it?" Jay flops on the bench over Igor's head, making it creak.

Matthew says something, which Igor can't make out because Matthew's on the other side of the gazebo and his voice is quiet.

"Never know what?" Jay replies. "Yeah, okay, so it may fill some gaps, but—"

"We could fill one gap really easily," Bender interrupts, "if you could just find out what happened to your uncle."

Igor's ears perk up. They actually tingle. Might "your uncle" be Uncle Troy?

"I *told* you," says Jay. "My dad said he slipped on some marbles and fell down a flight of concrete steps."

"We all know there's more to it than that—" Bender gets no further because Igor has popped out of the bushes and run around to the gazebo entrance.

"Is *that* what you want to know?"

"Where'd you come from?" Bender demands.

"You want to know what happened at high school graduation? Class of '85?" They're all staring at him in surprise, an expression that usually turns to impatience or worse. But he has something they want, for the first time since he can remember. He's received all kinds of attention in his life—laughter, mockery, anger, and frustration—but this is the best.

He says, "I know exactly what happened."

Early Dismissal

By 1:30 that afternoon, here's what they know:

Jason Stanley Hall is hiding out very close. Bender has seen him.

Matthew has his pewter eagle, picked up behind the bus shed.

Jay knows where one of his hideouts is, or at least he could probably find it.

Somebody in the house has tried to communicate with them, or at least with Bender—

Possibly somebody in a wheelchair. Spencer saw the tracks.

The person in the wheelchair has been injured. A small person? Yes, if the chair was taken from Pasternak Senior's back porch—which is kind of a wild guess, but Jay's grandmother is also a small person. But how could the thief have known the chair was there?

The property where the bus shed sits is owned by Mrs. B. That explains why one of the shouting voices Jay heard that night sounded familiar. From what he remembers of the argument, Mrs. B suspected someone was there who wasn't supposed to be.

The person she was arguing with might have been renting the house and letting an extra person stay there who wasn't supposed to. Like Jason Stanley Hall?

And, thanks to Igor, they now know that if JSH is hiding out, it's because he's not welcome in the community. At least not by certain people who may have never forgiven him, including the Pastnernak Seniors and maybe even Myra Bender Thompson. He's a persona non grata, says Spencer.

While he's in a sharing mood, Igor goes maybe further than he should and shares what Miranda told him about her poem—torn from the book and sent to her by someone who knew she wrote it, even though Shelly's name was on it. Almost certainly the same someone who sent Bender a Christmas card, even though it's harder to figure out how that person could have known who wrote the poem, when Miranda and Shelly were the only ones who did.

Somebody knows more than he or she should. That's the link they're missing, but they may have a way to find it. The plan Igor interrupted was for an overnight camping trip and stakeout. They were trying to figure out how to get four individuals with different schedules together on the same weekend.

"You mean five," Igor says.

Bender sighs, exasperated.

Spencer asks, "What's the big hurry anyway?"

After a pause, Bender says, "I want him to be at the reunion. First weekend in June."

"What reunion?"

"The class of '85. My mom was in that class, also every frickin' senior who carried those marbles. I'll bet none of 'em ever owned up to it. I think they should. JSH is the only one who knows who they all were. He should be the one to call them out."

Spencer scoffs, "How do we make him do that—lock him up? Besides, it was twenty years ago. Water under the bridge and all that."

"For *some* people," Jay says. "Some of us are still dealing with it."

No one comes up with a reply to that, even though they're all thinking similar thoughts about the potential stored in a handful of marbles. Maybe Bender's right. Somebody needs to own up.

May

Alice began the school year with two expectations that turned out to be wrong. First, she expected that for one reason or another, her family would have to move between September and May, because they always did. Second, she expected to finish up the school year as solitary as she began. A friend—that is, a flesh-and-blood friend to sit by on the bus and go over to her house in the afternoons—never figured in her plans for the year. Except for Darla in kindergarten and Amanda in second grade, all her friends are in books. Book friends are easy to take with you when you have to move (especially if you kind of forget to return them to the library), and they don't argue when you make a place for yourself in their story.

But now she has a real friend, and what's good about that is a whole lot better than what's bad. It started because of Kaitlynn's new idea. "Want to hear what my next story's about?" she up and asked right after Christmas vacation.

Alice looked up from her book, startled. Kaitlynn had talked to her before, in a hit-or-miss kind of way, but never actually stopped for an answer until now. "What's it called?"

"'The Mystery of the Empty Bus Stop.'" Alice's jaw must have dropped or something, because as soon as Kaitlynn saw a reaction, she swooped down on the bus seat beside her. And stayed there for the rest of the school year.

"Here's what I've got so far," she began. "There's a magic bus that takes kids away to the world of their imagination, where everything they dream about comes true. So every morning, the bus makes its rounds and picks up all the kids who had dreams the night before, only not all of them, because we all have dreams but we don't always remember. I'm thinking maybe the bus picks up the kids who wake up in the morning with the dreams they had still on their minds. The ones they can't quit thinking about. What do you think?"

"Well…" Alice wasn't used to being asked what she thought. She had to cough once and clear her throat. "That might not be so good. What if you have bad dreams? Like…your parents are missing or somebody died or gets really hurt?"

Kaitlynn considered this. "Okay, I'll work on it. Maybe only *some* dreams come true, after they run them by headquarters or something. Anyway, the bus comes by this one bus stop every day because somebody's signed up to ride it, only he's never there. And that's because he's a prisoner of his wicked stepmother who locks him up every time the bus comes around. But one of the riders is this really brave girl who uses her own dream-come-true to get into his dreams and—why are you staring at me like that? It's just a story."

Alice knew about stories. But she knew other things too, and what Kaitlynn was telling her was a reflection of those things, totally rearranged. It was like going through the looking glass, for real. "Why does the stepmother lock him up?"

"*Why?* Because she's evil."

"But…" Alice started to get the hang of objecting. "Suppose the boy is sick, or…can't walk or something like that, and the stepmother—or maybe just mother—thinks she's doing the right thing by keeping him home?"

"Do you want to hear this story or not?"

"Sure." Alice mentally zipped her lips. "Go ahead."

But Kaitlynn had lost momentum. She pulled a strand of hair from behind her ear and twirled it around her finger. "See, somebody has to be evil, or else it's not a good story."

"I know. But people can do the right thing for the wrong reason, or the wrong thing for the right reason, and sometimes that's more interesting."

Kaitlynn stuck the strand of hair in her mouth and chewed on it. "You think so?"

"Uh-huh. Like, what if the boy was crippled in a—a tragic accident, and he lives in an underground hideout, and his mother won't let him out because she thinks he'll only get hurt again, only somebody—like his grandmother, maybe—thinks he should get out and toughen up, and they're always fighting over it?"

Kaitlynn kept on chewing. "Hm. What kind of tragic accident?"

* * *

Actually, the accident would have been a lot more tragic if Ricardo's seat belt wasn't buckled, but it didn't have to happen at all. Daddy had driven their old Ford Galaxie to the convenience store in Arrowhead Rock to buy a half-gallon of milk. They couldn't afford a whole gallon—Alice remembered her parents fighting about that before her father stomped out of the house, taking Ricardo with him. They took the long way home (what they called home at the time, an abandoned farmhouse on a foreclosed cattle ranch) so Daddy could cool down. This being Oklahoma, where roads were straight as ladders, he was already going a little too fast when he came to the top of a long steep hill. There was a creek bridge at the bottom, and the only other traffic was halfway down the hill, a single tractor carrying a round hay bale.

"I hate it when tractors hog the road like that," Daddy said. "What if we throw a little scare into him, make him move over?"

"Go for it, Daddy," Ricardo said. At least, that's what Daddy said Ricardo said. They flew downhill in the Galaxie, laying on the horn, and were rewarded by the sight of the tractor lumbering to the shoulder. Daddy laughed before noticing the patrol car in the opposite lane.

He stomped the brakes, forgetting the right front brake shoe had a way of seizing up. The vehicle scissored across the highway and slammed into the concrete bridge abutment.

* * *

Friendships were best, Alice discovered, if each person brought something different to it. She and Kaitlynn were the same in the kind of stories they liked but different in what they got out of them. Kaitlynn wanted action: one thing after another, *bam-bam-bam*. Alice wouldn't mind the story going a little slower, because she wanted to know about the people: How did they grow up? What were the saddest or happiest things that ever happened to them? And (especially) why did they do the things they did?

"Because," Kaitlynn would explain frustratedly, "it's time for something to happen."

"But…things happen because of people, don't they?"

It led to some interesting discussions (okay, arguments) that made the bus rides go faster and helped them both determine what they were working toward. Before either of them realized it, the story became Alice's as much as Kaitlynn's. The magic-dream-bus idea was abandoned—or rather, it kind of drifted away while they were deciding who the missing boy was and why he couldn't ride the bus.

Albert (as Kaitlynn decided to call him) was crippled (Alice's idea) because of experiments by his mad-scientist uncle (who should have just used mice). Having an uncle that cruel was almost too much for Alice, who objected when Kaitlynn wanted the mad scientist to lock the poor little boy in a snake pit. (Kaitlynn was probably more spooked by her experience with Cornelia on the bus than she cared to admit.) "We'll need more obstacles for the hero to overcome on her way to rescue Albert! And snake pits are about the worst kind of obstacle there is!" Alice thought it was way too creepy, but they compromised by leaving the pit in and taking Albert out. That is, the uncle didn't actually throw him in there but was always threatening to. That ought to be evil enough.

＊ ＊ ＊

Actually, Alice could see the need for obstacles—in real life, they sort of happened anyway, whether you needed them or not. After the accident, their whole life became an obstacle. First the hospital, where surgery saved Ricardo's life but couldn't save his legs. Then Daddy disappearing because he felt so bad. Then GeeGee's arrival to take care of things (which Mama wasn't too good at).

GeeGee was the only person they could call on, being Mama's mother, but her coming meant terrible arguments, during which GeeGee called Daddy a screwup who was better off gone and Mama screamed that she just wanted to be left alone to make her own mistakes. But she couldn't be left alone with two kids to take care of, could she? That's when GeeGee made her an offer, and Mama had no choice but to take it.

The offer was to move to GeeGee's old house, which was empty and needed a little fixing up, and use her truck when she didn't need it, and get Ricardo into physical therapy. All that, in exchange for one thing: that Daddy stayed gone. Mama said okay. But after they moved, one of the first things she did was get a library card so Alice-the-little-reader could check out books. But also so Mama could use the library computer to get in touch with Daddy and let him know where they were.

Somewhere in north Texas, he got the message. Then he hiked and hitched his way right to them, arriving after midnight on August 16.

"What did you expect?" he asked as he was explaining into the night. "Did you think I'd skip off to Mexico? Family's family, Brenda Kay; no moral dilemma there. And we're staying family, and we can look after each other with no help from anybody."

It stunned him to see the shape Ricardo was still in: no strength, few words, had to be carried everywhere. Alice saw Daddy blink and swallow hard before saying, "But we can't turn the clock back, can we? First order of business is a wheelchair—we've got to get him out of bed ASAP."

"We're waiting," Mama said. "They haven't got us in the system yet."

"Phooey on the system. We're staying out of the system as much as we can. Anybody know where we can get a wheelchair?"

Alice did.

She's the one who told him about the one the Pasternaks had. She knew what Daddy would do, and stealing was the only name for it, no matter that the Pasternaks weren't using their wheelchair and he meant to return the item as soon as Ricardo didn't need it anymore. That made her accessory to a crime, but it felt good to have somebody in charge again.

But he wasn't in charge of where she lived and where she went to school. His mother, Mary Ellen Hall Truman, had offered to let Alice live with her so she could ride the school bus to Centerview. Daddy was dead set against it: government schools were for government drones. He could teach her everything she needed to know or how to find out what neither of them knew. They'd done it before, hadn't they? She'd missed big chunks of second, third, and fourth grade and never saw the inside of kindergarten at all. However, this time the only person on his side of the argument was Alice. Both grandmas were against him (even though they didn't know it, because they didn't know he was around), but so was Mama. Like it or not, Alice was going to school.

She found a way to show her appreciation to Daddy, though. One Saturday afternoon in September, she and Mama stopped by the library on the last day of the semi-annual book sale, and Alice noticed five boxes left under an *Everything must go!* sign. She whispered to her mother, and her mother talked to the desk clerk, and the next minute, they were loading boxes of books in the pickup to take home and be rewarded by one of her dad's huge smiles: "These'll get me through the winter!"

Daddy read everything: old westerns and romance novels and biographies of people you'd never heard of; college textbooks and county histories and seldom-read classics like *Moby-Dick*. But the real find was *Basic Principles of Physical Therapy*, third edition. Besides giving Alice the idea for her science fair project (which won a first-place ribbon for her age-group), that book helped prove Daddy's point that anything you want to know, you can teach yourself (exactly why school is such a big fat waste of time). Using a few *Basic Principles* during the fall, he almost got Ricardo on his feet and walking again, or so he claimed. Daddy was positive that if the unfortunate incidents of late January hadn't happened, Ricardo could have kissed his wheelchair good-bye.

* * *

Their story got more complicated over the winter. Kaitlynn wanted to hurry up and get to the rescue by the really brave girl on the bus, but Alice was more interested in Albert and his family and exactly why he was a prisoner. They decided that the uncle wasn't all bad, because after crippling the boy, he now wanted to cure him. But maybe that wasn't so good either. Kaitlynn insisted that the uncle wanted to claim all the credit for himself, which meant keeping Albert a prisoner so he could continue his experiments. And she still wanted Albert to spend one night in the snake pit. "But just one. It's an accident. And they're supposed to be healing snakes, not poisonous. Uncle Ralph didn't *mean* to leave him in there."

* * *

And actually, Daddy didn't *mean* to crash Ricardo a second time. That happened on a nice January afternoon—the day before the science fair, in fact—when the weather broke at sixty degrees and he pushed Ricardo up to the bus stop while Mama was taking a nap. Daddy wasn't supposed to do that, because GeeGee could show up at any time. But he'd been reading about the healthy effects of natural sunshine, and a warmish, sunny afternoon in January was too good to pass up.

Ricardo stood up. In fact, he actually walked a few steps, which made them both so giddy they started a game of tag—with Ricardo back in his chair—that got a little wild. It ended when Daddy ran behind the shed and Ricardo followed in his wheelchair and got so excited he overbalanced and fell over. He made a grab for Daddy while going down, but only broke off the belt buckle that was specially engraved with his high school logo. Ricardo hurt his back again, leading to a big fight between their parents and other complications.

Daddy never found his buckle either.

* * *

Once or twice per week, Kaitlynn would climb aboard the bus with a new idea that had just *popped!* into her head the night before. Like giving Albert a talented but snotty big sister who sucked up all the family money to launch her showbiz career. One of Kaitlynn's best ideas was having the little prince send messages to the outside world by a friendly bluebird named Blackie. (Why Blackie? Because it sounded better than Bluey.) That's how the hero of the story (a girl bus-rider who sounded suspiciously like Kaitlynn) came to know of his predicament and decide to rescue him.

"Don't tell anybody," she confided to Alice, "but Bender got a Christmas card from the bus stop—I mean, from somebody in the house. He wrote this dumb note to their address, and the kid who lives there wrote back."

"How did Bender know it was a kid?"

"You would too if you'd seen it. He showed it to me: big letters, a little shaky, like a second grader would write."

* * *

Actually, Ricardo would be in fourth grade if he were going to school, but the accident messed up his brain a little. Or so the grown-ups thought. Alice didn't think so—he'd misplaced some words and took longer to say anything while searching for them, but his brain was working fine otherwise. And he was as fond of practical jokes as ever, especially after he'd learned to get around in the wheelchair. Alice was the one who gave him the pompom that Shelly left at the nursing home back in September (the one she should have returned except she knew Ricardo would love it). She should have guessed what he would do with it. And who would help him.

What happened with Bender was even worse—or better, depending on how you looked at it. Ricardo wanted to know everything about the kids on the bus, so Alice told him about the rolled-up papers Bender liked to stick behind his ear. When she saw that paper rolled up in the mailbox, she was so surprised she tried to distract Bender with a spitwad, which totally didn't work. Then there was the Christmas card—actually two Christmas cards because Miranda got one too. Alice read the poem to Ricardo (which she knew was Miranda's because of an overheard conversation on the bus), and Ricardo figured out a way to let her know he liked it.

Sweet, in a way, but it was probably a good thing GeeGee finally surrendered in her campaign to get Ricardo in school. If she'd kept on turning down Farm Road 152 every morning, he would have been discovered sooner or later, and Mama just wanted everybody to leave them alone. Daddy wanted the same thing, especially since no one was supposed to know he was even there.

* * *

In March, Kaitlynn had the idea that a pet would be nice to add to the story: a little dog Albert could find under a bush or hiding in a tunnel. "Like where you found Panzer! How did you think to look in the culvert?"

Alice shrugged, even though she'd explained already: holes are great places to hide.

Actually, she knows this from experience.

Friday and Saturday nights were some of her best memories of the winter just past: her family sitting around the wood-stove like a scene from *Little House On the Prairie*, Daddy with his book and Alice with hers, Mama with her needlework or a crossword puzzle and an open box of Cheez-Its, Ricardo with his sketchbook and pencils. Ricardo didn't read so well. Mama could read perfectly well but said she couldn't concentrate when Daddy was in the room. He'd always have to share whatever he was into. "Hey everybody, listen to this," he'd say, then he'd read out loud about the great blizzard of 1934 or how gold mining got started in South Africa.

"Wow!" said Ricardo almost every time.

"Um," said Mama, stubbing out a cigarette. "What's a five-letter word for 'cured meat'?"

The sappy wood popped in the stove, Ricardo's pencils clicked softly on the wheelchair tray as he swapped colors, Mama hummed as she erased a word, and Alice wedged a bite out of her apple, crunching it to tall slivers of tangy-sweet juice. It was the kind of scene to make Kaitlynn jump up and down and wave her arms and say *What's happening?!*

Good memories are stitched together from plain materials.

However…if an outside sound invaded their cozy little scene, namely the mash of rubber tires on gravel, Ricardo would say "Hark!" Her parents would lay aside whatever they were doing and calmly but swiftly stand up. Daddy—without a word—would move his chair back to the table, put on his coat, tuck his book under one arm, and look around to make sure he left no visible clues behind. Mama, meanwhile, would go into the bedroom, flip over the rug beside the bed, and tug on the rope pull under the rug to lift up a slab of floor. She held it up while Daddy let himself down into the crawl space (stocked with food and blankets and a flashlight), and then let it carefully down. He pulled the rope back through the hole, she replaced the rug, and by then it was just about time to answer the door.

The visitor was usually GeeGee, stopping by to visit or

drop off some groceries. But once it was a social worker, and another time a truant officer, wanting to know why Ricardo wasn't in school. Mama handled that visit all right, because Daddy was right there under the floor. She couldn't handle things too well when he was gone, and he was gone for two whole weeks in February.

That was after the big fight following Ricardo's spill, when Daddy stormed out of the house and hitched rides to Oklahoma to see his buddy Ed. After a week or so, Ed gave him the money for a bus ticket back.

The whole incident was silly; he didn't have to lose his temper and take the risk of catching pneumonia while hiking over the countryside in dead winter. But risk-taking was in his nature—one of the reasons GeeGee called him a screwup. GeeGee began to suspect he was hiding out in the neighborhood but didn't know for sure until she found a box of library-sale books in the bedroom closet. That led to a fight between her and Mama, which Alice didn't hear but Ricardo told her about.

One good thing about living with her other grandma: she missed most of the fights.

* * *

Kaitlynn couldn't make up her mind about how to rescue Albert. Or rather, she had lots of ideas but couldn't settle on just one. Maybe his sometimes-crazy uncle could go all the way crazy, like poor Mr. Pasternak Senior, and be sent away to a nursing home—asylum, that is—but of course that wouldn't leave much room for a heroic rescue. The brave girl on the bus could train a commando team to overpower the bus driver and storm the underground lair. Or she could outwit the bus driver, castle guards, sorcerers, dragons, snakes, and whatever else stood in her way to reach the prisoner and fetch him out. "What do you think?" she asked Alice. "Strong or sneaky?"

"I think sneaky is better. It's more interesting."

Alice never thought of herself as sneaky, but eight whole months of keeping a huge secret was making her think again. GeeGee found out through her own investigations, but Grandma still didn't have a clue that her son was hiding out within five miles of her house. As to exactly why he was hiding, that's what Alice can't figure out. True, he was breaking GeeGee's one condition for helping Mama and Ricardo and herself, but she has an idea there's more to it. GeeGee never liked Daddy, but you'd think his own mother would. And you'd think he would want to see her, if only to say "Hi, I'm okay, but I'm not supposed to be here and I know you can keep a secret."

Grandma had arranged her life pretty much the way she wanted it—which probably didn't include having a granddaughter move in with her. But she'd agreed it was best the girl go to school and have a normal, routine life for a change.

And that's what Alice had, if "normal" meant the meals came on time and the floors were swept and dishes didn't stack up until you had to wash a few or else eat out of the box.

As for "routine"—it sounds good until you have to get up

at 6:30 just because Grandma volunteers at the hospital from eight to noon Monday through Thursday and needs that time to get her chores done so she can golf in the afternoon if the weather's nice or play bridge with the gals if it's not.

"I lead an active lifestyle," says Grandma. "I'm not one to sit around watching the tube and griping about the world." This was often said after dinner, while watching the tube and griping—about food prices, politicians, nice linen slacks that shrink in the wash, shoes that don't fit right after you buy them, greenskeepers, TV quiz show contestants who don't know enough to pass eighth grade, bread that goes stale, and fish that tastes fishy. And sons who never take advice because they think they know better, and daughters-in-law who just let things happen to them and may not be all that bright.

And what about neighbors who don't let you borrow stuff because they say they might need it again? As if they thought you'd never return it! When old Mr. Pasternak turned down Grandma's request to borrow their wheelchair for poor little Ricardo, Alice had heard her complaining about it to one of the gals on the phone. "This is all about what happened twenty years ago, mark my words. As if I had anything to do with it! I haven't been able to control Jason since he was nine, so what could I do with a high school senior?"

That was the first Alice had ever heard about something happening twenty years ago. Grandma seemed to think it served the Pasternaks right when the item was stolen. Nor did she put two and two together when Mama told her they'd found a wheelchair for Ricardo anyway.

Grandma wasn't speaking to GeeGee—from both her grandmothers' random comments, Alice gathered it was because each blamed the other for how their kids turned out. One thing they agreed on was that Ricardo should go to school where there were qualified teachers and assistants who could help him. But Mama turned out to be more stubborn about that than anyone expected. Nobody knew that Daddy was right there, backing her up.

Nobody knew that Ricardo was smarter than he let on.

Nobody knew how long Alice's parents could keep their secret, but surely not forever.

* * *

By May, Daddy is becoming very edgy after too many nights spent outside in the rain because of nosy county officials and mothers-in-law. "It sounds like something in a book," Alice tells him. "Like a fugitive hiding from the law." Grandma has just dropped her off for the weekend, and she's got two brand-new books from the library to read.

"It belongs in a book," he sniffs. "*The Count of Monte Cristo* meets the great outdoors." He sneezes twice in a row. A damp, chilly spring is hanging on and so is his cold. "But wait'll you hear my escape plan. Got a surprise for you, Lissa. Let's take a walk."

It's a beautiful sunny day, with more in the forecast. As they hike a threadlike path that leads up from the house, Daddy seems to expand, like one of those sponge creatures that swell up when you drop them in water. Except in his case, he's finally drying out.

The path leads to the top of a limestone bluff overlooking a little valley. The view opens up like a postcard: branches clothed in fuzzy green, white blossoms blowing like wedding veils, a deep cleft in the ground where Drybed Creek runs—when it's running, which it only does in rainy seasons. A red-tailed hawk circles at eye-level, wings spread like he's hanging on invisible strings.

"How about that?" Daddy asks.

"It's beautiful."

"You like it? It's yours." Daddy opens his hand and sweeps it over the view, like one of those girls in evening dresses showing off a prize in a game show. "Slip it in your pocket to take with you when we go."

"What?" She's not sure she heard those last few words correctly.

"It's time to say adios, Lissa-girl."

Her voice seems to fall off the bluff. "Say wha-a-a-t?"

"It's time to go. Don't you think?"

She realizes, of course, that they've seldom stayed in one place even this long, but the when-where-why questions are coming so fast, she can hardly hear his explanation.

They are starting a new life (again!) up north—way up north. Daddy is going first, hitching a ride with a friend of a friend who drives a truck and has a regular run from Tulsa to International Falls, Minnesota. The truck driver will pick him up just outside Centerview and (after a little money changes hands) keep on truckin' north, while Daddy takes it easy in the bunk. The following weekend, Mama will borrow the pickup and fail to return it.

"But that's GeeGee's truck! And it's stealing."

"No, it's borrowing. We'll get it back, uh, sooner or later."

"When will all this happen?"

"Next week."

Alice can't speak for a few minutes, during which Daddy lays out a time line: the trucker picks him up on Wednesday morning and gets to International Falls on Thursday night. Daddy has a prepaid cell phone and a calling card so he can be in touch with the family, and as soon as he finds a place, he'll let them know—maybe by Friday night. Then Mama will hit the road with Alice and Ricardo.

"But..." Alice begins.

Daddy isn't listening. "That was my mistake all along, coming back here. To make a new start, you need a totally new place where nobody's ever heard of you and you can make your own reality out of whole new material. After a year or so, we'll be settled. I'll have a job and start working Ricardo's therapy again, and we'll be taking care of ourselves, just like we were before—"

"But I don't want to go."

Now it's his turn to be dumbfounded and speechless.

"I—like it here," she goes on. "I like my teacher and my school and...and I have a best friend and our story's not finished yet and—"

"What story?"

"The...the one I'm writing with Kaitlynn. My friend."

"You're not spilling any beans to Kaitlynn, are you?"

"Of course not! It's just a story."

"Lissa, you want stories? You've already got more'n you know what to do with. Stick with me, kid, and you'll never lack for stories."

"But, Daddy, that's not it. It's just—"

"Just what? You're family's not enough for you anymore?"

"No!"

"You want your old man to be a loser all his life?"

"*No!*"

"What's it going to be then? We stick around so you can go to some government school where they stuff your head with crap and you can have some cookie-cutter friend who'll probably drop you like a brick next semester or—"

"Daddy!" She throws herself at him, but he's already backed away.

"*Or* you can go with your mom and brother and me. Unless you'd rather stay behind. If that's the case, we may just have to do what's best for *us.*"

That little word goes right through her. Until now, she was always part of *us,* but he said it like she wasn't—like she was cut off, a lonely arm waving futile fingers.

He starts down the skinny path she can barely make out in the fading light. "Daddy!" she sobs as he disappears. Running after him, she cries again, "I'm sorry! I didn't mean it!" Patches of his red plaid shirt flicker through the brush. "*Don't leave me!* Please!"

He stops long enough for her to catch up but doesn't say

another word as they wind down the path toward home. And barely speaks to her all weekend.

* * *

So this week will probably be her last at school.

Alice feels her wheels slowing down, crawling to a stop. Now they've begun to turn—very slowly—in reverse. After settling down in one direction and feeling pretty confident about it, now she has to change back. Forward or reverse? It's hard to say. And it's harder to *do*, especially since she can't tell anybody.

Her family is going to just disappear, like always.

But this time, it's different. This time it's going to be hard. Never before has she walked through her remaining days in a particular place with thoughts like, *This is my last spelling test, my last book report, my last game of kickball. I hope Kaitlynn won't think I don't like her—maybe I should give her some kind of going-away present on Friday? Without telling her I'm going away?*

On Tuesday night, she goes to bed but can't sleep. *Daddy's leaving tomorrow* is the main thought that crowds out her other thoughts. She won't have a chance to tell him good-bye, but if all goes according to plan, she'll see him next week, in a brand-new place that has no place in her mind yet. Mama's been packing, sorting out the essentials and deciding how much will fit in the pickup. The wheelchair is essential, of course. Daddy only intended to borrow it from Mr. Pasternak Senior and return it as soon as Ricardo could walk again, but his plans didn't quite work out. So that will be one of the first things to pack.

Alice sits up in bed and looks out the window. A round steely moon spreads light like butter on a white-bread landscape. She has to pack soon—just what she can carry in her gym bag and her backpack, because she's only supposed to be going home for the weekend. What about the coat Grandma bought for her, the only new coat she's ever had? Probably no room for it.

She's never had so much to leave behind.

Toward dawn, lightning flickers on her eyelids. She remembers the weather report last night: morning thunderstorms likely. But the constant light pulsing nervously in the sky comes with no thunder and no wind.

"Feels like tornado weather," says Grandma as she locks the front door on their way out. Pausing by the calla lilies near the garage, she adds, "Look at their droopy heads, when they usually stand up straight. Everything's too still. I don't like it."

Fat drops are spattering the windshield by the time they reach the bus stop. "I'll wait," Grandma says. "Terry won't be long." Grandma hardly ever refers to GeeGee by her real name—usually avoids referring to her at all. What does that mean? Within two minutes, the sprinkle has become a shower, then a cloudburst, slicking the cars and setting windshield wipers a-swish.

Igor and Little Al streak across the common to the gazebo, where Bender, Matthew, and Jay are already waiting. Shelly runs from the opposite direction. On the east side of the loop,

Mrs. Haggerty stops to pick up Miranda, who's hurrying along in an oversize yellow rain slicker.

"There she is," Grandma says as the bus curves over the hill and rolls toward them. "May as well wait till she stops. No hurry." The bus pulls into the Y and backs up by the gazebo. Grandma taps the steering wheel fretfully. "I'd almost drive you to school myself, except I've got to go the other way this morning."

"It's okay." Alice pops open the door. "Bye, Grandma."

She slams the door and runs toward the bus, thinking, *My next-to-next-to-last morning bus ride…*

As she squeezes in line, Kaitlynn's first words to her are, "I got a great idea last night! I figured out how to get our hero out of the dungeon—"

"Move it!" Spencer calls behind them. "We're getting soaked!"

"Quack-quack," GeeGee is saying to hurry up the littles. She smiles briefly at Alice, then glares out the rearview mirror. "Just hold your horses, lady," she mutters to Mrs. Thompson, who's fuming behind the STOP sign again.

"It's too wet to go to school!" Igor complains as he climbs aboard.

"You're not sweet enough to melt," GeeGee says. "Move along, folks! Find a seat and let's get this show on the road!"

I may never hear her say that again, Alice thinks.

Shelly shakes her head as she starts down the aisle, showering the littles with raindrops from her hair. ("Hey!" "Hey!" they protest.) Spencer unwraps his guitar case from his jacket, and Miranda slides into the seat across from Igor, sneezing.

Matthew and Bender are the last to board, dashing from the gazebo and leaping the steps, one after the other. GeeGee slams the door and puts the bus in gear as the two boys head for the back. She forgets to pull in the STOP sign; behind them, Mrs. Thompson lays on her horn.

"Cool it, Mom." At the back window, Bender makes a calming motion with both hands, which probably just irritates her more. GeeGee belatedly closes the sign, but a van is coming toward them on the road and Mrs. Thompson is still stuck behind the bus. There won't be any more places to pass until they reach the highway. Bender laughs. "You learn patience by being patient. That's what my mama always told me."

He and Matthew have been in fine spirits ever since the state science fair—in which they didn't win the chance to go to nationals but were ranked third from the top, so they "go out in a blaze of glory," as Bender says.

I wonder if he'll be a math professor? Or a comedy writer?

"Let me tell you my idea," Kaitlynn begins eagerly. Alice listens, though she can't keep her eyes from roaming. Directly behind them, Spencer has taken his guitar out of the case to check for water damage. Once it's out, he strums a few chords.

"This land is your land!" Jay sings, clapping off-rhythm. "This land is my land!"

"Can it, dork!" Spencer laughs.

Is Jay going to be an Olympic runner some day? And Spencer a musician, like his dad?

Two rows ahead, Miranda scoots toward the center aisle. Igor is waiting on the opposite seat. She takes an envelope out of her backpack and passes it over. His eyes are big as quarters as he takes it.

I hope Miranda writes more poems. I hope Igor graduates.

Shelly turns around halfway in her seat. "I have an announcement! Only sixty-three days, seven hours, and two minutes until I leave for camp!"

"You mean five hours, one minute, and thirty-two seconds," Bender corrects her.

Only two more days of Shelly's announcements.

"So how about this," Kaitlynn is saying. "Instead of knocking the guard out with a rock from a slingshot, what if she gets Blackie to slip the keys from his pocket while he's sleeping?"

"Umm…" Alice hasn't been paying attention.

Behind them, Jay says, "Holy cow."

The cloudburst has become a gully washer. The rain is pouring down in sheets, torrents, buckets. They've started down the hill toward Drybed Creek, and GeeGee has slowed almost to a crawl. The windshield wipers barely make a dent in visibility, even going full speed.

From the back, Bender says, "Oh no." And he's not kidding.

"No!" he says again. "Don't try—Mom, NO!"

Bender is moving up the aisle, yelling out the left-side windows. "Sit *down*!" GeeGee calls sharply, but not loud because she's focused on keeping the bus on the road. Alice catches a glimpse of an SUV passing them in a wedge of water, its roof gleaming like a seal's back.

Bender stops in the aisle, five rows from the driver, and stares out the front window. All talk, all eyes are frozen as Mrs.

Thompson's SUV slides across the yellow lines into the lane in front of them—and keeps sliding, across the line, onto the shoulder, and completely off the road.

One little girl screams. Bender drops like a rock, right there in the aisle, gripping the seat backs on either side.

GeeGee is struggling with the bus. All at once, everyone realizes it's floating, caught in a strong current that's about to carry them away. The back end swings dramatically to the right until they're almost sideways.

"Oh my goodness!" Kaitlynn gasps, clutching Alice's hand.

"Everybody hold on!" GeeGee yells. "Move to the right!" The screams begin: high yelps from the littles, shrieks from the girls, startled shouts from the boys. Alice sees Bender grab two kids and disappear between seats on the right side; seizing Kaitlynn's other hand, she ducks to the floor.

Get down, get down! somebody—or everybody—is saying. *On the right!*

She pushes Kaitlynn in that direction, but the bus is already tipping. As it goes over, the two girls slide between seats like pinballs, bouncing as the bus slams on its side in the churning ground, sliding fast and then slow until it shudders to a stop. And everything is quiet.

The Beyond

The first thing Bender notices is the roof, which is now on the side. There's a big dent in it; he guesses it was made by a tree. A tree probably stopped them from sliding into the creek. They are in a new dimension where down is up—or actually, sideways, for the bus has come to rest at an angle, right side windows mashed into mud and brush, front end angled down. The place where the ceiling curves is now the lowest point of the bus, a trough where everything slides. Rain lashes the opposite windows over his head; wind and water roar all around them, but the interior of the bus is still strangely silent.

"Ow," says a little voice under him. He's on top of Simon Killebrew, with Marilu Wong on top of him. "Are you okay?" he whispers to the girl, who dumbly nods.

"Get off me," sputters Simon.

Bender pushes Marilu until she can steady herself, then grabs the seat to pull himself up. Simon squirms out from under him and slides to the curve of the ceiling like a fried egg. "Do you think we might be dead?" he quavers.

Bender looks around, unsure how to answer that question. The silence, which seemed to be miles deep, is starting to break up in whimpers and moans. The darkness is pulling back from a dim gray light crisscrossed with leafy branches and thrumming rain. Yellow hazard lights pulse against the back window: blink, blink, blink. It's like a heartbeat. They're not dead—at least not all of them—but he's not sure they're all the way alive.

It feels like some kind of in-between place, where they've come to the end of one thing but don't know how to get to the next thing. The blink of the hazard lights reminds him of that string of dots at the end of a paragraph when the author wants to leave you guessing...

"Bender!" Jay's head is poking up from the tangle of arms and legs and backpacks in the rear. "You okay?"

"I think so. You?"

"Maybe. My foot feels...I don't know. How's Mrs. B? Can you see her?"

Bender squints in the dim light. The driver is tumbled more or less upright in the stairwell, limbs twisted like a puppet's. Something about her doesn't look dead, but she's out like a light. That means...?

"I see her. She's not moving."

Jay swears emphatically, then asks, "You know how to get the emergency door open?"

Bender flexes his ankles and knees. They seem to be working. He begins a slow crawl toward the back of the bus, walking sideways along the ceiling, stepping carefully over whimpering kids and moaning kids and kids who remain ominously still. He tries not to recognize faces until he comes to one he can't help but recognize: Matthew's, eyes wide open and staring at him from the ceiling.

Funny—he can't remember Matthew ever looking directly at him. "Hey!" he whispers.

Matthew is between two seats, on top of a window. His eyes flicker downward, at a spear of glass jutting out of his thigh.

Bender takes a deep breath, sucking in every four-letter word he knows. "Um. You…need help pulling that out?"

"Better not." Matthew's voice sounds surprisingly calm though even softer than usual. "It's in the neighborhood of the femoral artery. I could bleed to death."

"Right." Bender swallows the dry lump in his throat. "Sure. Don't go anywhere."

Matthew smiles thinly. "Okay."

"Bender!" hisses Jay. "Help me with this door."

He climbs over the next-to-last seat and grabs the emergency handle. "There's a second latch…right here…" His fingers go right to the latch as though they still remember from last fall, and the door pops open, making a flap they can crawl under to get out.

"Nice," says Jay.

"Guys!" It's Igor, balancing on the upturned seat five rows ahead. "What do we do?"

"How're you?" Jay calls back. "Anything broken?"

"No—I landed on Miranda."

Miranda pushes herself up from the corner, hair tumbled and eyes bleary. "At least I'm good for a pillow."

"We're going for help," Bender says, though he wasn't sure until then exactly what they were going to do. "Y'all see who's hurt. See if anybody's got a phone that works. We'll be back as soon as we can."

"It's still raining," Jay says.

No—it's pouring. If the emergency door had opened uphill instead of down, the bus would have been a swamp by now. Rain is cascading down the hill, and Bender suddenly remembers what he saw just before the bus left the road.

"My mom! I've got to find her!"

"What'll I do?" Jay asks.

"Run up to the road—flag the first car—"

"I'm not even sure if I can *find* the road!"

"It's uphill, you idiot!" Bender climbs through the opening, squeezing under the heavy door. "Come on, everybody says you're a runner—run for your life!"

He drops to the ground, and a burst of wind almost knocks him flat. He staggers to the lee of the bus, where the overhanging roof offers a little shelter, and tries to get his bearings. It's about 0.4 miles to the bridge from where they left the road. Near as he can remember, his mother's SUV had skidded off a little closer to the bridge. If it continued straight, at a thirty-six degree angle from the road (more or less), and nothing stopped the car...she'll be in the creek now. Oh God—no time to lose. "Oh God," he prays, and plunges into the watery world.

✳ ✳ ✳

After only three steps, Jay realizes there is something wrong with his right foot. Something broken or sprained. Rain streaks his glasses; he rips them off and lurches into a half-crawl, half-climb, his right foot shrieking in pain at every step. He pushes through brush and grass and chest-bumping wind, and it doesn't feel like he's making any headway at all. Branches snag his shirt and face, whip his bare arms. After what seems like hours, he trips on a root and sprawls in the mud, drained and disoriented. What now?

Go long, Jay—go long!

Sunlight gleams on his grandfather's silvery hair and outlines the backward arch of his quarterback arm. "We faked 'em out, boy—clear shot! Get your butt in line: here it comes!"

In his mind's eye, a football sails overhead. He backpedals, arms out, fingers spread—

Splat! How come the ground here is so muddy? And…flat? Like a path. Like maybe even the old railroad bed he'd discovered only five weeks ago. The one he knows where it goes.

Pass completed! Run for it!

He pulls himself up. The monsoon is slacking off to a downpour. He takes a shaky breath and sets off at a lopsided jog, heavily favoring his left leg. His pace blurs the spatter of rain until it sounds a little like cheering crowds, with Poppy's voice in his head providing the play-by-play: "Look at him go! He's at the seventy-yard line! The sixty—the fifty—the forty—can nobody stop this demon of speed?"

Nobody's stopping me, he thinks. *Nobody can stop me.*

Pain joins his team, like the block at his side. They could do this together. Half-crippled, half-blind, he runs and runs and runs, each step an electric shock that jumpstarts the next one. He runs as though he will never run again, and maybe he won't. But never mind: *it's for you*, he thinks; *for you*. "For you!" he cries out loud. And keeps on, to keep going: "You! You! You!"

The gravel road leaps at him, like a rope stretched across the finish line. It almost trips him, but he recaptures his balance. Almost there! He can blurrily make out the bus shed. He turns without hesitation to his left, even though that part of the road goes downhill and the extra jolt of gravity jars his injured foot so badly he could scream. And maybe he does. By the time he reaches the door of the house—on a little porch, under a little roof—it's already open, and Jay is not surprised to see a boy in a wheelchair framed by the doorway.

✳ ✳ ✳

"The letter!" Igor gasps. "I lost my letter!"

Miranda is looking at him like she just woke up. "What letter?"

"The one you gave me!" He feels frantically around his pockets, searches for his backpack. A stream of water from the cracked emergency door is making its way down the trough where the windows curve into the ceiling. There's just enough light to see how dark the water is.

"Blood!" he screams. "It's going to get all bloody!"

As if he'd turned on a faucet with that scary word, the screaming and crying begins, mostly from the littles. Igor can barely hear them for the clamor in his own head. Just a few minutes ago, he was holding it in his very hand—a letter from Bobby Price. To him. He didn't have time to read anything but the signature: *Dad*. Now it's like the man himself is torn away, and he feels like a little kid lost in a mob. "I've got to find it!"

Something charges up at him from the depths and cracks him on the head.

It's Miranda.

Did she just *headbutt* him? "Ouch," he says.

She's rubbing her head too. "Get a *grip*." He's never seen her so mad, not even when she yelled at Shelly. "Forget the stupid letter! We've got people hurt here—maybe worse. You can move easier than I can—go see about Matthew and Spencer while I check on the littles."

Pain restores Igor to his senses. He chokes back his loss, squeezing his hands into fists. Then he climbs up to balance on the seat and look around. The floor—or what's floor to him now—is like a horizontal ladder, its rungs made of the edge of each seat back. With that image in mind, he climbs it, loping like a monkey from one rung to the next.

Spencer is peacefully nestled beside a broken guitar. There's a gash on his head that's bleeding a lot, but it doesn't look deep. Igor moves on to Matthew—and confronts a bloody slab of glass.

"Don't touch it," Matthew says. No way is Igor touching

it—in fact, he barely makes it to the emergency door in time to hurl.

***

Matthew understands that all he has to do is keep still. It doesn't hurt yet—his legs feel almost numb. It's like a matter/antimatter state, the instant before one wipes out the other. He could just go to sleep right now, and maybe not wake up. It could happen. He's always felt a little not-here anyway. Suppose he never was here, just a dream? He's thought about that before, but it's not a comfortable thought because you always had to wonder, whose dream?

He feels his mind start to tip and drift away from the present, as it's inclined to do when chasing some idea into limboland. Except for the glass.

The glass is pinning him down. For the first time, he can't just float away; he has to stay here. He's got to concentrate on right here, right now, or…there might not be a here and now for him. "For me," he whispers. His leg begins to tingle with little pinpricks that will soon command all his attention, mind and body both, pinned to the moments as they pass. Staying alive will command all his attention. "Don't move anybody unless you have to," he says to Miranda.

"I know," she replies, staring at him.

***

His face is *gray*. Miranda is slow to move, not because she's hurt but because (her brain takes its own sweet time figuring this out) her yellow rain slicker is caught in a crack made by the dented-in roof. Wiggling out of the raincoat takes so much time that Igor completes his mission and passes her on his way to the front with a quick reassurance: "I'm okay now."

He scrambles forward to check on his brother and the others, reporting back at intervals: "Katie's leg hurts—may be broken!" "Evan's scrunched up under the seat—Evan, are you okay?" Pause. "He says he's okay! Ally, can you get up? Way to go! Now stay right where you are. Where's Diana…? Are you sure she didn't come today?"

"Mrs. B's phone is ringing!" a little voice calls out.

"I can't get to it," Igor says. "She's laying on it."

"Is she breathing?" Miranda asks.

"I think so. Crystal Applegate's out cold!"

"Don't move her!" Matthew warns.

"*I know!*"

Miranda bites her lip. Her whole body feels like it was run over, but she climbs carefully over the seat in front of her.

"Kaitlynn?" Simon's voice quavers from the front two seats where Igor is corralling the kids who can move on their own. "Can you hear me, Kaitlynn?"

"I'm headed her way," Miranda tells him. "Give me a minute. Everybody stay calm!"

The littles seem to take that as permission to panic. A fresh wave of screams rises from the front. "Quiet! Hush!" Igor keeps saying. Miranda climbs over a seat and hears someone whisper, "Help me up." One arm waves feebly—Alice's.

"I think my other arm's broken," she says when Miranda leans over her. "I stuck it out to keep from crashing into Kaitlynn…she's under me. Help me up?"

Very carefully, Miranda leans down to tuck her fingers around Alice's waistband, pulling up while the girl grabs the seat back with her good hand. She chokes off a little scream as her broken arm swings loose, and Miranda can feel tears soaking into her T-shirt. "It really hurts," Alice whimpers.

"I know." Miranda is using her gentlest voice. "Can you use your legs? Climb over the seat back here and slide next to the window. The boys went for help—everything will be—"

She's stooping down to Kaitlynn and suddenly realizes that the blackish water underneath her is actually blood! "How is my friend?" Alice asks between sobs.

"Just a minute…wait just…a minute." Miranda is feeling around Kaitlynn's head. The window underneath has shattered and left about a million cuts—but none of them look too deep. She picks up Kaitlynn's limp wrist, feeling for a pulse. Mom showed her how to do this a few times, but she goes through some long anxious seconds before finding it, strong and fast.

"Simon!" Miranda straightens up and calls toward the front. "Kaitlynn has a lot of cuts but I think she's okay. Just stay where you are!" Noticing a change in the noise level, she looks over to see Igor, hanging upside-down with his toes wedged into the seats overhead, chuffing like a monkey. The littles, if not exactly laughing, are at least distracted enough to stop screaming.

"I want to try that!" says Little Al.

Now that it's quieter, Miranda can hear a raspy noise from the seat ahead. Shelly!

* * *

The boy in the wheelchair soon gives place to a woman in a bathrobe, fuzzy green slippers on her feet and a frightened look on her face. "Who are you?"

Jay doesn't hear the question too clearly for the noise of the storm and the wheeze and thud of his own lungs and heart. "Gotta use your phone—the school bus—went off the road—"

"What?" she gasps. "The school bus *wrecked*?"

There is a scuffling behind her, which Jay senses rather than hears. The little overhang on the porch is no shelter at all—why don't they ask him in? A man pushes into the crowded doorway. Even at his present extreme, Jay recognizes Jason Stanley Hall from Bender's yearbook picture.

"What bus?" the man shouts. "When? Where is it?"

"Can I come in?"

He sees the man nod to the woman, and they back up to allow him just enough room to get inside and close the door. Dripping on the welcome mat, he gulps out his story. Mr. Hall's eyes bore into him—green, with startling pale eyelashes that remind Jay of somebody. He's barely begun when the man utters a strangled cry. Then he grabs a jacket and bolts out the door.

Jay wasn't expecting that. You'd think he had a kid on the bus or something.

"Stan!" the woman calls sharply after him. A stampede of emotions charge across her face, but by the time she turns back to Jay, it's empty.

"I need the phone," he reminds her.

All they have is a cheap cell phone that barely gets a signal, but after a few desperate tries, he gets through to a 911 operator who keeps telling him to stay calm. The call breaks up before he's finished. He feels like throwing the phone across the room but takes a deep breath and gets hold of himself. "I'm not sure she got that. The operator. I'd better run up to the highway and try to flag somebody."

"Let me wrap your leg first," the woman says. "It's starting to swell."

She's pale, with fluffy blond hair and light blue eyes. While he was gasping out his story about a wrecked school bus, she'd stared at him like he was an alien life-form. But the look she gives him now is firm and direct. The sight of his lower right leg, puffing up under his jeans like an overstuffed pillow, makes him sit down and shut up while she goes hunting for supplies. The house is topsy-turvy—stuff pulled out of drawers and closets and stacked up like a garage sale.

As she cuts off the lower leg of his jeans and winds his ankle with strips of gauze, her mouth clamped on three safety pins, Jay notices the boy watching him. He's sitting forward in the wheelchair with a weirdly happy smile on his face, staring hard enough to gobble him up. The kid is so small, with his stick-thin legs and arms, that his age is hard to guess. Leaning so far forward he's almost falling out, he says, "You're Jay. Aren't you?"

✳ ✳ ✳

Shelly dreams that someone is strangling her. Or a vampire has her by the neck and is closing in with his fangs. Or maybe it's not a dream. She can't move her head—the more she squirms, the more stuck she gets. No scream can get past the grip on her throat: "arggle" is the best she can do. Her right arm is wedged beside her body, and the other is feeling around but can't make sense of all this woody, twiggy stuff—*branches*? In a *bus*? That squeeze on her throat is tightening...she is shading into unconsciousness, a black frame around her thoughts getting thicker and heavier—"Help!" she shouts, but it comes out "aggh..."

"Shelly!" Miranda's voice, hands under her head, relieving the pressure a bit. "Can you hear me? It looks like a bush came through the window when the bus turned over and your hair is—Igor!"

Shelly hears an answering call.

"See if you can find some scissors, or a knife!"

She's glad it's Miranda. Miranda's a good friend...smart too...

"Shelly! Your neck is caught in a fork of this bush. You're choking, 'cause your weight's pulling you down and your hair's all tangled up in the branches..."

What's she saying…wait? For what? Or was it weight? You're a good one to talk about weight, girlfriend…Did she say bush? In the bus?

Somebody is scrambling over the back of the seat, which is now sideways, and everything is upside down and she's just now starting to realize that her throat really, *really* hurts and Star Camp is less than two months away and she can't sing like this…

"Simon had scissors in his backpack," says Igor. "Wow! She's pretty scratched up!"

What?

Miranda: "See if you can hold her head up." A pair of hands fumble around the top of her head—how did anyone get up there?—and a sound bites down right next to her ear: chomp, chomp. Like her hair is being chewed off.

Miranda: "These are *terrible* scissors. Like from kindergarten."

Igor: "First grade. They won't let little kids have anything sharp. You'll have to cut a little at a time."

The crunch of the scissors is kind of soothing. Shelly could go to sleep if it weren't for the iron clamp on her neck. And the pain. Yes, the pain, which is slowly bearing down on her now along with a rising panic. Does anybody know they're out here?

* * *

Spencer is slipping away even from his dreams. While turning over with the bus, he bounced off the side of the opposite seat

280

just before slamming the window frame headfirst. He doesn't feel anything and appears to be peacefully sleeping. But there's plenty going on inside his skull, none of it good.

Blood vessels have sprung like fountains, and brain cells are dying for lack of oxygen. He shouldn't be asleep. Sleep is the last thing he should do. He needs to wake up, needs to have people asking him questions, snapping their fingers in front of his face, slapping him even—anything to stop his long downward slide into that place where brain cells die and muscles forget how to move. Somebody needs to say *Hey, Spencer! Wake up!*

But there's nobody to say it.

* * *

The first thing Kaitlynn is aware of is a tingling in her back, then a pressure in her ears, as if all the ideas she's ever had are breaking up and shaking together. The first thing to do is remember who she is, then why she's here, then where she needs to be. As the feeling in her back comes alive, the pieces of herself are jumping, finding each other, snapping together, and aiming upward. Next minute, she's launched.

Up, up, *up*—arrowing straight for the surface, even though it's a long way and the higher she goes, the louder the buzz and the tinglier the tingle—though actually, she realizes now, it's more like pain. Each little quiver on her back is growing spikes and digging in and making her pay for things she doesn't even know she did…Up! Up! and the more she tries to outrun it, the worse it gets. She breaks, at last, upon a watery plain where the steady rain pummels her and the sobs of little children surround her and the outraged cries right beside her are the ones she's making herself.

* * *

Alice's jaw is sore from clamping down on it, trying not to scream. The rain, which had been hammering on the windows with watery fists, has lessened to a steady drumbeat that helps hold the panic down. Alice is trying to worry about Kaitlynn and Shelly and Spencer and everybody else, but pain is wrapping her up in the tight cocoon of herself. It's just one arm, but it's swallowed up her whole body. Tears track down her face and sobs jump in her throat, but she's holding them down. So far. If she gave herself up to them, she'd shake to pieces. She thinks of little Albert in their story, finding courage to hold on—and that makes her think of Ricardo, coming to after smashing into that bridge abutment…

"What's going on!" shouts an indignant voice beside her— Kaitlynn's. She sounds so mad, Alice somehow knows she's going to be okay. "Where's all this *blood* coming from??"

"Kaitlynn!" yells Simon from the front. "Are you okay?"

"NO, I'm not okay! I've got, like, a million cuts on me—is this *glass*?"

That sparks another uproar; Alice sees Igor climbing back toward the front and hears a moan from Matthew—

"Hey!" comes a voice from the back of the bus. "Lissa! Lissa-girl, are you in there?"

She can't believe it. *"Daddy?"*

Her father swings his legs over the emergency door opening and drops into the aisle, climbing over the seats on his hands and knees to get to her. "Sweetheart! Babydoll! You're alive—are you okay? Anything broken?"

"Just an arm—NO!" She stops him just before he can catch her up, jangling bones and all, in a big bear hug.

"Jeez!" He recoils as though stopped by an invisible hand. Then he reaches out to touch her good shoulder. "What can we use for a splint? Do you have anything we can wrap it up with?"

"Sir?" It's Miranda. "Do you happen to have a pocketknife?"

"Sure thing. Here you go—" He fumbles it out of his hip pocket and tosses it to her. "I might need it back, though." He slips off his jacket and is now unbuttoning his shirt. "I've got to cut some bandages."

"Daddy!" Alice is whispering. "Did anybody call 911?"

"Yeah, your mom. When that guy showed up at our door. What can we use for a splint?"

"I think we should wait for the ambulance," she says, still whispering. "Why aren't you gone?"

"We were waiting for the rain to slack off. Who else is hurt in here?" He's looking around distractedly. "Are y'all all accounted for?"

Miranda pops up again. "Could you see about Matthew? And maybe Spencer? And we don't know about Mrs. B—or Crystal—"

"Matthew? Where's Matthew?" He's stretching his neck, searching the forward seats.

"He's toward the back," Alice says. "Daddy! The ambulance'll be here soon. Hadn't you better go?" He's not supposed to be here, but she can't remember why.

"Plenty of time," he replies absently, crawling back the way he came. "Whoa! Are you Matthew?" Alice hears a murmur in reply. "I dunno, man, looks like you've lost a lot of blood already…"

"There!" Miranda exclaims triumphantly. "You're free! Careful, Igor. Let's pull her up…hold the branch steady while I get her untangled…"

"Is somebody coming to get us?" wails a little voice from the front.

"Mrs. B's awake!" comes another.

Alice hears a groan from that direction. She turns her head in time to see Shelly rise from between the seats like—well, maybe like a vampire from his coffin. It sure doesn't look like Shelly, her head bristling with tufts of black hair and her face red as a berry. She tries to talk but can't squeeze out a word. Her painful smile twists into a grimace of terror.

"Somebody please come get us," whimpers a voice.

All the littles start crying again, and Igor throws up his hands. "I give up!" Alice tries to call out to GeeGee, but her voice won't carry.

"Hey!" her dad's voice rings out sharply. "Hey, kid! Wake up! What's his name?" (Matthew mutters a response.) "Spencer! *Listen* to me, man! His eyes aren't right—one pupil's bigger than the other. Bad news—*Spencer!* That's right, stay awake. Stick with us, man—No! Don't check out on me. Open your eyes! Don't do this again, Ricardo. *Open your eyes!*"

Ricardo? Alice wonders. The rain is lighter but still loud enough, with the crying and shouting, that she can barely hear the scream of a siren as it lurches to the top of the hill and abruptly cuts off.

"Daddy?" But her father doesn't seem to hear, either her or the siren. He's holding Spencer up, supporting his head with one hand, putting words directly in his face ("What's your last name, son? Where do you live? What's your mom's maiden name? C'mon, Spencer—focus!"). Smiling, encouraging...

* * *

The bandage helps for the first twenty yards or so. Then it's back to grinding torture for every step until Jay reaches the highway. A patrol car, lights flashing, passes before he can flag it—he could have stomped in frustration. At least somebody knows, meaning his call got through, meaning more help was on its way. He can take it a little easier. But now that the urgency has let up, the pain sweeps in like water under a floodgate. He bites his lip and puts one foot in front of the other, limping.

The patrol car pulls over to the side of the road. Jay notices another vehicle on the opposite shoulder, headlights peering through the gray curtain of rain. A patrolman, just a blur from this distance, seems to be waving his arms. As Jay hobbles closer, he can make out the words the man is yelling: "Are you from the bus?"

Jay nods, noticing that the speed limit sign, which he'd

passed thousands of times in his life and never really seen, is now at a cockeyed angle. He points: "It went off right there!"

But the patrolman is no longer facing his way—he's yelling in the other direction. Limping closer, Jay recognizes Bender as though he were somebody he knew a long time ago.

"Are you sure?" the patrolman asks, and Bender is nodding. The cop reaches into his car for a radio and speaks into it urgently: "Dispatcher 7, this is Car 38. I'm at the bus scene on my way to check for injuries. We have an occupied vehicle in Drybed Creek, underwater. Repeat, *underwater*. Please dispatch another ambulance to the scene. Over—"

He tucks the radio inside his poncho and nods to Jay. "You guys watch for help." Then he's gone; it's like he dived down the slope headfirst in his hurry to get to the bus.

Jay limps a little closer. "What?"

Bender looks like he just went through a car wash: soaking wet, his clothes askew, and his hair every which way. "I couldn't do it—I just—" His voice sounds funny, and it takes Jay a moment to realize he's sobbing. "I tried—to save her—I—"

"Who? Your mom?"

"The—the—the current's too fast. I stepped in—and—it knocked my feet out from under me! I almost didn't get out."

"Is her car in the creek, is that what you're saying? And she's in it?"

"Couldn't even *get* to it." Bender is waving one arm mechanically, like the handle of a car jack. "I tried—I tried—I—"

"Good Lord!" The driver of the other vehicle, an old guy in overalls, has joined them.

Squinting down the slope, Jay can make out something white crunched up next to something gray. In a flash, he interprets this as a top of an SUV partly wedged under the bridge. "Dude," he says.

"I hear a siren," says the old man.

The noise is coming at them like a distant parade, a sound that makes your ears stretch and your eyes strain to see it. The violent flash of LED lights show first—red, blue, white—as a patrol car and an ambulance sweep around the curve, as fast as they dare. They slow down on the descent to the river. The water seems to have boiled over the bridge. At its edge, the lead car pauses and a highway patrolman gets out with a stick. Wading carefully into the water, he stretches forward to measure its depth, then waves to the ambulance driver to proceed with caution.

"I'll tell 'em about your mom," the old man says, starting down the hill. "You show 'em where the bus is."

Jay suddenly feels awkward, standing next to a boy he's known all his life and never liked, whose mother is in peril right before their eyes. It's even worse when the boy makes a noise like a calf stuck in a cattle guard and drops in a heap on the highway.

"I *tried* to save her!" he sobs again.

Jay remembers how he tried to pull his grandfather back from the brink and failed. The memory heaves up a mound of sorrow inside him and he doesn't feel awkward anymore, just sad. He sits beside Bender, clutching his swollen ankle, and discovers he's crying too.

"Hey, dude. I know you tried. I believe you. I tried too."

"I *should* have saved her," Bender chokes out and then adds, "Thorn would have."

"Who?"

Jay remembers Thorn—his sister Jessica had a crush on him all through high school. He just can't figure what the guy has to do with anything. Bender gives him the strangest look—did he think his brother was the center of the universe or something?

"Hey," Jay says, "it's probably better you didn't get to her now. That car's the safest place to be, as long as no water's getting in—"

"It shouldn't be there!" Bender kicks at the asphalt. "It's *stupid*! It's Myra Bender Thompson, the real estate go-to gal out to be number one in sales. Stupid! Always. Crash and burn. Knew it would happen someday. Wanted to tell her, but—we never *talked*."

Jay isn't sure he wants the whole backstory. "Yeah, well, talking…that's hard."

"So what? Everything's hard. Everything real, anyway. Big frickin' deal." It sounds like Bender is mad at *him* now.

"Okay, okay." Jay wipes his nose on his sleeve and stares down at the raging water with the SUV stuck in it that they can't do anything about.

Funny to think that on a normal morning, they'd be at school by now, starting another day that feels a lot like the previous day. But for all the motion that doesn't seem to take them anywhere—back and forth on the bus, around and around the track, on and off the honor roll—there's this huge current, carrying them forward. And just now, almost, swallowing them up. Almost.

The bumpy asphalt is digging into his butt. Everything is hard—and right now, he's glad of it.

He shouldn't feel this—should he?—but something like ecstasy is tingling in his bones. The accident that swept over them didn't kill him. It opened his eyes. For one endless moment, he can see the years ahead of him, taking him someplace real, not fuzzy and fading like the NFL. It doesn't matter if he ever plays football or runs again: *life itself*, the throb of his ankle and the cold rain in his face and the thump of his eager heart, is totally amazing. And it's just been handed back to him on a silver platter as wide as the world. For a moment, he's dizzy with gratitude.

The first ambulance has crossed the bridge and is now heading slowly toward them, lights blinking. Jay painfully stands up again, using Bender's shoulder for leverage and knocking pebbles off his shorts. He points repeatedly to the bent speed-limit sign. The vehicle pulls over and stops.

He wants to pass some of his gratefulness on to Bender but isn't sure how. "Look…" he begins. "I'll bet your mom's all right. I hope so. But whatever… We've got things to do."

Bender heaves a huge sigh and pulls himself up. Jay reaches out to him, lays a hand on his shoulder—and since Bender doesn't shake his hand off, it stays there, and anybody approaching would have thought they were the best of friends.

* * *

Within a week, they were all famous, in a way.

Kids on Wrecked School Bus Rescue Themselves was the local headline written by Maribeth Grand and picked up by Associated Press. It was an exaggeration, of course; nobody was really "rescued" until the emergency vehicles arrived. But the kids had to take care of each other until then because their driver was unconscious. What made their story grow and sprout wings and fly to news outlets all over the country was a very important fact: they all survived. Some, like Spencer, had to spend a lot of time in therapy. Some, like Matthew and little Crystal Applegate and Myra Bender Thompson, came close to actual death. But all survived, and none were ever quite the same.

One more interesting sideline to the story was how Jason Stanley Hall raced to the scene to rescue his daughter and stayed to pull Spencer back from oblivion and revive Mrs. B—who happened to be his mother-in-law! His very name heaved up unhappy memories of the class of '85 and their infamous graduation ceremony. No wonder he didn't want to be seen or recognized, but putting personal concerns aside to lend a hand made him a hero. For a while, anyway.

All the riders were heroes, for a while. But their fame quickly faded.

Mrs. B's, however, grew and grew.

First, she was fired—not for the accident so much as for all the other little irregularities that came out during the investigation. Irregularities like making an unauthorized stop every day for four months, allowing Christmas decorations on the bus, failing to report the snake incident, and (possibly) going a little too fast on the downhill slope just before going off the road, even though she swore she wasn't.

The good thing about being fired was it gave her time to devote to her secret project. By November of next year, it was done: a book. A novel for children based on her experience as a school bus driver and titled *Somebody on This Bus Is Going to Be Famous*.

There is just enough fiction in it not to be sued and to keep readers guessing about how much of it really happened and how much not. Only her former riders knew for sure.

And they're not telling.

* * *

No fair! you say. *You tricked us!*

We thought all along it was going to be one of the *kids* who'd be famous, but it turns out to be the only grown-up.

But wait a minute (I say). They've got lots of time to be famous. Or not. And anyway, fame isn't all it's cracked up to be. I still have to get up and get going and deal with aches and pains and grown-up children who can't seem to make up their minds and furnaces that stop working and drivers who cut me off in traffic and repairmen who don't show up and booksellers who don't return my calls and librarians who forgot they asked me to come and talk to their students. Being famous doesn't fix any of that.

As for Shelly, Bender, Miranda, Kaitlynn, Spencer, Matthew, Jay, Igor, and Alice—they have plenty of time for becoming who they are.

That doesn't happen by accident.

It'll take a lot of thought and experience, of charging down the wrong path and backing up again, of screwing up and then doing what they can to get unscrewed. Mainly it'll take years of bouncing off each other and their families and the important people in their future, because that's how you find your limits. And your potential.

But they'll get there. Oh, they're going all kinds of places! This world has its bumps and falls, and nasty surprises too. But it's not boring, unless you stop looking.

Everybody on this bus got picked up and shaken pretty hard on their way to school one May morning. It changed their lives—it changed *them*, but now they're on the road again and closer to becoming who they really are. The good Lord willing and the creek don't rise (excuse the expression), they'll get there.

And so will you.

Don't Miss the Bonus Chapter...

Next August

The gazebo needs a paint job and the loose railing still needs to be fixed, but it's ready. The kids are ready, too. Some of them have been through a long, difficult summer, and for others, the three months went by like a bullet train and sparkled like a firecracker. But one unchangeable fact of life seems to be that you're always ready for a change. Seven miles away, school buses are lining up outside the barn to turn on to the highway, and doors are opening all around the loop at Hidden Acres. The first person to reach the gazebo is...

Are you wondering what comes next for Shelly, Bender, Miranda, Kaitlynn, Spencer, Matthew, Jay, Igor, and Alice? Visit books.sourcebooks.com/somebody-on-this-bus OR www.jbcheaney.com/SOTB-epi for an EXCLUSIVE additional chapter and educator materials to go with it!

But first: you know these kids pretty well by now. What do YOU think happens?

Acknowledgments

I've never ridden a school bus in my life—except once, as an adult. In my early drafts, I imagined them as having a front entrance and a rear exit, like a city bus, but then someone mentioned that school buses only have one door.

Oh.

So I stopped along my rural highway about two miles out of town at the house where I'd sometimes been stalled by school buses going in and out. There I talked to Russell Martin, part-owner and all-operator of the buses that prowl our local R-I school district. He answered all my questions and allowed me to walk around and take pictures, so I know exactly what Mrs. B's bus looks like, inside and out. And he hasn't heard from me since, until now. Thanks, Russell!

This manuscript took its own sweet time finding a home, during which I tried it out on my long-suffering critique-mates, Vicki Grove and Leslie Wyatt (both outstanding authors in their own right). Our critique sessions always included food—as they should!—for which Vicki was mostly responsible, while Leslie slogged through an entire early draft and pointed out some major weaknesses I'd missed. They were both on hand when I decided to put the ending at the beginning, and both gave the idea a thumbs-up. "Like *The Bridge of San Luis Rey!*" remarked Vicki and promptly handed over her own copy of Thornton Wilder's classic. She mentions a book and it (almost) magically appears! Thank you both, sweet friends.

Dr. Julie Bryant at Southwest Baptist University was the first to read the revised copy. I had emailed it to her in three parts, and somehow she didn't get the last one. After reading parts one and two, she frantically tracked me down (I was on vacation) and begged for part three, *now*. Such unfeigned enthusiasm at that point was a shot in the arm for me.

After I signed with Erin Buterbaugh at MacGregor Literary Agency, she had a publisher on the hook within four months. And speaking of publishers, Aubrey Poole at Sourcebooks/Jabberwocky generously shared her encouragement and enthusiasm while whipping this manuscript into shape. I've been surprised and delighted by the whole team at Sourcebooks, who know how to get behind a book. High fives all around!

Thanks most of all to God, from whom all blessings flow.

About the Author

J.B. Cheaney was born sometime in the last century in Dallas, Texas. She did not want to be a writer—all the years she was growing up, her ambitions belonged to the theater. But since a life onstage didn't pan out, building a stage in her head, where she gets to play all the parts, has been a pretty good substitute. She's the author of two theater-related novels (*The Playmaker* and *The True Prince*), as well as *My Friend the Enemy* and *The Middle of Somewhere*. She resides in the Ozarks of Missouri with her husband and no dogs or cats.